PRAISE FOR SOPHIE'S VOICE

"Ms. Hardt has a way of writing that makes me forget I'm reading a book. It's more like slipping into a world she created and getting lost for a while."
~Tiger Lily, Whipped Cream Reviews

"Helen writes these books with such grace and finesse that you feel as though you've been transported back in time and are walking among the characters. You feel every bit of passion, anguish, and love emanating from the pages. It envelops you and leaves you grasping at the hopes that these two wonderfully in love couples get to have the HEA they both deserve."
~Bare Naked Words

"Flawlessly written, and in my opinion a work of art..."
~Girly Girl Book Reviews

SOPHIE'S
VOICE

A SEX AND THE SEASON NOVEL

HELEN HARDT

WATERHOUSE PRESS

Copyright © 2016 Waterhouse Press, LLC
Cover Design by Waterhouse Press, LLC
Cover Images: Shutterstock

PRINTED IN THE UNITED STATES OF AMERICA

ISBN: 978-0-9905056-4-8

SOPHIE'S
VOICE

HELEN HARDT

In memory of my grandmother,
Helen Marie Hardt Betcher,
from whom I took my pen name.

OVERTURE

Women are whores. They're born that way. Such is the fault of their original mother. Eve was the one who tempted Adam into eating that forbidden fruit. That's what women do. They tempt. That we men cannot resist temptation is not our fault. The fault lies with the women.

My own mother was the empress of the whores. She fed us by lying on her back, letting men stuff their cocks into her dirty cunt while I kept my brothers quiet in the next room. I have no idea who my father was, and I doubt any of my brothers were my true full-blooded brothers. Every year or so, another brother came along. Mother never gave birth to girls. Just as well. I'd have to see that the dirty little hussies were fed.

Man after man filtered through our small shack, sometimes tossing a biscuit to my brothers and me. We'd scramble to see who could get it first. Usually, I let Liam have the biggest piece. He was small and weak for his age.

"I'm hungry, Brian," he used to whine.

"I know, lad," I'd say, my heart breaking.

That little boy was the only thing I ever loved in my life. Until...

Liam died when he was six. Mother laid him outside in the gutter among the piss and shit. Eventually his little grey body disappeared.

I didn't cry for Liam.

I don't cry. Crying is for filthy women cunts.

I never thought I'd find a woman who wasn't a dirty whore. Until her.

Lady Sophie MacIntyre.

She is quiet, reserved. A cross or profane word never leaves her rosy lips. She is the opposite of her bitch sister. She is perfection, an angel, with long blond hair and beautiful green-gold eyes. She sings to herself, and when I can, I sneak into the conservatory and listen to her.

A young man used to visit her, but I made quick work of him. Finding a common harlot to seduce him and pretend she was with child was almost too simple.

She will be mine soon. The day of reckoning comes.

My graceful Sophie now sits in the conservatory, her fingers dancing over the piano keys.

Sing for me, Sophie.

But she does not. Her elegant face is in turmoil as she plunks out random notes on the pianoforte. Something disturbs her, but what?

I will kill whatever it is.

I've only killed once in my life—my own hussy of a mother. I left her in the street as she had left Liam, among the human and animal waste. She was no better than filth, after all. Then I took my brothers to orphanages and workhouses. I found work at the townhome of an English lord and quickly made myself indispensable to the family. Years later I moved to their estate in the country and worked like a dog, renting a small dwelling at the edge of the estate for my brother Harry—the only one of my brothers I could find after searching, a giant who wasn't right in the head—to live in.

I never killed again. Oh, I've wanted to, but I've held my desires back. What good would rotting in Newgate do me?

For Sophie, I would kill.

I have watched her from afar for so long now, and she never leaves my thoughts, tormenting me, haunting me. I dream of her day and night.

When I claim her, I will keep her safe from the outside world. She needs to be kept, secluded, locked up, so nothing will spoil her perfection. I will take care of her.

Always.

ACT I
CHAPTER ONE

Brighton Estate, Wiltshire, England April 1854

Was it possible for one's heart to fill to bursting yet break at the same time? For that was what Lady Sophie MacIntyre felt as she held her cousin's infant. In her arms cooed Morgan Daniel Charles Crispin Farnsworth, Marquess of Gordonshire and heir to the Lybrook dukedom. Morgan's mother was Sophie's cousin, Lily Jameson Farnsworth, the Duchess of Lybrook. The tiny marquess was beautiful, with his mother's dark hair, and blue eyes that had begun to turn an exotic emerald green, just like his father's. His little fist clasped Sophie's pinky finger, and her womb skipped a beat.

Such a splendid feeling, holding a baby. Holding one's own baby would be even sweeter, but that would probably never be. Sophie's sister, Lady Alexandra Xavier, was large with a child of her own, and Lily's other cousin, Rose Jameson Price-Adams, held her infant daughter, Lady Joy Lily Price-Adams, who had bright blue eyes and the coal-black hair of her father, Cameron Price-Adams, the Earl of Thornton and heir to the Marquess of Denbigh.

Alexandra's baby was sure to be just as fair as her cousins'. Ally's chestnut hair and golden-brown eyes combined with her husband's wheat-blond hair and warm brown eyes would surely produce a handsome or beautiful young nephew or niece for Sophie.

Alas, a baby was not in Sophie's future. The only man who had paid her any attention in the last several years was Lord Marshall Van Arden, and even he had never formally courted her. After several months of visits, during which she'd allowed no liberties at all, Van Arden had broken off their friendship and married a commoner.

"Goodness gracious, Lily," Ally was saying, "the poor child will grow ill from all those names."

Lily smiled, her brown eyes shining. "We didn't want to leave anyone out. This is the future duke, after all. In fact, I suggested five names, adding Thomas."

"I'm sure our brother will understand why you didn't include him in the mix," Rose said, cuddling baby Joy.

"Yes, he did," Lily replied. "In fact, he forbade me giving the child five names. So we settled on four." She let out a chuckle.

"I do hope you all know how lucky you are," Sophie said serenely.

"Of course, Sophie," Rose said. "We are all thrilled. But why so glum?"

"It's just that... None of this will ever happen for me, I'm afraid." Sophie snuggled baby Morgan just a little closer to her. The baby had fallen asleep and resembled a cherub in her arms.

"For goodness' sake, Sophie, of course this is in your future," Ally said. "Just because Van Arden didn't have a clue what was good for him doesn't mean some other gentleman won't come along for you. You are lovely, and any man would be lucky to have you."

Sophie sighed. "I'm four-and-twenty years old now, Ally."

"I'm your sister. I know when your birthday is. Why you chose to forgo this season is beyond me. With Lily, Rose, and me all helping you, you would've been the belle of the ball."

"I didn't want to impose on the earl's generosity."

"The earl's generosity? He's our stepfather. He's happy to do it. Anything for Mother. He adores her. He even gave us dowries."

"Yes," Sophie said, "which you didn't need, since you married his son."

"All the more reason for you to let him spend his money on you. He could have given you a lavish season, and you would have had so much fun. I'm positive you would have met someone perfect."

Sophie shook her head. "Honestly, Ally, I have no interest in a season, and I never have, as you well know. We must all face it. I am an old maid—the oldest of the four of us and the last left. I am too old to marry now. I have accepted my lot in life. I'll be the spinster auntie and spinster first cousin once removed to all of your children. It will give me joy to watch them grow."

Rose smiled. "We will all adore watching them grow," she said in her gentle way. "And I promise you that you will enjoy watching your own children grow as well, Sophie."

Sophie returned Rose's smile, though she wasn't really feeling it. "Let's do talk about something else. My spinsterhood is hardly a subject for such a fine afternoon as this. What is happening in your lives?"

"Well, my breasts are the size of watermelons," Lily said dourly.

Ally let out a loud guffaw, and even Rose chuckled, but Sophie gasped.

"Goodness, Lily."

"I'm sorry to offend your delicate nature, Sophie, but that little marquess you're holding gobbles up milk like there's no tomorrow. And let me tell you, I make it like there's no tomorrow."

"As do I," Rose said with a sigh. "But it does give me such joy to know that I am feeding my child from my own body. Wouldn't you agree, Lily?"

"Of course, I love the little lad. He's everything Daniel and I had hoped for. But I can tell you that I'm looking forward to the day when I'm not carrying around two cannonballs in my corset."

"I can't say this is the subject I was hoping for when I asked that we talk about something else," Sophie said.

"I have some news," Rose said. "Cam says Mr. Newland is looking for some new talent for his upcoming musicale."

"Thank the good Lord," Lily said. "I am so tired of that prima donna Nanette Lloyd."

"Yes, she does think quite highly of herself," Ally agreed. "But she sings beautifully. However, Sophie, as enchanting as her voice is, it does not hold a candle to yours. You should consider auditioning for Mr. Newland."

Sophie let out a laugh. Imagine, her auditioning to be a public spectacle. Absolutely not. She was a lady of the peerage, after all—and fairly much fearful of her own shadow. "Ally, that is absurd. How could you even think such a thing?"

"Because you're so talented, my dear. Don't you agree, Lily, Rose?"

Their cousins both nodded.

"Absolutely, Sophie," Lily said. "The fact that you never sing for anyone besides us is a crime."

"I have to agree with Lily." Rose nodded. "Your voice is so unique, so delicate. Nanette is talented, but your voice has an ethereal quality, something I've never heard in one of Mr. Newland's musicales."

"Really, Rose, you aren't suggesting I audition as well?"

"I agree with you it's not exactly...standard conduct for women of our station, but why not? You have the talent. You have the time. And singing gives you such joy. Why not let it bring joy to others, as well?"

Sophie smiled at her gentle cousin. Of the four, Sophie and Rose were most alike in demeanor and personality. Ally and Lily were much more flamboyant and unconventional. "I do appreciate the confidence all of you have in me, but I'm afraid I am never going to audition. Singing in public is about as much in my future as marriage and children."

Ally smiled, her eyes gleaming. "Would you be willing to make a small wager?"

Sophie gasped. "You're suggesting that I gamble? What would I have to gain?"

"I'm simply suggesting"—Ally pulled a sovereign from her reticule and placed it on the marble-topped mahogany coffee table in front of the divan where she sat—"that I can place a glove atop this coin and move it without moving the glove."

"For the love of the Lord, I have no idea what you could be talking about," Sophie said.

"Lily, may I borrow one of your gloves?" Ally asked.

"Of course, dear." Lily rose and placed a glove on the table next to the sovereign.

"Give baby Morgan back to his mother, and come here."

Sophie stood. Whatever did her conniving sister have up her sleeve? She handed the baby back to Lily and sat next to Ally on the gold brocade divan. "So you have a sovereign and a glove. Now what?"

"You see the sovereign is showing the image of St. George killing the dragon."

Sophie nodded.

Ally placed Lily's white glove on top of the coin. "And now, Sophie, I bet you that I can turn that sovereign over to the side showing the head without moving this glove."

★ ★ ★ ★

Zachary Newland let out a yawn. Nanette Lloyd's painted lips held his cock.

Since when do I yawn during a cock sucking?

Since he had grown damned tired of Miss Nanette Lloyd. She was a decent actress with a nice voice, but bedding her had become dull. Her eagerness bored him. Zach enjoyed the chase, the conquest. He had fucked Nanette standing, against the wall in his office, the first time they met. What some women would do to get a part... Of course, he hadn't been complaining at the time. Who was he to turn down a romp?

Nanette assumed she would be his lead soprano forever. For now, she was the best Zach had, and he did want to keep her...as an actress at the theatre.

As a lover? He was done.

How long had she been sucking him? Shouldn't he be ready to release soon? Regarding fellatio, some women had it and some women didn't. Nanette was a decent enough fuck, but as much as she enjoyed sucking cock, she did not have the gift. He wasn't going to come this way. He'd have to turn her around, spank her arse until it was pink, and then fuck her. The thought didn't arouse him much.

He gently grasped her head and moved her lips away from his cock. "I need to fuck you."

"But I love sucking you, Zach. Please, I want you to come down my throat."

Wasn't going to happen. He was going limp already.

"Sorry, honey, I've just got a lot on my mind. Auditions for the new musicale start on the morrow. I've got so much paperwork to do yet."

"All right," she said, "you can fuck me."

But the moment had passed for Zach. He was no longer looking for a fuck, and certainly not one from Nanette. He pulled up his drawers and trousers. "I'm afraid, Nanette, that we're not going to fuck this afternoon."

"But you were so hard for me just minutes ago."

Zach sighed. He hated breaking off with women. Though he had never been serious with a woman and didn't have any plans to do so in the near future, he still didn't like ending things. He had no desire to upset any woman. But he and Nanette were a ship that had already sailed. He had been taking her to his bed for over six months—a long time for him. He had enjoyed himself—even though the cock sucking hadn't gotten any better over time—and so had she, as far as he knew. He drew in a deep breath.

"Listen, you know I love your voice and I'm thrilled to have you here as part of the theatre. But I think that the sun has set on this little affair of ours."

Nanette stuck out her bottom lip in a pout. "You can't mean that, handsome."

"I'm afraid I do. But please, do audition for the musicale. I value you as a member of the theatre and as"—he swallowed—"a friend." So that last part was a little lie. Wouldn't hurt anyone. Zach was not against having women as friends, but Nanette was not the type he wanted to be friendly with. She was a decent soprano and a decent fuck, but intelligence was not her strong suit.

"Well," she said in a huff, "perhaps I will not audition for you. And then you'll be less one soprano."

"As you wish. If you change your mind, I'll see you at auditions tomorrow." Zach wasn't worried. Nanette had no other job in town, so unless she wanted to lie on her back to earn money, she would be at auditions.

"Well, I never..." She adjusted the bodice of her gown and flounced out.

Oh, yes, you have, honey. And you haven't learned much.

★ ★ ★ ★

"That's the most ridiculous thing I've ever heard," Sophie said. "There is no way you can move that coin without touching the glove. Last time I checked, you're not telekinetic."

"I say I can."

Sophie rolled her eyes. "Good for you, then."

Ally smiled. "Are you willing to bet that I can't do it?"

"I don't believe in gambling, as you well know."

"This is not gambling, Sophie. This is just a fun game. I say I can move the coin without moving the glove. You say I can't. If I can, will you audition for Mr. Newland?"

Her sister had gone stark raving mad. That was the only explanation. Fine, Sophie would humor her. "If you insist, Ally.

Yes, if you can move that coin to its other side without moving Lily's glove, I will audition for Mr. Newland's musicale."

"Excellent!" Ally smacked her hand down on the table. "The coin has now been moved."

"You've gone dotty. What is this pregnancy doing to you?"

"I assure you I'm far from dotty. And as for the pregnancy, why, I feel in perfect health. Once those few months of dreaded sickness were over, I've never felt better. In fact, you can ask Evan. I've been rather...*insatiable* lately."

Sophie's cheeks warmed. The way Ally talked about her bedroom antics with Evan had made her blush on more than one occasion. "Ally, really..."

"Let's not get off the subject, shall we? I say the coin has been moved. If you don't believe me, check for yourself."

Sophie let out a laugh. "If you say so." She removed the glove only to find that the sovereign had not moved at all.

Before she could say as much, Ally flipped the coin over onto its head side. "Ha! You lose. You must audition for Mr. Newland."

Yes, her sister had definitely gone dotty. "You need to have your head examined, Ally."

Ally erupted in giggles. "I fear it might be you who needs your head examined. I bet you that I could move the coin to its other side without moving the glove. And I did."

Lily let out a loud guffaw. "You're too much, Ally! Oh, Sophie, she did get you good."

Sophie shook her head. "That is ridiculous, both of you. She said that she had moved the coin when she slapped the table."

Ally shook her head. "I did say that, but if you recall the terms of the bet, what I said had nothing to do with them. I bet you that I could turn the coin over without moving the glove. You moved the glove, not I. Then I turned the coin over. Case closed."

Lily continued to laugh uproariously until little Morgan stirred in her arms and she quieted. "Where on earth did you learn that trick? I've got to use it on Daniel."

Even Rose joined in, smiling. "It was all in good fun, Sophie," she said. "And you do have such a lovely voice. Why don't you audition?"

Sophie wasn't one to get angry, but a bit of passion stirred within her. They'd made her look like an idiot. How had she allowed herself to be duped like this? "I'm afraid it's absolutely out of the question."

"Don't be angry. It was all in sport," Ally said. "I am your sister, and I love you. I would never ask you to do anything that wasn't for your own good. You need to get off of this estate. You need to have something to do that you enjoy. You love singing, and auditioning for the musicale will at least get you out for a few hours tomorrow."

"Cam can give you a ride in when he goes to the theatre tomorrow," Rose said.

"Oh, no, I wouldn't want to be a bother."

"You're no bother."

Sophie shook her head. "Why am I talking about this as if I'm going to do it?"

Ally smiled. "Because, dear Sophie, you are the finest lady I know, one who would always pay her debts. And I'm afraid you lost a bet to me, and payment of your debt to me is to audition for Mr. Newland tomorrow."

"I..." Sophie looked away. Ally might have tricked her, but she had fallen for it. "Fine. I shall audition for Mr. Newland.

But I know I will fall flat on my face, so can you all promise me one small thing?"

"Of course," Rose said. "What?"

"Once I make a fool of myself at this audition, can we please never speak of me singing in public again?"

CHAPTER TWO

Sophie gulped. The scone she had forced down at breakfast had tasted like sawdust, and now it was threatening to reappear. Rose's husband, Cameron, had driven her into Bath this morning for the auditions. Cameron was the composer for the Regal Theatre and spent his time at his townhome in Bath during the theatre season. The upcoming musicale was an original work written by Cameron, and he had told Sophie during the drive to Bath that she was perfect for the leading female role.

Not possible. A woman who vomited on stage couldn't be perfect for anything.

Before Sophie knew what was happening, Cameron had ushered her through the lobby of the theatre, around a few winding hallways, to an office.

She gaped. A man stood behind a desk reading a news journal. Auburn hair graced his shoulders, and his light brown eyes glowed. He was splendid, with exotic looks that she might not have considered classically handsome had they belonged to anyone else. But this man? Oh, how they worked. Her heart beat rapidly.

Zachary Newland. She had actually seen the gifted actor perform once nearly a year ago as Puck in *A Midsummer Night's Dream*. Then he had been costumed as a wood elf, a wreath of twigs on his head and his glorious chest bare. His acting had been so true to character that she had begun to think of him as a wood sprite, despite his immense and golden masculinity.

Not so anymore. The man was not as tall as her stepfather or brother-in-law, Evan, but his presence filled the room. Broad shoulders were clad in only a billowy-sleeved white blouse that belonged several centuries ago. Tight britches gloriously hugged his hips and thighs. Her heart nearly stopped. The man belonged on a pirate ship, carrying a maiden down to his quarters—a maiden with blond hair and hazel eyes. The image came alive in her mind, and the maiden had Sophie's own face.

"Newland, I'd like you to meet my wife's cousin, Lady Sophie MacIntyre," Cameron said.

Sophie looked up, her pirate vision vanishing. Cameron had been speaking, introducing her. *Open your mouth, Sophie. Say something.*

"It is indeed my pleasure, my lady." Zach put down the paper, walked around his desk, and offered his hand. "Thornton, here, speaks highly of you and your talent."

Sophie warmed from her hair follicles down to the tips of her toes. Surely she was turning beet red. She held out her hand limply. Mr. Newland took it in his own, raised it to his lips, and brushed a light kiss over it.

Sophie squirmed. Her skin erupted in tingles, and new sensations skittered within her. What was going on?

"It is indeed my pleasure, sir." She drew her hand away.

"Cameron tells me this is your first audition."

Sophie nodded.

"We'll try to make it easy on you," Mr. Newland said. "Cam will be right there, playing the pianoforte for you. What will you be singing for us today?"

Sophie held out the wrinkled paper she had been

clenching in her hand. She willed herself not to stammer. "'Deh Vieni, Non Tardar.' Susanna's aria from *The Marriage of Figaro*. By Mozart."

"Yes, yes, quite familiar with it. A beautiful piece. Let's go out into the theatre, and we will begin your audition. I hope you don't mind. I'm doing auditions in the theatre this time instead of the green room."

Green room? No need to show him what a novice she truly was. She nodded. "That's fine."

"I want to hear everyone with the theatre's acoustics. Just give your music to Thornton."

The paper rustled quietly as she handed it to Cameron.

"Don't be nervous," Cameron whispered as they left the office. "I've asked him to let you audition first so you don't have to sit around all day and wait. I have to stay for the duration, though, so I'll hire a hansom cab to drive you back to the estate."

Sophie gasped. "I have to go first?"

Cam nodded. "Trust me, it's for the best. This is your first audition. If you went second or third or, God forbid, last, you would sit here all day and your nerves would get the best of you. You would have to hear all of the other singers, and you would find something better in their voices than what you have in your own. You would be wrong, of course. Your voice is unique and engaging, Sophie. But I know how timid you are, and it would not be good for you to listen to the other auditions."

She nodded, her tummy gurgling. He was undoubtedly right...but first? "Cameron, I don't know that I can go through with this. I honestly...feel quite ill at the moment."

"That's just nerves. Trust me, I have been to my share of auditions in my lifetime. The belly flutters never go away. But you can do this. Just breathe deeply, concentrate, and pretend you're at home, singing alone in the conservatory."

"I don't know..."

"I will be here with you. I'll be playing for you. If you feel yourself losing focus, just look over to me, and I will get you back to where you need to be."

Sophie inhaled and let her breath out slowly, willing her heart to stop stampeding. "All right. I will do my best. Ally really wants me to do this, and she must know what she's doing. Maybe."

"She does." Cam nodded. "Newland is ready for you. He's sitting out in the theatre where the acoustics are best."

Sophie glanced out. Yes, there he was, looking as amazing as ever. She wished she hadn't looked. Perhaps if she could pretend she was singing to empty space, this would be easier.

She turned back to Cam. "One more thing. What is a green room?"

Cam smiled. "It's a room off the theatre for the performers when they're not on stage."

Sophie nodded. Of course. She should have known that. She should know a lot of things if she was going to go through with this. She was so out of place here.

"Walk out on stage now," Cam urged.

She swallowed, gathered as much confidence as she could muster—which wasn't much—and strode onto the stage.

"Everything all right, my lady?" Mr. Newland said from the audience.

Sophie cleared her throat softly. "Yes, sir."

"Excellent. Whenever you're ready, then."

Sophie glanced at Cameron, who had sat down at the pianoforte. "Are you ready, Sophie?"

She inhaled again, more deeply this time, and blew out

her breath in a slow stream, closing her eyes. She loved the aria, knew it by heart, and could sing it in her sleep. Slowly, she opened her eyes, looked over at Cam, and nodded.

Cameron began the introduction to the song.

Sophie opened her mouth, ready to sing, but at her musical cue, nothing came out. Her cheeks warmed, and she trembled all over. She looked back at Cam, pleading with her eyes. He stopped playing.

"My lady, is anything wrong?" Mr. Newland asked.

Goodness gracious, now what? Sophie opened her mouth to say, "Yes, something is wrong. I have no business being here," but Cam spoke first.

"It's my fault, Newland. I made an error during the intro, and Lady Sophie wasn't able to begin at the correct time. Let's just try it again."

"Very well," Mr. Newland said, smiling.

Cameron had not made a mistake. Sophie knew he was covering for her, and no doubt Mr. Newland knew as well.

She swallowed. Ally had bested her in that bet, even if she had been sneaky. Naïve little Sophie would just have to do better next time. Still, she was not a dodger. She had lost the bet, and she would pay up. Time for the audition.

She turned to Cameron and mouthed, "Thank you." Then she nodded.

Cameron began playing again.

This time, at her cue, Sophie opened her mouth and her singing words emerged. She sang of fearful anxieties, of amorous fires, of little flowers laughing, calling her love to her, and soon she was back in the conservatory at the estate, singing for no one's pleasure but her own. The notes on the pianoforte hummed in her ears as she became one with them.

Her voice soared, and with it so did she, to a better place, the place she always escaped to when she sang. The music took her away—the melodies, the harmonies—and she floated upward, onto a cloud, a cloud where no one could harm her. All fueled by her own voice.

When the last word of the song dripped from her lips, she bowed her head, closing her eyes. Nothingness enveloped her, and peace surrounded her.

Until the clapping of Cameron and Mr. Newland and the rest of the actors in the audience thundered into her ears.

"Brava!" a gentleman yelled from the audience.

Soon more "bravas" echoed throughout the theatre. When the excitement died down, Mr. Newland stood, speaking from his seat in the audience.

"My lady, that was profound. Your voice is captivating and unique. May I ask where you studied?"

Sophie's lips trembled. "I didn't."

"Really, you don't say? Another self-taught prodigy, then, like our own Lord Thornton here."

"When I was quite young, I had lessons on the pianoforte, and my instructor coached me on vocal technique. But before long..." She couldn't go on. The truth was, before long, her mother had no longer been able to afford her lessons. Sophie didn't like to think about her childhood. Her father had been abusive to her, Ally, and their mother. Each year they'd had a little less, due to his negligence in handling estate affairs, and eventually they hadn't been able to live on the estate at all. They moved into town and lived in near poverty. When her father, the Earl of Longarry, passed away three years prior, they had come to England, where their mother's sister, the Countess of Ashford, had set them up in a townhome in

Mayfair. Soon thereafter, their mother, Iris, had met the love of her life, David, the Earl of Brighton.

"And before long...what?" Mr. Newland asked.

She cleared her throat. "Before long...I guess I just lost interest in music." *Oh, Sophie, what a horrendous lie.* She hated lying. Especially to Mr. Newland, although she wasn't quite certain why. Something about him...

"Well, despite your loss of interest, I can see you excel at it nonetheless. I thank you very much for singing for us today. Auditions will go on today and tomorrow. Parts will be posted here at the theatre two days hence."

Sophie nodded, unsure what to do. She looked to Cameron, who gestured with his head for her to leave the stage.

A few seconds later, Cameron joined her. "That was brilliant, Sophie. Truly."

"I'm afraid I made a horrible fool of myself. I had no idea what I was doing."

"You did fine. Everyone is nervous at the first audition. Actually, everyone is nervous at every audition. You sang beautifully, and I could tell that Newland was impressed. I have to get back to auditions, but I've arranged for a cabbie to meet you at the front of the theatre. He will take you back to the estate."

Sophie gulped. "Thank you, Cam. Having you here made it a little less nerve-racking."

Cameron smiled and walked back onto the stage.

Sophie heaved a sigh of relief. Whether roles were posted two days hence was irrelevant. She had fulfilled her bargain with Ally and auditioned. She was now done. Back to her life of spinsterhood. The thought calmed her.

Calm was good.

★ ★ ★ ★

Zach squirmed in his theatre seat.

What was it about that woman? She had dressed conservatively in a dark-green day gown, plain and simple. Small wisps and curls of blond hair feathered out from the severe bun holding the rest of her coif tight. Her eyes—brown. Or were they green? Brown with green flecks, a few golden sparkles too. Eyes that could hold a man captive. Such a delicate little figure, but lush in all the right places.

Yes, she was beautiful, but she didn't know how truly beautiful she was. Something held her back. She trembled as though she wished she were invisible—like a wood sprite who had appeared from another realm and might vanish in an instant. She lacked confidence and courage—that was clear.

But that voice... He had never heard anything quite like it. Angels had come down from heaven and sung through this nervous woman.

Nanette was up next for her audition. She was also a soprano, and though quite talented, her voice was nothing compared to Lady Sophie's. Zach had to see her before she left, had to tell her how moved he had been by her audition.

"Ladies and gentlemen," he said, standing, "we're going to take a short respite. Miss Lloyd, you're next. Go ahead and use this time to warm up with Lord Thornton at the piano."

"But Zach..." Nanette whined.

Zach didn't respond. Instead, he rushed out of the theatre and into the lobby. No sign of Lady Sophie. Looking out the door, he spied her getting into a hansom cab. The cabbie had taken her hand and was helping her into the coach.

He pushed the heavy glass door open and ran forward.

"My lady, wait!"

Lady Sophie turned around, her face flushing a lovely raspberry color. She arched her eyebrows.

"If I may have a moment?" he said.

"I'm sorry. I am getting ready to leave for the Brighton estate, as you can see."

"Yes, yes." He turned to the cabbie. "You may go on. I'll arrange for Lady Sophie's transport in a few moments."

"Yes, sir." The cabbie tipped his hat.

"Mr. Newland"—Sophie cleared her throat gently—"what is this about? This is highly irregular, not to mention improper."

"Yes, my lady, and I offer you my apologies. However, I could not let you leave without telling you how thoroughly I enjoyed your audition. I would like to offer you a leading role in the new musicale."

"How are you able to offer me anything? You haven't heard the other auditions yet."

"I am familiar with all of the other actors and actresses who will be auditioning today. I know their voices. None of them can come close to you, my lady."

Sophie fidgeted with her reticule. "I'm afraid, Mr. Newland, that I will be unable to accept a role in the production."

What? Not able to accept? Did this woman have any idea of the talent she possessed?

Her pink lips trembled ever so slightly, and her cheeks deepened from raspberry to aubergine. Zach gulped, his pulse quickening. Had anyone kissed those lips? How they beckoned him. Sophie was of average height, coming up to his chest. He again eyed her dazzling blond hair swept up tight with only a few wispy curls free. How might it look flowing freely over her milky-white shoulders? Over her pert breasts?

"If you would be so kind, Mr. Newland..."

Zach stood, mouth agape. She had said something after his name, but he had heard no words. Only that voice, that voice from an angel, swirled around his head. He could not get enough of it. Still those rosy lips trembled, calling to him.

He couldn't help himself. He gripped her shoulders, lowered his head, and pressed his lips to hers.

CHAPTER THREE

What is happening?

Mr. Newland was...*kissing* her.

Sophie gasped, the air suctioning Mr. Newland's lips even more onto hers. She hardly knew this man, and indeed, it was her first kiss. But...

Heaven.

He nibbled at her lips, his tongue pressing along the seam. He wanted her to open her mouth. She knew a bit about kissing, mostly from Ally telling her things she hadn't really wanted to hear. And now... She was in the middle of a kiss with a most handsome man, and suddenly, she wanted this kiss more than she wanted to breathe. No worries there, because she couldn't breathe. Her skin tingled all over, and her heart thumped.

She parted her lips.

And all thought fled. Only feeling remained—pure raw feeling. He swept his tongue inside of her mouth, seeking hers, and she responded, letting her own tongue drift outward and touch his.

Oh, the sparks! Such sparks tickled her skin. Her skin heated, her belly fluttered, and a strange pulsing began between her legs.

Dear Lord... The tickle, the fresh desire. Her nipples tightened against her corset, two hard little berries aching to be let free of their confinement. Between her legs... She wanted something between her legs... Something hard...

Something hard? What was she doing?

With all of her strength, she pushed against Mr. Newland's chest, breaking the kiss with a loud smack.

"Mr. Newland, please!" She placed both her hands on her cheeks. How red must they be! "In the middle of the street. And I...I hardly know you!"

"We can certainly remedy the latter, my lady." Mr. Newland arched his eyebrow and smiled. An adorable dimple appeared on his left cheek.

Sophie attempted to back away from Mr. Newland but stumbled, her knees like jelly.

Mr. Newland caught her, gripping her upper arm. "Easy, my lady. Let's get you inside for a moment." He led her back into the theatre lobby.

Sophie yanked her arm away. "I can look after myself." But she stumbled again.

Mr. Newland chuckled and took her arm again. "Please, come with me."

He led her back into his office and helped her sit down on a lush leather chair. "Sit here for a moment. I will get you a drink of water." He returned seconds later and handed her a cup.

She drank thirstily, the water soothing her parched mouth. What had gotten into him? More importantly, what had gotten into her? Why had she allowed the kiss in the first place? In broad daylight? In public?

Zach sat down in the chair next to her. "Are you feeling better?"

Sophie was certain she was turning twelve shades of red. "Yes, thank you."

"Good. Because I meant it when I said I wanted you to

take the lead role in my new musicale. You have such an exquisite operatic voice, unlike anything I've ever heard. I can make you a sensation."

A sensation? Sophie had no desire to be a sensation. She wished only to stay at home, doting on tiny cousins and a soon-to-be-born niece or nephew, reading, singing, walking about the grounds. It might not be a glamorous life, but it was hers, and she was used to it.

She knew firsthand how wretched life could be when she had a man's attention. Ally had shielded her from most of it by taking their father's punishment for her. Sophie had tried to repay Ally in the past, but had finally come to the conclusion that she just couldn't. The best she could do for Ally was stay out of harm's way, be a recluse, a spinster.

"I do appreciate your confidence in me, sir, but I must decline."

"You have no idea how much it pains me to hear you say that, my lady."

Sophie winced a bit. She hated causing anyone pain, especially this man who had just given her the amazing gift of his kiss—something she never thought she would experience—no matter how inappropriate it was. "I am not meant for the stage, sir. I am meant for a simple life, a life at home helping to care for my loved ones. That is my destiny, and it is one I am happy to fulfill."

Mr. Newland took her hand. Shivers ran through her at his touch. She tried to draw her hand away, but he held fast.

"A voice such as yours should be shared, my lady. I don't believe for one moment that your destiny is to remain on the sidelines, watching your life trickle by day by day, moment by moment. I believe your destiny is to share your gifts with the world, to become who you were meant to be."

"I know very well who I am meant to be, sir." And she had made her peace with it.

He leaned toward her, their faces becoming closer, his full pink lips glistening. Her heart nearly stopped. He was going to kiss her again, and dearest Lord, she wanted him to.

But Mr. Newland was a rake, well-known in his circles as a seducer of women. She had heard the tales from Cameron and Rose. Though they both thought very highly of Mr. Newland as a businessman and as a performer, they both admitted that he enjoyed bedding many women. Sophie had no intention of being one of them.

Before his lips descended on hers, the door to his office opened.

Sophie turned, gasping, and beheld a pretty blond woman, her hair cascading down over her shoulders. She wore a simple peasant dress. Blue eyes pierced Sophie's own. Nanette Lloyd—or the prima donna, as Lily would say.

"Zach? Are you returning for the auditions, or are you not?" Miss Lloyd whipped her hands to her hips and tapped her foot impatiently. "There are over twenty people waiting for their chances to audition."

Zach cleared his throat and stood, his face pink. "Yes, yes, of course. But before we resume auditions, I would like you to meet the Regal Theatre's new star soprano, Lady Sophie MacIntyre."

Sophie stood, gasping. "Mr. Newland—"

Miss Lloyd dropped her mouth into an O.

Mr. Newland grabbed Sophie by the hand. "Lady Sophie, meet Nanette Lloyd, another gifted soprano in our company."

"And the lead soprano," Nanette said.

"Dear Nanette, you are a true talent, but Lady Sophie, I'm afraid, is just a little bit better than you are."

Sophie warmed down to her toes at the compliment. But goodness, she did not want to be the star soprano of his company. She just wanted to go home. She had fulfilled her bet with Ally, and now she was finished with this. "Miss Lloyd, I assure you I am not the new star soprano here."

"Then what is the meaning of this, Zachary?" Nanette asked, her hands still glued to her hips.

Zach opened his mouth, but Sophie spoke over him.

"Mr. Newland, I told you that I am not taking this post. I do thank you for the opportunity to audition, but I have no interest in the stage."

"Well, that's a very good thing indeed," Nanette said, shaking her hair so that it tumbled in waves over her bosom, "because I can assure you I would make both of your lives miserable." She turned and flounced away.

Sophie curtsied politely to Mr. Newland. "And now, sir, if you will please excuse me." She left the office and ventured back into the lobby of the theatre. There she asked the doorman to hail her a hansom cab. A cabbie couldn't get here fast enough. She was so ready to leave the city and go home, to her own chamber, where she was safe and nothing could harm her.

★ ★ ★ ★

Zach returned to the theatre and apologized to the performers waiting to audition. They were all very gracious except for Nanette, who glared at him. Well, so be it. Nanette was a fine soprano, but Sophie was an angel. Somehow he would talk her into taking the role.

Several hours later, after all the auditions were finished, Zach headed back into his office, his mind racing with ideas of how to get Sophie to perform. He walked in, and then dropped his jaw nearly to the floor.

Nanette lay, stark naked, on the Oriental rug covering the floor of his office.

"What took you so long, handsome?"

Zach closed his mouth and cleared his throat. "What are you doing here, Nanette? I told you it's over between us."

"You didn't really expect me to believe that, did you? We've had so much fun between the sheets, and the thought of never having you again... Well, I just can't bear it."

"I'm afraid you're going to have to bear it. I was not kidding. We are over."

"But won't you miss me?"

Miss her? She was lovely to look at. But Zach grew tired of women easily. It was his way, and he certainly wasn't going to settle down anytime soon...especially not with the likes of Nanette Lloyd. She was a talent, it was true, but she had gotten her start as a saloon girl. That's where Zach had found her. Her voice was good, and under his tutelage, it had gotten even better, but she was still a saloon girl. Not that there was anything wrong with being a saloon girl. Zach had had plenty of fun with saloon girls over the years. But although Nanette was a competent actress and singer, she was not destined for greatness.

Lady Sophie, however, was.

Nanette stood, her blond tresses tumbling over her breasts. She was a little thing, smaller even than Lady Sophie. Her body was curvy and soft.

A sudden jolt of déjà vu hit Zach in the gut. This was the exact scenario that had occurred when he first met Nanette. He had asked her, after hearing her sing at a local saloon, to audition for him. After the audition, he had found her naked in his office, and that is how their liaison had begun. How fortuitous that it would end the same way.

Nanette strode forward, her hips swaying, her lower lip protruding. "Surely you don't want to give all this up." She wrapped her arms around his neck, her own neck craned to look up into his eyes. She bit her lower lip.

Normally when a naked woman was this close to him, Zach's cock reacted. This time? Nothing.

Nanette fumbled with the buttons on his shirt. Soon his chest was exposed, and she rubbed her breasts into him.

"This feels so good. My nipples get so hard against your chest. I want you so much. I want you to eat my pussy. Would you eat my pussy for me, handsome?"

Few things existed in the universe that Zach enjoyed more than eating a sweet pussy. And Nanette's was quite nice, but today Zach was not interested—at least not in this particular pussy.

What might Lady Sophie look like between her legs? Plump and red and luscious? How might her nectar taste against his tongue? Would she have a beautiful dark-blond bush he could bury his face in? And what would her breasts feel like against his chest? From what he could tell, they were slightly larger than Nanette's. Probably with delicate carnelian nipples begging to be sucked.

Zach loved breasts and nipples almost as much as pussy.

But Sophie's mouth... He didn't have to imagine that perfectly formed piece of art. Her sweet pink lips were just plump enough, just moist enough, and shaped almost like a heart. That kiss had stirred him like no other. Had he been the first to kiss those glossy lips of hers? He was pretty sure he had been, and the thought filled him with a primal joy. His cock stirred.

"There we go. Can little Zachary come out and play?" Nanette fondled him through his trousers.

Why not? He could fuck Nanette and pretend she was Sophie. He frequently fantasized about other women during sex.

Nanette dropped to her knees and began unbuckling his britches. If she meant to suck him, he would have to stop her. He wanted her up against the wall, from behind. If he didn't see her face, he could imagine that her hair was a darker blond and that she was slightly taller. Sophie...

He gently pushed Nanette away and lowered his trousers.

"Place your hands on the wall, Nanette," he ordered.

"But I want to suck your cock, handsome. And then I want you to eat my sweet pussy."

Hell, no. This was a fuck. A fuck with a purpose. A fuck to ease his discomfort and think of that fetching woman whose lips he couldn't get out of his mind.

"No. This way. I want to fuck you up against the wall. Pound my hard cock into you."

Nanette smiled. "I suppose, if you put it that way..." She stood and moved to the wall, bracing her hands against the guilt-edged wallpaper, her legs parted slightly.

Zach moved behind her, his cock at attention. He bent his knees and rubbed it against the wetness of her slit. Yes, she was ready. Nanette was always ready.

As he prepared to plunge into her, he conjured a vision of

Lady Sophie in his mind. Lord, would she ever offer her pussy to him like this? Would he get the chance to make her his?

Make her his? Where had that thought come from? He had never deluded himself that the women he bedded were his. He had no desire to make any of them his.

He backed away from Nanette, his cock already beginning to lose its erection. "I'm sorry, Nanette. I clearly lost my head for a moment, but I meant what I said earlier. It is over between us."

"I don't believe that for a moment." Nanette slapped him across the face.

The smack stung, but it was nothing he hadn't endured before. Nanette was far from the first woman he had offended.

"I am indeed sorry," he said again.

"I suppose this means you no longer want me in your productions."

"To the contrary. I appreciate your talent and would be happy to have you on my stage."

"So I have talent. But I suppose I'm nothing compared to your new protégé, Lady Sophie."

Zach let out a sigh. How could he explain this? "Lady Sophie has a gift."

"And you don't feel I have that gift?"

"You have a lovely voice. You're a good actress and a good singer. But Lady Sophie... It's as if the angels themselves come down from heaven and sing through her."

Nanette shook her head. "Did I really just hear you correctly? What utter nonsense! You want to know what *I* think? I think this 'gift' you speak about is your way to get into her drawers."

"For God's sake, Nanette. Get dressed and get out of here."

Nanette gathered her garments and walked out of the office, still naked.

"Good riddance," Zach said under his breath. He readjusted his britches quickly, pondering. Did Nanette have a point? Was he enamored with Sophie's voice just because he wanted to get beneath her corset? Because he couldn't deny it. He wanted Sophie. Something about her called to him.

Was it her voice? Her voice was angelic, and he did want to help her develop it. He truly did believe he could make her a sensation. But something more tugged at him. She was lovely—lovely in a way more understated than usual. She was a beautiful woman who didn't know she was beautiful. Zach wanted to help her find her beauty and appreciate it.

He had to get her to agree to perform in the musical. It would not only help him and his production and be a gift to all audience members who heard her, but he had the distinct feeling that she needed it.

★ ★ ★ ★

Sophie had no sooner returned to the estate than Ally pounced on her.

"Tell me all about it! How was the audition? How did you find Mr. Newland? Isn't he just magnificent to look at? Were you nervous? What did he say about your singing?"

Sophie drew in a breath. "My goodness, how many questions did you just ask?"

"I counted five. Answer whichever you want first. It's no matter to me." Ally took Sophie's hand and drew her into the parlor. "Now sit here right beside me." Ally pointed to the divan.

Sophie sat—or rather, Sophie collapsed. Her energy was drained. First singing in front of Mr. Newland and others, and then the kiss, and then dealing with that other actress—all of it had sucked the energy right out of her.

"So come on, tell me. How did it go?" Ally patted Sophie's hand.

Sophie opened her mouth to speak but was interrupted by the Brighton butler, Graves, and his apprentice, Bertram.

"I do beg your pardon, my ladies," Graves said, "but a message has been delivered for Lady Sophie."

CHAPTER FOUR

Sophie arched her eyebrows. A message for her? She never got messages. She hadn't had one since Lord Van Arden had broken off their friendship, and even before that, messages from him had been few.

"Yes." Bertram strode forward, his cheeks rosy, and handed her the parchment.

"Thank you, Bertram."

Graves's apprentice had been a footman up until a few weeks prior, when Graves had announced his intention to retire. The Earl of Brighton had conferred with Graves and the other lead servants, and they had decided to groom Bertram to be the new butler. Bertram was shy and awkward, but he was learning quickly.

Graves and Bertram bowed politely and left the parlor, closing the door behind them.

"Whatever could this be?" Sophie broke the seal on the parchment.

"Perhaps you have an admirer." Ally smiled deviously.

Sophie's cheeks warmed as she remembered her kiss with Mr. Newland. Of course, it meant nothing. Mr. Newland only wanted her to sing in the production. "That is highly unlikely." She unfolded the paper and read the message.

You were wonderful today.

"I'm on pins and needles here," Ally said. "Who is it from? What does it say?"

Sophie handed the paper to Ally. "It's not signed."

"That is odd," Ally said. "But someone must have enjoyed your audition. Tell me, how did it go?"

"It went...well, I guess. Cameron said I was brilliant, and Mr. Newland wants me to be the new lead soprano in his company."

Ally shot up from the divan and then clutched at her stomach. "Goodness, I should know better than that."

Sophie stood and guided Ally back down. "Yes, please, remember the child." Sophie sat back down beside her sister.

"But aren't you excited, Sophie? This is your big chance to get off of the estate. To make something of yourself. There is so much more to you than you even know, my dear sister. I hate to think of you wasting away your life just sitting in this house."

"I am quite content with my life, thank you." But was she? The audition *had* thrilled her. Once she got over her nerves and started singing, only she and her voice had existed.

"What exactly are you saying?"

"I'm saying that I refused the post."

Ally's eyes widened into saucers. "You cannot be serious. This is an incredible opportunity for you."

"It's an opportunity that I have no interest in, Ally. I'm quite content with my life the way it is. I don't wish to put myself in the public eye. I'm not meant for that life."

"Sophie, you are meant for more than knitting, crocheting, and singing by yourself in the conservatory. The world has so much to offer you, and more importantly, you have so much to offer the world."

"I just don't know..."

"Don't be ridiculous. Now, who might have sent this note?"

"If I had to guess, I would say Mr. Newland. He was very determined to have me join his company. He even told the present lead soprano, Miss Lloyd, that I would be taking her place. She was not thrilled, to say the least."

"That cheap floozy? Why, you can sing circles around her, and she no doubt knows that. Mr. Newland obviously does."

"That's quite beside the point. I'm not taking the role."

"Oh, yes, you are." Ally's eyes gleamed. "Would you care to make a wager?"

Sophie shook her head, letting out a little chuckle. "Oh, no. I've learned my lesson the hard way. You don't play fair."

"Fair? What is the meaning of fair, anyway? I got you to go to an audition that I knew would be good for you. And it *was* good for you. You proved to Mr. Newland that you have an amazing voice, and he wants you. Seems pretty fair to me."

Sophie opened her mouth to speak but then pressed her lips together. Did Ally have a point? She *had* been gloriously happy on stage. And though she did love her life, it became tedious at times. But the public... If she put herself out there, she could get hurt. And Sophie had endured enough hurt already in her short life. She couldn't bear anymore.

"Don't you have anything to say, Sophie?"

"Ally, you just don't understand. We are two different personalities. You enjoy being flamboyant, being the center of attention. That has never been my desire."

"But your voice, Sophie. It should be shared with the world. *You* should be shared with the world."

Sophie shook her head. "I have no desire to share myself with the world, Ally. I have nothing to give. Father saw to that."

Ally's facial features softened. "Oh, dear, dear Sophie, how I used to think the same of myself. I considered myself broken, which is why I wanted to marry for money and not love. But then I found Evan, and Sophie, I'm not broken. Someone wonderful loves me, and someone wonderful will love you too, if you open yourself to it. Not only that, you have the chance for thousands of people to love you when they hear you singing."

Sophie let out a sigh. If only it were that simple. She was not like Ally. Ally was strong.

Ally continued, "Can't you give it a try? For me?"

Sophie gulped. "You know I would do absolutely anything for you, Ally. I owe you."

"Pishposh, you owe me nothing. It is not for me that I'm asking. It's for you."

Graves entered, Bertram behind him. "Pardon me, my ladies, do you wish for tea this afternoon?"

Sophie nodded. "Yes, Graves, thank you."

Ally turned toward the two men. "Graves, you've known Lady Sophie for a while now. And you've heard her sing in the conservatory."

"Yes, you do have an incredible voice, my lady." Graves adjusted his cravat.

"Don't you feel she should share her voice with others? She could sing at the Regal Theatre in one of Mr. Newland's productions."

Graves cleared his throat. "I'm not sure it's my place to have an opinion on the matter, my lady."

"Actually, Graves, I should like to know what you think," Sophie said.

"May I speak freely, then?"

"Of course. I would appreciate that." Sophie smiled. Graves was such a proper servant.

"To be honest, I've never thought much of young ladies

making a spectacle of themselves in front of an audience. If I may say so, Lady Sophie, you're much too good for that type of endeavor."

"Well"—Ally petted her growing belly—"I don't know what on earth you know about it anyway."

"Now, Ally, that isn't fair," Sophie said. "You asked his opinion. There is no law in England that says everyone has to agree with you."

Ally chuckled. "There should be."

Graves even let out a laugh at that one, though Bertram stood behind him, awkward and cowering.

"Indeed," Graves said, "I did not mean to offend either of you ladies."

"We know that, Graves," Sophie said. "My sister will just have to get over herself."

"Very well, then." Graves turned to leave. "Tea will be served in a few moments."

"It serves you right, Ally," Sophie said. "You see? Not everyone agrees that I should be on the stage."

"Graves is old school, Sophie. He's retiring soon, after all. How old must he be, anyway? Sixty years old? Times have changed. We women have voices now—not as loud as we should be, but things will continue to evolve. This is your chance to give something back to the fairer sex."

"You have faith in me where none is warranted. I have nothing to give."

Ally started to speak, but they were interrupted by two footmen bringing in the tea tray. Sophie poured tea for Ally and herself, and they each took a plate of finger sandwiches.

"Sophie, I—"

Sophie held up her hand to stop her sister. "Please, let's no longer speak of this today. You wouldn't believe how fraught with exhaustion I am after the audition this morning." And after the kiss with Mr. Newland, but Sophie wasn't quite ready to talk about that.

"All right." Ally took a few more sips of her tea and then rose. "If you'll excuse me, dear, I must lie down. Afternoons are so tiring for me in this condition."

"I completely understand," Sophie said.

Ally took leave, and Sophie finished her tea and sandwiches. After the tray had been cleared, she curled up on the divan to read, but soon her eyes fluttered closed.

★ ★ ★ ★

Zach rapped forcefully on the door of Brighton Manor.

The door opened. An older gentleman said, "Yes, sir, may I be of assistance?"

"Yes, if you please," Zach said. "I'm here to call upon Lady Sophie."

"I will see if she is receiving guests. Your name, sir?"

"Zachary Newland."

"Yes, the actor. You work with Lord Thornton at the theatre. Do come in, and I will see if Lady Sophie is available."

Zach paced the marble hallway for a few moments until the butler returned.

"Lady Sophie will receive you. Please follow me to the parlor."

Zach's heels clicked upon the marble flooring until they came to a door, which presumably led to the parlor. The butler opened the door, and there sat Sophie, perched on a divan along the back wall.

She looked like an angel, those pink lips slightly moist, her cheeks that bewitching raspberry. His groin tightened.

"My lady," Zach said. "Thank you for receiving me."

"You're quite welcome." Sophie nodded to the butler. "Thank you, Graves."

The gentleman left the room and closed the door behind him.

"What is it that I can do for you, Mr. Newland?"

"You no doubt already know why I am here, my lady. I must have you for my new production. Now that I've heard you sing, I can't imagine this role being played by anyone but you. You did know that your cousin-in-law, Lord Thornton, wrote the music?"

"Yes." Sophie nodded. "And I do adore his work. He is a gifted composer."

"I couldn't agree more, and only your voice will do his music justice."

"Mr. Newland, I—"

"Yes, my lady, I know exactly what you're going to say. But before you say it, might I persuade you to take a late-afternoon walk with me? You could show me around your estate. I have not visited the Brighton estate before."

"I see no reason for us to go walking, sir," Sophie said. "It would be quite improper without a chaperone, as you well know. Plus, I will not change my mind about appearing in the production."

"My lady, I hope I don't offend, but a woman of your... age...no longer requires a chaperone."

Sophie's cheeks reddened further. Zach wished he could bite back his words. What had he been thinking? He didn't want to insult the lady. In fact, at the moment, all he could think about was undressing her. But that was not the reason for wanting to walk about the estate with her. If he could get her outside, show her the wonders of creation, perhaps she would agree to share her voice with the world.

"Please, my lady, I meant no offense. All I ask is an hour of your time on this late afternoon. Allow me this one chance to try to persuade you to sing for me."

Sophie rose. Oh, how he wanted her. That a woman so fetching could know nothing of her charms confounded Zach. Those lips, those raspberry cheeks, the radiant hazel eyes laced with green and gold...

He walked slowly toward her, his feet moving independently. When he reached her, he cupped those berry cheeks, bringing his own head down and pressing his lips to hers.

CHAPTER FIVE

Oh, the pleasure... His kisses... After this morning, she had never dreamed she would experience another one. She parted her lips eagerly this time, her body taking over. His tongue twirled with hers, and she tingled all over. Her nipples tightened against her corset. They were so hard she felt for sure he could feel them as she pressed against his chest.

Dear God... Difficult to get her breath... She was...going... to...

Had to break away... Couldn't breathe...

As if he had read her mind, he ripped his lips from hers and trailed tiny kisses across her cheek to her earlobe. He bit and sucked the small lobe into his mouth, and Sophie's knees nearly gave way.

Sophie gasped for air. Such sensation... Truly... *This is why Ally let all those gentlemen take liberties...* She let out a sigh.

"Do you like that, sweet? Does it feel good to have my lips upon you?"

Sophie couldn't find her voice. *Yes, yes!* she shouted inside her head.

"Tell me, sweet Sophie, how does it feel when I kiss you?"

Again, she was without words. After all, words had limitations. How on earth could she describe the ethereal feelings flowing through her? She knew only one way to show her true emotions—through singing.

"Tell me," Zach whispered in her ear, "do you enjoy kissing

me as much as I enjoy kissing you?"

"Yes," she murmured. "Oh, yes."

Zach backed away from her slightly and looked into her eyes, burning two holes in her with his bronze gaze.

"Let us walk together. Show me your estate, and perhaps I can convince you what a grand experience it would be to sing on stage with me."

Sophie swallowed a lump in her throat and nodded. She would walk with him. After all, they would be outside in full view of anyone on the estate, so she didn't have to worry about him taking more liberties. And what was the harm in spending time with a man who intrigued her? If she asked her sister, Ally would say there was no harm at all.

"Yes, Mr. Newland, I shall walk with you."

★ ★ ★ ★

They walked about the estate, Mr. Newland educating her on the theatre and how he got his start in acting. He'd offered Cameron a job a year ago as the house composer. Cameron, like her, was self-taught, having grown up poor as Sophie had. The stories fascinated Sophie. Mr. Newland himself was a self-made man, having gained a benefactress in Cameron's great-grandmother, the dowager Marchioness of Denbigh.

"Did you..." Sophie warmed all over, embarrassed by the question she couldn't help asking. "With the marchioness...?"

Mr. Newland chuckled. "No, no. She was in her early sixties at that time, and I was a mere lad of nineteen. She didn't expect it or ask for it. Some benefactors do expect, shall we say, benefits, but most don't. Most people do it out of the goodness of their hearts."

"I see." Sophie looked down. Her shoes were scuffed with dirt. Drat, she'd have to have Hannah clean them.

Soon they came to a secluded area, one of Sophie's favorite places on the estate. Often she wandered out to the little area to read or sing or just be alone.

"What is this place?" Mr. Newland asked.

"Just a little alcove. I come here often. No one ever bothers me here. It's private from the servants."

"Would you mind showing it to me?"

Sophie had a brain. She might be naïve and untried, but she knew if she took Mr. Newland into the alcove, he would kiss her again. She should turn around, walk away, go back to the estate, and tell him in no uncertain terms that she was not that kind of woman—no matter that her body was telling her to drag him into the alcove and kiss him senseless.

"It would not be proper, I'm afraid. I hope I haven't given you the wrong impression, Mr. Newland, but I'm not at all—"

"Sophie"—he locked his brown gaze on hers—"please."

Her skin rippled. Those eyes... She floated into them, losing herself. "Mr. Newland..."

He smiled—a dazzling smile. No wonder he captivated his audiences. "I do wish you would use my given name. Zach."

"It would not be proper."

"Who's to say what is proper? Is this proper?" He clamped his lips over hers.

Again, Sophie's legs threatened to collapse beneath her, but Mr. Newland—Zach—held her fast. He ate at her mouth, giving, taking, kissing her with a passion she had never known existed. When they both were nearly devoid of breath, Zach broke the kiss.

"The alcove, Sophie. Now."

In a pink haze, Sophie led him into the secluded area. The grass was soft as moss under them as he pulled her down onto it. He kissed her again, sucking at her lips, her neck, what was exposed of her shoulder.

"Your skin is so soft, Sophie. I want to touch every inch of it, feel it under my fingers, under my tongue."

He turned her around and deftly unbuttoned the back of her gown. She stood, petrified, powerless to stop him. Icy fear coursed through her, but no words escaped her lips. Part of her wanted this, wanted him.

Once he had finished with her dress, he gently brushed it over her shoulders until it landed in a dark heap on the grassy floor. He turned her around. Her bosom swelled over the tightness of her corset.

"My God, you're lovely." He kissed her décolleté, the rounded tops of her bosom.

She shuddered. No man had ever seen this part of her, let alone touched it and kissed it. Boiling honey surged through her veins. She should stop him. But the cold hard fact was...she didn't want to.

Everywhere his lips touched, a trail of fiery sparks followed. He kissed her shoulders, her upper arms, and then back to the tops of her breasts.

He inhaled. "You smell heavenly. Like mulled wine, spicy. And vanilla."

Her breath came in rapid puffs against the top of his head. Surely she would swoon any moment.

"Please, Sophie, may I loosen your corset?"

She couldn't speak. But she nodded. She was defenseless, paralyzed.

He smiled and then turned her around again. He deftly

loosened her corset and removed it, leaving her in her chemise and drawers. He turned her toward him and brushed the filmy chemise off her shoulders until it landed in a plop on top of her gown and petticoats.

There she stood, her breasts exposed to his gaze. Would she please him?

The blaze in his green eyes indicated she did.

"So beautiful." He cupped her breasts and ran his thumb over the tips of her nipples.

She gasped. A jolt shot straight to that foreign place between her legs. Her nipples ached, and her forbidden heat throbbed.

Yes, this was what Ally, Lily, and Rose had experienced, why they hadn't been able to resist. This was bliss. Pure bliss.

"Such sweet pink nipples." Zach gazed up at her, continuing to rub her erect buds. "Do you have any idea how beautiful you are?"

Sophie looked down, unable to meet his fiery eyes. Ally was beautiful. Lily and Rose were beautiful. She, Sophie, was merely acceptable.

"Look at me, Sophie." Zach tipped her chin so that her eyes met his. "Look at me and tell me you're beautiful."

Sophie hadn't thought her skin could heat further, but it did. She could not say the words. They were untrue. She was not beautiful. She was not desirable. She was nothing. Her father had seen to that. She shook her head, casting her gaze downward again.

And again, he tipped her chin upward. "It's a disgrace that someone so beautiful has no idea how beautiful she is. Will you let me show you, Sophie? Will you let me show you how beautiful I find you?"

Before she could answer, he bent down and took one pink nipple between his lips.

And she thought she had experienced bliss before... Every new pleasure he showed her opened up new feelings inside her, like a flower blooming in the sun. As he sucked the first nipple, he fingered the other one and then gave it a tiny pinch.

"Oh!" The lightning went straight to her core.

She knew about the sexual act, and she couldn't imagine that it could top what she had experienced so far. The kisses, his mouth and his hands on her nipples... What could be better than this? He was consuming her bit by bit, and she didn't care. She wanted to be consumed. She wanted to be consumed until she was a part of him and no part of Sophie remained.

Yes, no part of Sophie remaining. That was what she truly wanted. If she could only meld into Zach, become part of him, perhaps she would like herself more, be able to respect herself.

Zach continued to nibble at her nipples. She arched her back, mentally forcing him closer to her. Oh, the joy, the ecstasy. How could anything be better?

In a flash, Zach had gently pushed her onto the soft grass. He hovered above her, piercing her eyes with his own. Had a more handsome man ever been created? One auburn curl fell off of his forehead, and she resisted the urge to reach for it.

"You are delicious, Sophie. So very luscious." He trailed his fingers down her arm, across her abdomen, and then reached into her drawers.

Sophie gasped.

Zach nodded his head slowly. "Please, sweet, let me."

The softness of his finger against the most private part of her shocked and enlightened her. Her skin bristled and tightened, and lightning flashed between her legs.

"You are so wet. So wet for me."

Wet? What did he mean by that? She would need to talk to Ally later. Right now, she was overwhelmed with feeling, emotion, sensation. And then her breath caught as something slid inside of her most private place.

"Just a finger, love. Don't you worry. Your maidenhead is still intact. Please, let me pleasure you this way."

Sophie faded into the grass, becoming one with her surroundings. Yes, yes, this was it. No more Sophie, just the pleasure, just the marvelous torment. This was what she wanted... What she needed.

Slowly Zach slid his finger in and out of her while something else—was it his thumb?—teased a tight bundle of nerves at her center.

"Oh, my!" Although she lay still, her hips were moving of their own accord, reaching, running, wanting something more than anything else... What was it? What was she running toward? Her body yearned for something... Just out of reach... Just out of—

Holiness! Something inside her shattered, and tiny sparks started at her sexual center and radiated outward through every nerve ending to her skin, where she tingled all over. She was airborne, even though her body was still melted into the ground. She soared higher, higher, higher, reaching the precipice.

Oh, yes, holiness. Anything this beautiful and amazing had to be holy, didn't it?

What on earth had happened to her? She stretched, grasped, tried to seize the awareness and make it last. She held on, gripped the grass at her side, wanting more, more, more...

"Yes, yes, Sophie, that's it. Come for me. Come all over my

hand."

Come? Zach's words didn't make sense. But at the moment, she didn't care. She wanted to hold on to this sensation as long as she could.

She continued to climb, fly, spread her wings...

When she finally began to float downward, Zach was still caressing her most private place, murmuring words of comfort to her.

"That's it, my love. That's it."

Sophie smiled, completely sated, completely one with the earth beneath her. Though her eyes were closed, vibrant colors danced against her eyelids, and an ethereal sense of peace consumed her, unlike anything she'd ever experienced.

When she finally opened her eyes, Zach sat beside her, looking down at her, his eyes dancing.

"You're so beautiful, Sophie."

Suddenly, embarrassment overwhelmed her. She was lying here in nothing but her drawers, and his fingers had been beneath them. She sat up quickly and covered her breasts with her arms.

"A shame to cover such beauty," Zach said, smiling.

"My goodness," Sophie said, "I have no idea what's gotten into me. Why did I let you...? Why did I...?"

"I'm afraid I can't answer that, sweet, but I'm very glad you did. I thoroughly enjoyed myself. Did you?"

"Why... A lady wouldn't... I...I shouldn't say..."

"It's perfectly natural for a woman to enjoy such encounters."

"That is what my sister always says..."

"Your sister happens to be correct. Now tell me, Sophie love, did you enjoy yourself?"

"I...I cannot say that..."

Zach grabbed her, turned her over his knee, and landed a smack on her bottom. "My lady, for every lie you tell me, I will give this charming rump of yours a slap."

Sophie cried out, more from shock than pain. What was he doing? A jolt of energy rushed through her, surprising her even more. This was far from the first swat on her bottom she'd ever received, but... The others had been courtesy of a man she despised, a man who'd wanted to hurt her. But this? A handsome and kind man who had just shown her pleasure beyond reality was the perpetrator. It felt different, too. Oh, yes, it stung as any slap would, but the sting was oddly... pleasurable?

What on earth was she doing? Letting a man she hardly knew kiss her, touch her intimately, and now...spank her? Before she could voice her disapproval, his palm came down on her bottom once more.

And once more, energy coursed through her, culminating in that secret spot between her legs that was still sensitive and pulsating.

"Sir," she said, "I have not lied to you. I do not lie."

"Oh, my lady, but you did. You experienced a climax, and there is no woman in the world who doesn't enjoy a climax."

Climax? She would ask Ally about that. Whatever it was, she had enjoyed it—had reveled in it, actually—but a lady wouldn't admit to such things.

"No, of course I didn't enjoy any of this."

Slap! Another spank on her bottom, and oh, the sting, the pleasure, the pain... Tiny little convulsions launched between her legs... Could it be? Not the... Oh, yes! She soared again, spiraling out of control! Such a heady sensation! What was happening to her?

"My dear Sophie, you are a rare treasure indeed—the voice of an angel, and a woman so responsive to my every touch. You are something special."

As she came down from her high, she processed Zach's words. Special? She was far from special. A rare treasure? Zach Newland had obviously gone dotty.

"Let me up, please."

Zach helped her into a sitting position. "Absolutely, my dear. I will never make you do anything you don't want to do."

"Then why do you persist in asking me to sing on your stage?" Sophie asked, hastily pulling her chemise over her exposed skin.

He smiled, a gleam in his eye. "A fair question. I keep asking because you auditioned for me. And the fact that you auditioned means singing is something you want to do."

"I auditioned because I lost a bet with my conniving younger sister."

"Lady Xavier? Yes, I know of her. Quite the beauty."

Sophie nodded. So much more striking than she would ever be.

"However," Zach continued, "I find you infinitely more beautiful."

Sophie rose and fiddled with her corset. "You smacked my bottom when I lied to you. Should I smack yours now?"

Zach let out a laugh. "I might enjoy that, actually. However, whatever makes you think I'm lying to you?"

"Ally is far more beautiful than I. You *must* be lying."

"Beauty is in the eye of the beholder, sweet, and as I behold you, I see beauty as infinite as the stars in the sky."

Sophie warmed all over, turning her back to Zach so he

couldn't see her blushing. "Could you please help me with my corset?"

Zach stood. "Of course, though I must say you're far more enchanting out of it."

Quite the charmer, this one. Quite the fabricator as well. Once her corset was tightened, Zach helped her into her gown and buttoned it up in the back.

She said little as he walked her back to the house. What had gotten into her? Zach Newland was no gentleman. She would never be alone with him again. And she certainly wouldn't sing in his production.

How could she have been so self-indulgent? And how could she have let herself be so aroused? Gratified? A lady wouldn't...

No use crying over a broken teacup. It had happened.

But it could never happen again.

★ ★ ★ ★

After a brief nap before supper, Sophie strolled to the library of the Brighton estate. Ally was still resting, and Sophie didn't want to disturb her because of her condition. However, Ally had told Sophie many times about all the reading she had done...about...

Gracious, Sophie. You were just nearly nude in front of a man, and you can't even think the words to yourself?

Well, she didn't have to actually think the words to find the books, did she? The Brighton library was vast, and Sophie hadn't ventured into it often—only when she wanted a new novel to read. She read mostly from her own private collection of novels, and occasionally she would borrow from Ally, Lily, or

Rose. She adored having her nose in a book, and she frequently reread her favorites.

Where to begin? This room was wall-to-wall books, literally. She inhaled. The crisp scent of parchment and the rich aroma of leather bindings wafted toward her. Burgundy brocade chairs sat in each corner, flanked by tables and lamps. She drew a match and lit a lamp.

Where exactly did one look to find books on...those words she couldn't bring herself to form in her mind?

Novels... Yes, she knew where those were, as she had borrowed some previously. Books of history, religion, philosophy... Giant leather-bound tomes filled the shelves. However, those weren't what she was looking for. Biographies... Memoirs... A giant book of maps—an atlas... All fascinating, but not what she needed.

The sciences—botany, chemistry, zoology... Human anatomy... That might be a start. She grabbed the book off the shelf and began perusing it, finding only graphic depictions of the circulatory system and skeletal system. No, clearly not what she had in mind.

Yes! A book sat just out of her reach on one of the higher shelves, but she could read its spine. *An Introduction to the Marriage Bed* by Lady Margaret Mead. Sophie stretched, standing on tiptoes—

"Oh!" She lost her footing and fell.

CHAPTER SIX

"My lady!" One of the downstairs maids hovered above Sophie. "I was walking by, and I heard you take a fall. Are you all right? Can you get up?"

Sophie gathered her wits. "Yes, I'm fine. Thank you for asking. I'm afraid it's my own clumsiness. I was trying to reach a—" She could say no more. She couldn't very well admit which book she'd been reaching for. Of course, this maid was taller than she and perhaps could...

No. Absolutely not. Gossip among the servants traveled faster than the rail.

"Were you trying to reach a book, my lady? Perhaps I could help."

"Oh, no. Thank you for your offer, but I am no longer interested in reading material this afternoon. Do be on your way now."

The maid curtsied politely and left.

Should she try again? Why not? Sophie grasped the shelf for support this time, stretched upon her toes, and grabbed the book from the shelf. Now, how to get it to her chamber without anyone seeing her? Ally was still abed, and she didn't know where Evan was. Her mother and the earl had gone out for the day although they would be returning soon. If only she had a shawl with her to hide the book in.

Well, it couldn't be helped. She'd have to put the book back. As she stepped toward the shelf to return it, she dared to open it in the middle.

The sage wife will permit no more than one or two sexual experiences per week. Little by little, she should make every effort to reduce this frequency. A wife should not allow her husband liberties at all during the week of her courses.

Confusion muddled Sophie's brain. Sexual activity should be reduced? But Ally, Rose, and Lily seemed to like it so much. In fact, Ally had told Sophie many times that women had just as many desires as men. Was Ally mistaken? Or was Lady Margaret Mead?

Sophie closed the book and hugged it to her chest. She had to read more. She stole out of the library and down the hallway to the servants' staircase. As quietly as she could, she ascended and walked swiftly until she finally reached her own chamber on the second level. She silently closed her door and flopped onto her bed.

The book sat next to her, beckoning. Each time she reached for it, she drew her hand away quickly, frightened.

Oh, for goodness' sake, Sophie. It's a book. Just a book.

She opened it to the first page.

If you are reading this book, may I congratulate you on finding a husband. You have begun fulfilling your ultimate duty as a woman. Your duty now is to serve your husband, bear his children, and raise them. Your sole reason for existence revolves around this new man in your life. His needs are now your needs, his goals your goals, his likes and dislikes are your likes and dislikes.

The marriage bed is, unfortunately, now a part of your life. Do not delude yourself into thinking it enjoyable. Perhaps some women find it such, but most do not. But you must succumb to your husband's baser desires. To understand the male human, think of animals copulating in the wild. The male human is not unlike his creature counterparts. He has urges, urges that must be met or he will become violent. While you may have been lucky enough to find a man who is gentle in most areas of his life, he may not be gentle in the marriage bed. You must lie back and allow him to do as he wishes, especially this first night. Get through it by hoping that he gives you a child. Once you are with child, he will most likely sate his desires elsewhere until you have given birth.

Sophie shook her head, confounded. This sounded nothing like what Ally talked about. And what in the world was that phenomenon that had happened to Sophie today in the alcove—with feelings so intense and pleasurable she thought she must be drifting into the heavens?

She closed the book. She would wait and talk to her sister. Perhaps Ally could show her some of the books she had read.

She startled at a knock on her door. Quickly, Sophie threw the book under her bed and then casually—or so she hoped—walked to the door and opened it.

Her maid, Hannah, stood there. "Supper is served in ten minutes, my lady."

"Very well. Thank you, Hannah."

Sophie was far from hungry. Her body was... She couldn't find the words. Perhaps Ally would be at dinner. Of course, their parents and Evan would also be there—not the opportune time to speak of what she needed to speak of.

She descended and joined her family for dinner.

★ ★ ★ ★

"So have you all heard the good news?" Ally asked.

"And what good news would that be?" Her husband, Evan, cocked his head.

"Yes, by all means, Ally, tell us," the girls' mother, Iris, the Countess Brighton, said, smiling.

Sophie groaned inaudibly. She knew exactly what was coming.

"Our own Sophie auditioned for Mr. Zachary Newland for his upcoming musicale, which was written by our esteemed cousin, the Earl of Thornton. Mr. Newland was so impressed, he wants to make Sophie his new lead soprano."

Evan smiled broadly. "Why, Sophie, that's excellent news. I've always wondered why you keep your angelic voice to yourself."

"Indeed," the earl said. "Congratulations to you."

Iris simply smiled, nodding.

"When do you begin rehearsals?" Evan asked.

Sophie swallowed a mouthful of potage. "I don't."

"What do you mean?" Iris asked.

Sophie opened her mouth to respond, but Ally was quicker.

"Sophie doesn't want to take the post. She wants to give up this amazing opportunity."

"Ally, I'm still a lady of the peerage, and I shouldn't be singing for an audience."

"I agree," Iris said. "Of course, if it were something you

wanted to do, Sophie, I would support you. But as it's not, I think, Ally, that we need to support Sophie's decision."

"Evan, you agree with me, don't you?" Ally batted her eyes at her husband.

"I think Sophie would be wonderful, but I'm sorry, love. I have to agree with your mother that it's her decision. Not yours, and not mine."

Sophie gulped. "Thank you, Evan."

Ally pressed her napkin to her lips. "Sophie, you sit in the house all day. Don't you want something more? Wouldn't it bring joy into your life to know you are bringing joy into others' lives with song?"

"Ally, I would faint away on that stage, and you know it. Performing is simply not in my nature."

"You're being silly. You made it through the audition, and Cameron said you were brilliant."

"I nearly lost my breakfast during that audition," Sophie said. "If I have to feel that way every time I get on stage, I may starve to death."

"Don't be so melodramatic," Ally said.

Sophie ignored her sister and continued with her dinner, saying little. Part of her—a part of her she hadn't known existed until a few hours ago—longed to take the role. She had taken a risk this afternoon, and she had found pleasure unlike she'd ever imagined.

"Goodness, Sophie, you're blushing," Ally said. "What is there to be embarrassed about now? You got through the audition."

Sophie locked her gaze on the second course the footman set in front of her—salmon croquettes, one of her favorites. Yet she had no desire to eat. The warmth in her cheeks rapidly spread to her neck.

"Leave her alone, Ally," Evan scolded. "Let her eat in peace."

Conversation rambled on around Sophie, but she didn't join in. This day had turned into a conundrum. She'd auditioned for a musicale, gotten her first kiss from a man, and then let that same man molest her in broad daylight!

All very out of character for her. Who was Sophie now?

She did love singing, and if her voice could bring joy to others... But dear Lord, she would be ill every time she went on stage.

But being on stage... When she'd finally started singing, nearly forgetting anyone was watching her, and then the thunderous applause that followed—all of that had been truly heaven.

When supper had finally concluded, Sophie did not retire to the porch for tea with her mother and sister. Instead, she went back to the library. Surely she could find another book. Ally had told her of volumes that spoke of a woman's sexual desire, and the book about the marriage bed certainly did no such thing.

Sophie slowly perused the books again, taking in each one in the sciences section. Finally, she found one with promise. *Physiological Mysteries and Revelations in Love, Courtship, and Marriage* by Eugène Becklard. Perhaps this would be more interesting. She grabbed the book off the shelf, nearly losing her footing once again, wrapped it tightly in her arms, and stole up the back stairway to her chamber.

She sat down on her bed, opened the book, and began to read.

Chapter One

Must man be born of a woman?

Indeed not. Adrastus contends that every living species the world contains has been from all eternity; and hence, that the time has never been when there was no man or woman; so that, according to his system, the human race cannot be the offspring of one general mother. And he further insists that the meanest reptile that crawls, is the representative of an equally everlasting line of ancestry. The last assumption, however has been set at nought by experiments in modern chemistry, though without showing the necessity of original parents for they not only argue that living animals of perfectly original construction may be produced at pleasure, and independent of the usual modes of generation; but they have actually so produced them.

That was about as clear as tar. And who was Adrastus? The author couldn't be referring to the legendary king of Argos, could he?

Sophie flicked through the book quickly, looking for something, anything, to help her understand the physiology of men and women and their love. She stopped when the word "childbearing" caught her eye.

Period of Child-bearing.—Women may be ten, eleven, and even twelve months in a certain condition, the ignorance whereof, causes much domestic trouble, and has occasionally been the means of divorces. On the contrary, full grown children may be born in the seventh month after conception, and some say in the sixth, or even less, but I doubt them. At least, out of all my experience, I never had personal knowledge of a case of the sort, but one, and then I had my suspicions, grounded on various circumstances, apart from the main one, which were rather unfavorable to the lady's character. The law, which rarely, if ever, suffers itself to be guided by exceptions, holds it a proof of illegitimacy if the period of child birth is delayed until the tenth month after the husband and wife have lived together.

Even she wasn't so naïve to think a human pregnancy lasted anything other than about nine months. Those who came early were most likely conceived out of wedlock, and those who came late were most likely the result of a feigned pregnancy.

Still no help. She continued leafing through the book.

Marriage and Poetry.—Marriage blunts the imagination. A married writer of fiction must hold Hymen in check, or weary his readers; and poetry is almost irreconcilable with the state of wedlock. Schiller observes, that one cannot woo his wife and the muses; and there is, no doubt, much philosophy in the assumption. Thus it would seem that poetry is the escape of love when not otherwise directed.

Marriage blunts the imagination? This man was making marriage sound terrible. Sophie continued reading.

Ideas of Beauty.—Men of poetical or sanguine temperament prefer the beauty of the face. Those of stronger animal propensities, the beauty of form. The latter make the most attentive husbands, as they are most content with the realities in life.

Beauty of face? Of form? Sophie sighed. Ally had both. Sophie, though, was plain, in face and in form. Her hair was a dull gold as opposed to Ally's lustrous chestnut brown. And her body? Ally was tall, with curves in all the right places and a voluptuous bosom. Sophie was shorter, her breasts not nearly as large, and her figure lean, not curvy.

If what this book said was true, no man would want her.

Violation.—Conception cannot take place under feelings of horror or disgust. Hence, no woman ever became pregnant from a rape committed on her against her inclination.

Odd, that statement. Sophie knew of women who had become pregnant after forced encounters. Did this mean that those women had actually wanted the encounter? This man had written it, and although she knew nothing of his qualifications, the book had been published. She would have to ask Ally about that.

Matrimonial Regret.—Men are liable to regret their marriage on the morning after its consummation, and to sigh for the freedom they have lost. But this is only an evanescent feeling, partially attributable to the fact, that, at the commencement the realities of love are usually found to be unequal to the anticipations. A week corrects this uneasiness, and contentment mostly occurs before the end of the honey moon.

Matrimonial regret... Why did men marry if they were going to regret it afterward? Was it possible for women to regret marriage also?

Transfer of Passion.—Love is partially the effect of mental, but more so of physical feeling. This is especially the case with men; and hence, when they despair of the consummation of one passion, they can always relieve it, or escape from it altogether, by nourishing another.

Physical feeling? Physical feeling had dominated Sophie's afternoon with Mr. Newland. Did this mean she was falling in love with him? This book was not answering any of her questions. In fact, it was only giving her new ones.

Longing for Marriage.—Young unmarried ladies, from the time they arrive at the age of puberty, think and talk about little besides love, and its attributes. Young men, however, though they have other objects of pursuit, are more carried away by the passion. When crossed in love, a woman becomes melancholy, a man insane.

Sophie had no disagreement there. She'd been longing for marriage forever, even coming from a home where her only example of marriage was abusive and intolerable. Resigning herself to spinsterhood had taken a lot of strength. Now, after she'd accepted it, along came Mr. Newland.

She closed the book, and then, on a whim, opened it again in the middle.

Many physicians of high authority have maintained, that two-thirds of the diseases to which the human race is liable, have had their origin in certain solitary practices; or to call things by their proper names—for I wish to make myself, thoroughly understood, so that I may not weaken the effect of what I am about to say, by catering to an affectation of false modesty— in onanism and masterbation. Some writers use the terms synonymously; others apply the first to the act in males, and the latter in females; and for the sake of perspicuity I shall follow the second rule. I say that many physicians of high authority have maintained, that two-thirds of the diseases to which the human race is liable, have had their origin in these habits. I cannot go so far as this; but I am convinced that they entail great calamities on all who indulge in them to excess, and that consumption, impotence, and lunacy, are among their fearful effects.

Oh, she could read no more! How horrid that people might...*touch* themselves and, in so doing, destroy themselves.

She was now more confused than ever. Her mind was jumbled. Monsieur Becklard was certainly no help. She wanted to go back to the library to see if she could find a more helpful volume, but fatigue had descended upon her. This day had been...consuming.

As she prepared to summon her maid to help her ready for slumber, a knock sounded on her door.

CHAPTER SEVEN

Sophie opened the door to find Hannah standing there.

"Hannah, dear, I was just about to summon you. I wish to get ready for bed."

Hannah curtsied. "Of course, my lady, but I was coming to tell you that a message has been delivered for you." The maid held out a parchment.

Another message? Two in one day? Very odd. "Thank you very much." Sophie tore open the parchment.

You will be mine.

She widened her eyes, and her pulse quickened.

"Is anything wrong, my lady?" Hannah asked.

Sophie shook her head, biting her lip. "No, no. Nothing." She folded the parchment and laid it on her night table. Most likely it was Mr. Newland—Zach—indicating his hope that she would take the role in the musicale. No need to worry, despite the hairs on her forearms standing on end.

"Hannah, please prepare me a bath."

★ ★ ★ ★

The next morning, Sophie breathed a relieved sigh to find Ally in the parlor taking a light breakfast.

"Where are Mother and the earl this morning? And Evan?" she asked.

Ally stopped munching on her scone and swallowed.

"Evan and the earl had business to attend to early this morning, and Mother has decided to sleep late. I was planning the same thing, but Junior here kicked me until I woke up." Ally petted her belly.

Sophie smiled. "Only about a month and a half to go now. Are you still hoping for a little boy?"

"Well, Evan doesn't have a title to pass to a son, so it doesn't rightly matter what I have. I just want a healthy baby, but I know Evan would adore having a son, so for him, I'm hoping for a boy."

"If I know Evan, he'll be happy with a healthy baby as well," Sophie said.

Ally smiled. "You're probably right."

Sophie's cheeks warmed as she gathered her courage to ask Ally the questions she'd been thinking about since yesterday. She was more confused than ever after reading those excerpts from Monsieur Becklard's book.

"Ally..."

Ally looked up, continuing to chew on her scone.

"I was wondering...if I could ask you...a few things."

Ally swallowed again. "Of course."

"Well, before you and Evan married, you told me once that you had done a lot of...reading."

Ally's golden eyes gleamed. "Dear Sophie, are you finally blossoming?"

"Blossoming? What are you talking about?"

"The stirrings, my dear. Has a young man caught your fancy?"

Sophie blazed with heat. Yes, a certain man had caught her fancy—and had undressed her yesterday in a hidden alcove on this very estate. Not only that, he had breached her private place, and he had smacked her bum. She heated even further at the memory of those stinging little slaps.

"I have no stirrings, Ally. I am merely curious."

"What do you wish to know?"

"You know I've resigned myself to spinsterhood."

"Pishposh. You just haven't met the right gentleman yet. He will come along."

Perhaps he had already. "Ally, I'm four-and-twenty years old. Everyone knows the prime time for marriage for women is ages nineteen to twenty-five. I'm nearly too old already."

"For goodness' sake, where did you get such an antiquated idea?"

"From a book I found in the library—Monsieur Becklard's *Physiology*...or some such."

She remembered well the passage:

The proper age to marry, all the world over, is between twenty-five and thirty for men, and nineteen and twenty-five for women; and in fact, previous to the ages of twenty-five and nineteen they are, as a general rule, inadequate to the requirements of matrimonial intercourse.

"Becklard? That French fool? Why, that book is complete rubbish."

"You've read it?"

"Yes, a couple of years ago. I found a copy at the duke's estate. I couldn't believe what I was reading, but then I found other treatises that were much more accurate."

"Treatises? Which ones?"

Ally giggled. "Not so much treatises as...*literature*."

"Literature? I don't understand."

Ally smiled a devilish smile. "Come to my chamber after breakfast, and I shall show you."

Sophie's cheeks heated. "Can't you just answer my questions, Ally? I'm not comfortable reading this type of... literature."

"I'm certainly happy to do what I can. What questions do you have?"

"Well, I'm not exactly sure how to ask this..." Lord, she wanted to disappear.

"Go right ahead, dear. I used to write for an erotic magazine, remember? Chances are I will have the answers you seek."

Her sister was no doubt right. Sophie took a deep breath and let it out slowly. "Something happened to me—something that is very difficult to explain. I...felt like I was flying. Yet I felt one with the earth as well. A contradictory feeling, but an intense pleasure that...I can't adequately describe."

Ally clasped her hand to her mouth and gasped. "Sophie, are you saying you had a climax?"

"Is that the word for it? I'm afraid I just don't know what happened."

"It certainly sounds like a climax to me. How did it happen? Did you just stumble upon the right spot while you were...touching yourself?"

Sophie wilted, unable to speak. She was going to die an untimely death right here in the breakfast room.

"Was it with a man?" Ally smiled.

Sophie closed her eyes, still unable to force words from her throat.

"Don't tell me it was with a woman, although your maid is quite pretty."

Sophie's eyes flew open, and she inhaled a loud gasp. "Of course not with a woman. How could you even think such a thing?"

"There are some people who prefer the company of those of their own gender."

"I will assure you I am not one of those people." Though the thought was intriguing. Women were beautiful, and she appreciated their beauty... Goodness, she could not let that thought continue.

"Well, you obviously haven't been with a man, so I can only infer that you were touching yourself."

"Oh, my, no! Why, Monsieur Becklard's book says that can lead to all sorts of dangerous diseases."

"Sophie, dear, did I not just tell you that book is pure refuse?"

"Yes, but you must understand. It's all that I've read, other than a book on the marriage bed."

"That drivel by Lady Margaret Mead? She thinks all men are perverted creatures who constantly have sexual acts on the brain."

Sophie squirmed. "Don't they?"

Ally let out a guffaw, clutching her belly. "Well, yes, they do."

Sophie couldn't help smiling. The male was fascinating. Especially one as handsome, talented, and interesting as Mr. Newland—Zach.

"Tell me now, how did you come about to have your climax?"

Sophie dropped her gaze to the napkin in her lap. "This is absolutely embarrassing..."

"Sophie, we're sisters, the closest two people can be other

than husband and wife. You have nothing to be embarrassed about in front of me. After all, we survived a horribly abusive childhood together. Nothing could be worse than that. Especially not something that feels so good."

Ally did have a point. Still, Sophie had to will the words out of her mouth. "I've never been one to allow liberties, but Mr. Newland...er...Zach...accompanied me on a walk yesterday afternoon. We came to the secluded alcove where I enjoy reading or just relaxing, and then..."

Ally smiled impishly. "And then what?"

Sophie let out a breath of air that she hadn't realized she'd been holding. "He kissed me. And it was not our first kiss."

"What?" Ally's eyes turned into saucers. "You had kissed him before?"

"Yes, after my audition. I'm not quite sure how it happened, Ally, but it was...enjoyable."

"Enjoyable? Your first kiss? If it was merely enjoyable, you definitely need to experience more."

Sophie warmed at the lie she had just told. The kiss had been way more than simply enjoyable. It had been thrilling, heavenly, more than she'd ever anticipated it might be. Just the memory made her glow—at least she felt as if she were glowing on the inside. She opened her mouth to say so, but Ally continued speaking.

"My dear, it must've been more than enjoyable if you allowed him further liberties in the alcove."

Shuddering, Sophie nodded. "It was more thrilling than I could ever have imagined."

"Tell me what happened in the alcove, then."

"It started with more kissing, even more rapturous than our previous kissing, and then he...began to undress me."

"And?"

Sophie fidgeted with her napkin, kneading the linen with her fingers. Her nipples tightened and her core throbbed. Would Ally be able to tell she was aroused? "I knew I shouldn't be doing it. I knew I should stop him. But God help me, I didn't want to. I wanted him to undress me. I wanted him to see me nude. I was so...wanton! I was not ladylike at all, I fear."

"Succumbing to your baser urges doesn't mean you're not ladylike. We 'ladies' are equipped with a certain organ, the sole purpose of which is sexual pleasure. My guess is he introduced you to yours."

"It was a place near my...private opening. He touched it, and...I can't even explain the feeling."

"That is called your clitoris."

"My what?"

"Clitoris. The word originated in the seventeenth century. An Italian anatomist claimed to have discovered it in the sixteenth century. He called it *amor Veneris vel dulcedo,* the love of Venus."

"Love of Venus?"

"Yes, I have no idea what that was supposed to mean. I don't personally think any man discovered this organ. It was probably discovered by a female millennia ago. It was only just named in the seventeenth century."

"What is it exactly?"

"Most seem to think it's the female version of the cock... er...the penis. But unlike the latter, the only purpose of the clitoris is sexual arousal in women. The cock, as you know, has other functions."

Sophie's entire body burst into flames. If only a hole could open up and swallow her. "Ally, this conversation is getting...

uncomfortable."

"Dear, there is absolutely no reason for you to be uncomfortable. I am well versed in these things, and I'm happy to share my knowledge with you. Discovering your clitoris is a beautiful experience. That organ will give you intense pleasure for many years."

Sophie shook her head and heaved a sigh.

"Now tell me," Ally said. "What exactly did Mr. Newland do to make you climax?"

Sophie closed her eyes. If she was going to tell this story, she couldn't look at Ally. "Well, it all felt so good. It's difficult to pinpoint exactly what happened. He put his mouth on my... nipples. And then he put his hand inside my drawers, and..."

"I see what happened. He was massaging your clitoris when his hand was inside your drawers. That's how most women climax for the first time."

But what of the spanking? That had also brought Sophie to a climax, and she didn't know how to tell Ally. Was there something wrong with her? She had been beaten on the bottom as a child, and then she had watched in horror as her father beat her mother and Ally. She had cowered in a corner, letting them take the punishment for her. How could a smack on the buttocks feel good to her? She trembled, still squeezing her napkin. She was ill. Ill in the head. God help her.

"So tell me," Ally continued. "Do you intend to see more of Mr. Newland?"

"Well, I'm bound to, if I take the role he has offered me." She wasn't sure exactly when she had decided to join the cast of the musicale, but she had. Perhaps it would help her get her mind off of her illness. A role would keep her busy. Of course, it would also keep her in close proximity to Mr. Newland. How she would look him in the eye after what transpired between them, she didn't know.

Ally clapped her hands together. "That's fabulous! I knew you could do it. I'm so happy for you. This will bring joy to not only everyone who hears you but also to you, in your heart. You deserve joy, Sophie, more than anyone I know."

Joy. Sophie wasn't sure she'd ever experienced it. She'd been content, yes, but pure joy? Maybe during the bliss of her... climax, but that had been short-lived, and a lot of it was purely physical. Joy. How could Ally think Sophie deserved joy when she had let Ally take her punishment from their father for all those years? Ally was a strong, forgiving, and amazing person. And Sophie loved her more than anything.

"I just hope I don't freeze up. I hope I'm not making a gigantic mistake."

"You're not." Ally smiled, radiant with the glow of her pregnancy.

"I do appreciate your confidence in me, Ally. I hope it isn't misplaced."

"It's not." Ally shook her head. "I promise you."

★ ★ ★ ★

Sophie exited the coach that dropped her off at the Regal Theatre in Bath. She still wasn't quite sure when she had decided to take the part. Sometime during the conversation with Ally that morning. If Ally had confidence in her, she should have confidence in herself.

"Good morning, Lady Sophie," the doorman said, ushering her into the lobby of the theatre.

"Good morning. I'm here to see Mr. Newland. Is he in?"

"I believe he's in the back, in his office. Should I show you the way?"

"Thank you, but no. I know the way."

Sophie walked slowly, her nerves on edge, to Zach's office in the back. She stopped a few steps shy of the open door, breathing heavily. Her skin tingled, and her nipples were so hard she felt sure they'd cut right through her corset. *Relax, Sophie, relax.*

Gathering all her courage, she walked the remaining steps to Zach's open door.

And there stood Miss Nanette Lloyd, the prima donna herself, her arms around Zach and her lips on his.

CHAPTER EIGHT

Bile rose in Sophie's throat. She had let this man kiss her, touch her, bring her to...climax. And here he was with another woman in his arms. How could she have been so stupid and naïve?

She turned to walk away, tears threatening and anger simmering—anger at Zach, but mostly anger at herself for allowing him to take advantage of her. True, they were not courting, and he had not mentioned anything about courting, but really...only a day later?

Clearly, Sophie meant nothing to him. He truly was only after her voice.

As she backed away from the door, Zach called to her. "Sophie! Come back. Please."

Come back? Was he serious? Though she hesitated a moment, she then continued walking.

"Please!" Someone tugged at her arm.

She turned to look into Zach's chocolate eyes. Her face warmed, and she didn't want to think about how red it was. "I am very sorry to interrupt you, Mr. Newland."

"You didn't interrupt anything. Nanette came into my office and pretty much attacked me. There is nothing between us, I assure you."

Sophie dropped her gaze to the mahogany floor. "And I assure you that I do not care if there *is* anything between you. It is certainly none of my concern."

"Really? None at all?" Zach's voice was low, husky.

Sophie shook her head, her lips trembling. "That is correct. None at all."

"I'm sorry to hear that." He tipped her chin upward so their eyes met. "However, if you would please accompany me back to my office, I am happy to discuss whatever brought you here."

"I'm afraid the reason I came here no longer exists." She certainly could not take the role now. Though she had no intention of continuing any type of liaison with Mr. Newland, she couldn't watch him seduce every harlot in sight.

"Please, I truly want you to stay. I'm delighted that you came to visit."

Sophie yanked her chin out of his grasp. "I fear I cannot stay. As for the role you offered me, please give it to Miss Lloyd. It's clear that you two are...close."

"As I've told you, anything that existed between Nanette and me is now over. She is not happy about that fact, so she came to my office and attempted to seduce me."

"From where I was standing, she appeared to have succeeded," Sophie said.

"I promise you, she did not. She was kissing me. I was not kissing her. And even if there were something between Nanette and me, I would still want you for the part. You are so far above Nanette in talent and grace, and it would give me so much happiness to make you the queen of the stage that you were meant to be."

Sophie gulped. The queen of the stage? Timid, plain little Sophie? And was he truly telling the truth about Nanette? Not that it mattered, of course. Sophie had no feelings for Mr. Newland. None at all.

"Please, come back to my office, and we will discuss the

terms of your contract. It would give me great joy to welcome you to the theatre company."

Sophie relented. She had made a commitment to Ally and to herself to try to bring some joy into her life and into the lives of others. If singing in front of an audience could do this, she had to try.

She let out a breath. "All right, but only to discuss the role."

Zach nodded and led her into his office, shutting the door behind them. He sat behind his desk and motioned for Sophie to take one of the leather chairs facing him.

"The new musicale, written by our own Lord Thornton, is called *Love on a Midsummer Night*. The music was inspired by his wife, your cousin Rose. I would like you to play the female lead. Thornton's music is captivating, and I myself wrote the lyrics to the songs." He held out a piece of music to her. "Please, take a look. I believe you'll find it's well within your range, and I also believe you are the person to do justice to this role. It will be not only your debut, but the debut of this musicale."

Sophie bit her lip. She would love to perform in something that Cameron had written. He was remarkably talented as a composer. She looked at the song and the notes on the page. Yes, she could definitely sing it, and sing it well. And then she read the words...

Such fluidity in the poetry, such love coming through in the lyrics. She almost couldn't believe Mr. Newland had written them. Had he ever been in love? Surely he must have been at some point.

Sophie herself, of course, had never been in love and never could have described love in such a beautiful manner, having not known it personally.

"So do we have a deal, Sophie? Will you be my lead

soprano? My protégé?"

Sophie took a brief deep breath and nodded. "I am willing to try."

"Excellent!" Zach rose, walked around the desk, and pulled Sophie out of her chair. "You will be the belle of the theatre, Sophie. Your loveliness, your quiet demeanor, your angelic voice that comes from the heavens above—the people will fall in love with you."

He pulled her into a tight hug.

Sophie gasped. All of her senses went on alert. Her nipples hardened beneath her corset, pressing against the stiff fabric. And that place between her legs, that tiny little organ—the clitoris—began to pulsate.

Oh, not again. Would she be able to resist the lure of that incredible feeling?

Before she could think about how to refuse him, Zach's lips came down on hers.

And then she could no longer think about all the reasons not to kiss Zach. Because she wanted to kiss him. She wanted to explore so much more with this man. Was it wrong to want such things? Ally didn't think so. And Sophie couldn't think at all...

The kiss was firm and drugging, eliminating all rational thought from Sophie's mind. He nibbled around her lips, seeking entrance, and she granted it. He delved his tongue into her mouth, seeking hers. She met him, tangled tongues with him, kissing him with an urgency she had only begun to know.

When he broke the kiss and they both took much-needed breaths, he looked into her eyes, burning an inferno straight into her soul.

"Sophie, why do I want you so much?"

She had no answer for him. She wanted him as well, and she knew not why. He certainly was no longer attempting to seduce her so she would take the role. She had already taken it. Did he want her to answer? After a few seconds passed, though, he crushed his mouth down to hers once again.

They continued kissing with passion, their lips sliding over each other's, their tongues swirling, their teeth nibbling. Closer, she wanted to be closer. She desperately wanted to tear off all of her clothing, and then his, and writhe with him on the Oriental rug covering his floor.

Wherever were these thoughts coming from? They were not the thoughts of a lady of the peerage.

She ripped her mouth away from his, stepped back, and looked straight into his piercing eyes. "I can't do this."

He frowned. "I'm sorry. I thought... Well, never mind. I understand."

"It's just... I'm a lady. And you were just kissing..."

Zach trailed a finger down her cheek to her chin, again tipping it so she met his gaze. "I've told you, that meant nothing to me."

Sophie gulped. "Yes, but that's not really the point. This is all improper. This isn't me, Mr. Newland—"

"Zach. Please." His coffee-colored eyes burned two holes in her skin.

Her lips trembled. "Z-Zach. You must believe me. I'm not a loose woman. I'm not like this."

"Sweet Sophie, no one would ever mistake you for a loose woman. You are no doxy. You are as sophisticated a lady as exists."

"If you believe that, why do you want me to..." The words clogged her throat.

He smiled, his teeth like dazzling pearls. Sophie's knees weakened.

"My dear, did you enjoy what happened yesterday?"

Sophie shivered, her tummy fluttering. Surely he didn't expect an answer. Besides, her response had proved she'd enjoyed it immensely.

"Your blushing cheeks are lovely, my sweet," Zach said, cupping them and rubbing his thumbs gently over them. "No need to be embarrassed. I enjoyed myself yesterday, more than I even expected to."

"Well, of course you enjoyed it," Sophie said. "You're a man."

Zach let out a chuckle. "Point taken. I see you know a little about men, then."

Only what Ally had taught her. She didn't respond.

"I don't know when I've had quite as much enjoyment as I had with you yesterday, and I didn't even release." He grinned. "But *you* did."

Release? Another word for climax, maybe? A perfect word for the experience. She had been released from her shell, and she had soared, erupting in volcanic waves of pleasure, the sensation releasing every last shred of resistance, every last molecule of tension from her body.

Release...

Sophie melted. She had no strength left to resist this man. She knew better, but she wanted more of that freedom, that spontaneity, that...brazenness.

That *release*.

She turned her back to Zach, brushing the strands of curls that had come out of her coif off her shoulders with one hand. He took the hint and unbuttoned her gown. When he finished, he brushed it over her shoulders, and it landed at her feet. She turned her head at a faint click.

"Just shutting the door, love," Zach said with a wink, turning the lock.

Sophie's heart pounded as if a stampede of wildebeests were racing inside her chest. That elusive feeling, that delicious sensation she had experienced for the first time yesterday at Zach's hands—the release—beckoned her. She throbbed between her legs.

Zach returned to her and clamped his mouth to hers once again.

She parted her lips and bravely thrust her tongue into the moist warmth of his mouth. She kissed him with longing, intensity, lust. She poured her essence into this meeting of their mouths, making their previous kisses nearly meaningless. She tasted, she teased, she taunted.

Zach broke the kiss with a loud smack. "My God, sweet, you've never kissed me quite like that."

Sophie's cheeks burned. She didn't know how to respond.

Before she could, Zach turned her around, loosened her corset, and divested her of the tight garment. Then he brushed her chemise off her shoulders, her drawers over her hips and onto the floor. He removed her shoes and stockings. He was still fully clothed, and she stood before him, stark naked.

The urge to cover herself dueled with the desire for him to see her in all her nakedness. She fought the first urge, standing, her pert breasts and her triangle of dark-blond curls in plain view.

"You are so very alluring, Sophie. I could look at you all day and never get enough of your beauty."

Sophie cast her eyes downward. She was not beautiful,

and she did not delude herself into thinking Zach spoke the truth. He was merely playing his part, saying what she wanted to hear. He was a gifted actor, after all.

Truth be told, she did enjoy hearing it. It made her hot in places she had only recently learned of. She gathered her courage to speak.

"Am I ever to see your body? Or are you only to see mine?"

Zach smiled, his dimple apparent. "I will show you anything you wish to see."

She nearly unraveled and melted into a puddle right on his rug. Again, she fought dueling urges—the urge to run out and not look back and the overwhelming hunger to see him in all his naked glory.

Of course, she couldn't very well run out without clothes on, and right now, not a stitch covered her.

"Well, Lady Sophie, what do you wish to see?"

She quivered. "I suppose we can start with your chest."

Zach slowly removed his coat and hung it on the brass rack in the corner of his office. He loosened his cravat and discarded it.

He undid each button of his shirt at a maddeningly slow pace. Sophie tingled with every new inch of golden skin that was exposed. And those muscles... He was hard where she was soft.

When he pulled his shirt out of his waistband and removed it, Sophie gulped. Crisp mahogany hairs grew over bronze nipples. His abdomen was rippled with muscle. She clenched. Never had she imagined such beauty. Could men even be beautiful? Zachary Newland certainly was. Her fingers itched to touch the hard muscle.

As if reading her mind, Zach said, "Touch me if you'd like.

I would enjoy it."

Sophie cautiously strode forward. She reached out timidly and skated the fingers of one hand over his shoulder and down his upper arm. She pulsated between her legs. His skin was soft and smooth under her fingertips, but underneath, his muscles were hard and tense—the sinew, the corded muscle, so grand, as if he had been sculpted by the finest artist.

He shuddered softly beneath her caress. "That feels nice, Sophie. Tell me, did you like it yesterday when I touched your nipples?"

Sophie's lips trembled as she nodded.

"I'm glad you did. I adored touching them. I would love it now if you would touch mine."

Shaking, she trailed her fingers downward to one of his brown nipples. It hardened under her touch.

"Yes. That's nice, sweet."

Forgetting for a moment how frightened she was, she slid her other hand up his chest and fingered the other nipple. This time, when it hardened under her touch, a jolt arrowed to the wet place between her legs. She squirmed, fearful that her juices would drip down her thighs.

As she continued to graze his nipples, he reached forward and tugged on hers. And another jolt arrowed straight to her... Could she even think the word?

Pussy.

Pussy.

Yes, she could do it.

"Such beautiful breasts you have, Sophie," Zach said. "And so responsive to my touch."

He cupped her breasts, thumbing her nipples and then twisting and pinching them.

Sophie cried out. The pleasure-pain was exquisite. And, oh...the sensations in her pussy...

She needed more.

"Zach, yes, please... Squeeze my nipples."

Had such words left her lips? Yes, they had, and instead of feeling filthy and dirty, she felt...empowered. She dropped her gaze to the bulge in his trousers. Yes, this man had power over her. But she had the same power over him. She drew in a breath, embracing the power.

"What you do to me, sweet. Your words, they...make me so hard for you. How I yearn for you."

Zach had no doubt yearned for many women in his day, but at that moment, Sophie couldn't bring herself to care. She wanted him to continue playing with her nipples, and then she wanted him to suck them as he had yesterday, his firm pink mouth licking and nibbling on them.

God help her, she had become a slave to her own lust...and she was enjoying it.

Zach let one of her breasts drop and covered one of her hands, slowly sliding it downward to the bulge inside his trousers. "Touch me, Sophie. Please."

It was hard as stone. She could never have imagined. Though she had seen the bulge, she hadn't imagined it could really be solid like granite. Timidly, she squeezed just a little.

Zach jolted. "God, yes. Your touch excites me so much."

She squeezed him again, harder this time. His cock jerked. She trembled, her body sparkling with energy. Yes, the power.

"Sweet, you must stop that, or this will be over before it has begun."

Sophie wasn't sure what Zach meant, but she drew her hand away quickly.

"Easy, love, you've done nothing wrong." He bent his legs and helped her lie down on the Oriental rug. The fine fibers tickled her back. He spread her legs.

She squirmed. That secret part of her... "Are you sure..."

"Shh. Let me pleasure you." He crawled downward, his tongue meandering over her belly, pushing into her navel, and then stopping to rest on her blond curls. He inhaled. "You smell of the glory of spring, my Sophie. Your pussy will taste sweeter than the finest fruit."

When his tongue touched her...clitoris, Sophie melted into the rug, floating on something softer than a silken mattress. "Zach. We... We're..."

His breath tickled her wet folds. "Let me suck the honey from you." He stroked her pussy with one smooth swipe of his sleek tongue. "Red as a ruby, sweet, and succulent as a peach."

He forced his tongue inside her slit, and her body quaked. His strong hands pushed her thighs farther apart.

"More of you, Sophie. I need more."

Her body pulsated in fiery heat. He sucked on her folds, tugging them, his teeth scraping the delicate skin and threading jolts of delight through her. He kept sucking, taking her pussy lips between his teeth and tugging. Had anything ever felt so good? He licked her like a cat lapping cream, his tongue moving rapidly against her clitoris, against her folds, and then he sucked her entire wet pussy into his mouth. So good... Wicked longing permeated her. She tried spreading her legs farther, wanting to open to him completely. The slurping sounds he made as he sucked on her drifted to her ears, and she unraveled further. Her skin rippled.

"Mmm. So sweet," he said against her folds, still sucking.

He was enjoying this—having his face between her legs,

his tongue within the most secret part of her.

"Yes, Zach. That's so good. More. More!"

In an instant, he flipped her over to her hands and knees. His face was back down between her legs in a flash, his tongue vibrating over her pussy once more. For an instant, his tongue slid over her most secret and forbidden opening.

He turned her back over so she lay on her back. His lips descended to her pussy once more as he caressed her abdomen and breasts. Had anything ever felt so wonderful? He squeezed her breasts as he continued to suck her, finding her nipples, twisting them.

When his full, firm lips closed around her clitoris, she leaped into nirvana and spasms rippled across her flesh, taking her higher into the air. When she floated downward, she opened her eyes and looked between her legs. Zach floated with her, his fingers massaging her slick channel. His brown gaze locked on to hers, and he smiled, his pearly teeth a stark contrast against his swollen pink lips glistening with her cream.

She melted softly into the ornate Oriental rug.

"Zach..."

He kissed her pussy once, twice, and slid up her body, his tongue leading the way, until he found her lips and devoured them. Sophie opened, sucking his tongue into her mouth and tasting her own spicy essence. *Zach. Oh, God, Zach.*

Of their own volition, her hands slid to caress his shoulders and arms. The sinewy muscle was taut under her fingertips. How had she come to this? This sheer amazing experience?

When he finally broke the kiss, his lips and chin shone with her essence. "You are wonderful. Never have I tasted a pussy quite so sweet."

Sophie didn't know whether to be embarrassed or

flattered. That she had just let a man taste her down there still frightened her. But oh, how good it had felt. And it had led to another...climax.

Release.

Zach pulled her up until they were in a sitting position. "May I show you something?"

She gasped. Did he mean to take his...*organ*...out of his trousers? She wasn't quite ready for that. Still, she had come this far. "I suppose so," she said.

He rose and helped her into a standing position. He turned her around and leaned her over his wooden desk. "Brace your hands on the desk, sweet."

Though she had no idea what was going on, she did as he bid.

"Oh!" She gasped as his hand came down on her bottom. As it had yesterday, the slap stung but metamorphosed into intense pleasure that she didn't comprehend. Before she could think it through, another landed on her bare bum.

"So grand, Sophie. Such a pretty shade of pink on your arse."

"You must stop..." But even as the words crossed her lips, she knew she didn't mean them.

"Of course I will stop if that is what you wish."

When another smack didn't come, she found herself desiring it more than her next breath of air. But he was a gentleman. He would not spank her again unless she asked for it. *I should get up. I shouldn't lie here, bent over, my bottom exposed.* Yet she couldn't bring herself to move.

"If you want more, Sophie, you'll have to ask me for it."

She was immobile, numb. Oh, how she wanted to say the words... *Yes, spank me again, please. I need you to.*

Tiny sweet nibbles covered her buttocks. Zach was kissing the cheeks of her arse, kissing the sting away. How sweet and gentle he was.

She opened her mouth, gathering her courage and her wits. "Spank me, Zach. Please."

Smack! His palm landed on her bottom, and the jolt arrowed straight to her pussy. Shivers coursed through her. *More. More.*

"Again, please."

And again his hand descended upon her bare buttocks. Once more, the pain transformed into pleasure, and this time, something nudged her clitoris. His finger? She didn't know. She didn't care. All she knew was she was flying again, another intense climax overtaking her.

Release. Sweet release.

"You like that? You like coming for me?" Zach's voice was raspy with lust. "I like it when you come for me. You're so beautiful, and your arse is such an alluring shade of raspberry."

Sophie gripped the edges of the desk and braced herself. "Again."

CHAPTER NINE

His hand came down upon her, harder this time. She winced, clawing at the desk, wanting—no, *needing*—more. The pain... It was what she craved—the way it shimmered into pleasure...

"And again, please."

Even harder this time his hand came down upon her. God, such heavenly sensation... Bliss. Pure unadulterated bliss.

"Please, Zach... Again!"

The softness of his lips met her derriere. "No, my sweet, you've had enough for one day. You're new to this. I don't want to overwhelm you."

Sophie loosened her grip on the edge of the desk. Rationality flooded back into her brain. What had she been doing? Here she was, naked, bent over a mahogany desk, letting a man she barely knew spank her bare bottom. She should be ashamed of herself. Oddly, though, she wasn't. For some reason, what had just transpired felt very natural to her.

Zach was gently massaging her stinging bum. "I have some salve that will help the smarting. Of course, there is no broken skin. I would never do that to you."

Soon his warm hands were rubbing something oily and soothing over her buttocks.

"It's beeswax and oil of rosemary. It will help the stinging."

Sophie closed her eyes. Dear Lord, she didn't want to help the stinging. She wanted to remember it forever. "Truly, I'm fine."

"Yes, you'll be fine," Zach said, "but I don't want you hurting on the morrow."

"I promise you I am fine."

"Indulge me, then. I quite like massaging you." He continued to rub the sweet-smelling ointment onto her. His hands were warm and firm.

She tingled all over, savoring his touch.

"You were able to take quite a lot," Zach said. "Most women can't take that much their first few times."

Sophie stifled a sob. *Most women.* Others had come before her. Of course, she knew that. She just didn't expect him to tell her about them. Then again, he was not courting her. No reason existed for him to be faithful to her. However, a bit of her heart broke at that moment. She was having feelings she had never even imagined, feelings she'd never had for Lord Van Arden or anyone else, even Frederick McKenzie, a young man she had known when she was but a blossoming teenager. He had been majestic and refined, and she had longed for him to pay her the slightest bit of attention. He hadn't, but she dreamed of him for years. He'd been too old for her at the time, but the thoughts of him had given her pleasure. She'd needed the pleasure to escape the pain in her life.

"There you are." Zach removed his hands from her.

Immediately she mourned the loss of his hands upon her. He stood and turned her away from the desk to face him. Perspiration gleamed over his beautiful face and hard glistening body.

"Please, forgive me if I took it to an extreme. You're just so ravishing, and you seemed to want it so badly. I could never live with myself if I'd hurt you."

Sophie forced a smile. "You didn't hurt me. I...enjoyed it."

"I'm glad you did. I enjoyed it too." He brushed his lips over hers in the softest of kisses. "I've loved every minute I've spent with you, from listening to your sweet voice when you auditioned on the stage, to kissing your perfect lips, to having you touch me through my trousers, to spanking your lovely bottom. There's something about you, Lady Sophie MacIntyre, and I'm not quite sure what it is. All I know is I want to see more of you."

It wasn't an offer of courtship, but it was something. Zachary Newland was a talented and intelligent man. If she were Ally, Sophie would be thinking she could learn a lot from such a man. She was not Ally. But still, perhaps learning more in the art of pleasure and pain would not be a bad thing. In fact, the thought delighted her.

"You will see plenty of me when we begin rehearsals in a few days," she said coyly.

"Yes." He cleared his throat. "We will see a lot of each other. And we will be rehearsing together. I cast myself as your leading man."

Sophie warmed all over, suddenly very aware of her nakedness. "It will be my pleasure to work with you. You're very talented."

Zach chuckled. "Why so formal all of a sudden? Did you forget that you were just bent over my desk and I was spanking your gorgeous bottom?"

Fire spread to her cheeks. She clasped her hands over them. How could she have forgotten? It had been the most exciting thing that had ever happened in her life. "Zach...Mr. Newland... It's difficult for me to..."

"Speak of such things?" Zach nodded. "It is for most ladies. But I assure you, there are plenty of ladies like yourself who enjoy these types of erotic arts."

Yes, she had heard of such from Ally. She'd just never imagined she herself would enjoy such play. She resisted meeting Zach's gaze. If only she were more like her sister... But she wasn't, and right now, she needed to escape.

"I really must go," she said, dressing as quickly as she could. She turned and allowed him to tighten her corset and button her dress. "Thank you for..." For what? She could hardly say thank you for bending me over your desk, swatting my bottom, and giving me release. "Well... Just...thank you."

★ ★ ★ ★

"Please...stay!"

But she was already gone. Zach heaved a sigh. Something about her drove him absolutely mad. He wanted to mold her, help her find her voice...in more ways than one. Her singing voice captivated him, and with some proper tutelage, she would become the toast of Bath and maybe even London. Zach had formal training in voice, and he wanted to share it with Sophie, to teach her, help her become who she was meant to be.

And sexually... A long time had passed since he'd been as aroused as he was with her. Not since he was a mere lad of fifteen and lost his virginity to a servant girl four years his senior. Evangeline was her name, and she had tresses of fiery red hair and a personality to match. "Spank me," she'd begged. He had, and he'd found he was a natural dominant.

Some women enjoyed it. Others didn't. Those who didn't, he rarely saw more than once or twice. Those who did, he'd have longer relationships with. But never had he longed for something more... Something elusive...

Zach wasn't the type to fall in love. He considered himself married to the stage. But Lady Sophie MacIntyre brought out something in him—something new and almost frightening. Since the moment he first saw her onstage and heard her enchanting voice, she hadn't ventured from his mind. And once he'd kissed those lips, he'd been lost. Now he still ached for more. They had not yet consummated the relationship. He had no doubt that would happen, but he wanted to take it slowly with her. This was a new concept to him. Normally, consummation happened quickly, and if it didn't, he was no longer interested. But with Sophie... He wanted to indoctrinate her slowly, help her find her muse not only in her performance but also in the bedchamber. He imagined being with her for years, perhaps even a lifetime.

Truth be told, those thoughts troubled him.

Zach hadn't had an easy life. His father had run out on him and his mother when he was a babe, and his mother had found work as a maid. His mother was all he had, and he was very close to her. Unfortunately, she passed on from the consumption when Zach was young. He'd cried and cried, begging her not to leave him, but she had. Afterward, he begged on the streets, making his own way until he was old enough to find work. He scrimped and saved, determined to make his way in the world as a performer, something he had dreamed about since he was a young lad.

While he was performing at a tiny hack theatre outside of London, the Marchioness of Denbigh spotted him. She was so taken with him and his talent that she set him up as an apprentice at the Theatre Royale in Bath. He worked hard, trained in acting and voice, and became one of the top actors of his time. When he reached the age of one-and-thirty, just one year ago, he opened the Regal Theatre.

Sophie reminded Zach a bit of his mother. She had been timid and soft-spoken as well, and she was all he'd had in the world.

"Please, Mama. Please don't leave me," he'd begged through his tears.

The pain in her eyes still haunted him. She'd held on for days, and in the end, even at the tender age of seven, he could see that she was in agony. He told her to go ahead to a better place, that he had been selfish to beg her to stay, and she went, a serene smile on her face as the life drifted out of her.

Zach closed his eyes, willing back the tears that threatened to fall. He hadn't thought of his mother in ages. He had fleeting thoughts now and then, always wishing that she could see how far he had come in the world. She would have been his biggest supporter, and she would have been proud of every step he took toward his career.

Something about Sophie brought thoughts of his mother to the surface, but not in a strange sort of way at all. Her demeanor just reminded him so much of his mother's demeanor.

His attraction to Sophie—that was something different altogether. She was truly beautiful. Those hazel-green eyes were so big and doe-like, and her lashes so long. Her hair was a stunning darker blond, thick and rich, and her body... She may not be as buxom as some of the women he had been with, but she was absolutely perfect. She fit against him so well. When they finally joined their bodies in the act, he had no doubt the earth would move.

He tried shooing the thoughts away. After all, he had much

work to do. Rehearsal started on the morrow. He went about his work, but Sophie's face still hovered inside his mind's eye.

He feared he'd never be free of her.

★ ★ ★ ★

Sophie sucked in a breath, gathering every ounce of courage she possessed. Then she entered the parlor where Ally sat, alone, thank goodness.

"Ally?" she said timidly.

Ally looked up from the book she was reading. "Oh, Sophie dear, I didn't hear you come in."

Sophie eyed her sister's bulging tummy. "How are you feeling today?"

"Pretty good. Thank you for asking. Although, this baby seems to think my bladder is an enemy. I've had to use the convenience a dozen times already today."

Sophie let out a small chuckle. She loved that Ally could always find the humor in every situation. How had Ally, who had grown up in the same household as she and taken much more abuse, turned out so different? Ally wasn't afraid of anything, and she went after what she wanted, often defying convention to do so. Sophie wished she were more like her sister.

"Could I...talk to you for a few minutes?"

Ally put her book down on the table and patted the seat next to her on the divan. "Of course. What's on your mind?"

What was on her mind indeed? Sophie hoped she could get the words out without stumbling over them. But if anyone could understand, Ally could.

"I've...just come from the theatre."

Ally's eyes shone. "And I suppose you saw Mr. Newland there?"

Sophie nodded, her cheeks warming.

"And..." Ally urged.

"Oh, Ally, it's all so...complicated."

"Love is rarely uncomplicated, my dear."

Love? Sophie hadn't said anything about love. "I'm not talking about...love. At least, I don't think I am."

"Very well, then. Just tell me what's on your mind."

"I... I let him kiss me again, and we went...further again."

Ally's mouth dropped into an O. "Are you saying you actually...had intercourse with him?"

Sophie vehemently shook her head. "Oh, goodness no, no, no. But he..."

"Gave you another climax?"

Sophie let out a breath. More than one, actually. She nodded.

"Why do you seem so distraught?" Ally asked. "It was my understanding that you enjoyed the climax he gave you before."

"Well, of course, I did. And I...enjoyed them today."

"Them? You had more than one?"

Sophie nodded, gulping. "Several, yes."

"That's absolutely superb!" Ally smiled.

"Yes, it was...superb, of course. But..."

"But what? What exactly are you trying to tell me, Sophie?"

"What troubles me is that...he smacked my..."

"Your bottom? Did he spank your bum?"

Sophie nodded, wishing she could disappear into the gilt brocade of the divan. No such luck.

"Sophie, dear, many women enjoy playful spankings. In fact, there are clubs where people go to get such pleasure."

"Clubs?"

"Yes. Of course, I've never been to one myself, but I've read about them."

"So you don't think it's...*odd* that I enjoyed the spankings?"

"Not at all."

"But Ally, after all the two of us went through during our childhood, isn't it strange that I would enjoy having a man taking hand to me like that?"

Ally hesitated a moment before speaking. "Honestly, Sophie, I cannot say for sure. I do know that many men and women enjoy such things. I really don't think it's anything to be concerned about. You and he are both over the age of consent, and if you both enjoy those acts, why worry about it? Grab every bit of pleasure out of life that you can. You can't know how much it pleases me to know that you're finding some pleasure. You've always been quiet, and I know you're content with the simple life of being alone, reading, singing to yourself. But I've always felt you were meant for so much more. That's why I wanted you to audition for the musicale. And perhaps you're meant for more than singing as well. If you enjoy these acts in the bedchamber—"

"Well, not in the bedchamber exactly. First in the alcove, and then in his office at the theatre."

Ally chuckled. "It's just an expression. Sometimes those acts outside of the bedchamber are the most pleasurable."

Sophie smiled. Embarrassment warmed her cheeks and neck. "Perhaps."

"At any rate, grab every little diversion you can out of this life, sister dear. The tough times will come no matter what.

Seize the good when you can. *Carpe diem*."

Carpe diem, indeed. "Thank you, Ally. That helps. If you'll excuse me, I think I want to retire to my chamber for a small catnap before luncheon."

Sophie left the parlor and strode up the stairway to her chamber. She lay down on her bed and closed her eyes, waiting for blackness to take her away from her muddled thoughts.

★ ★ ★ ★

"Out of bed, lassie."

A strong arm yanked Sophie off of the hard cot she'd been sleeping on. Her father's rank breath reeked of Scotch and filth.

"Ye're becomin' a woman now, and a woman needs to learn how to take a good beatin'. That way I'll find a decent husband for ye, someone to take ye off my hands so ye're no longer my problem."

Father yanked her to the corner of the room. From the corner of her eye, she saw her little sister, Ally, open her eyes.

Sophie gasped, icy fear surging through her. She'd just started her courses—her first time—and her body was cramping with pain. The rag she wore in her drawers clung to her private parts, sticky with her blood. Her father had smacked her and Ally around before, but not anything to cause them lasting injury. Though they had witnessed him do much worse to their mother. Both of them wanted to help her, but they were not big enough or strong enough, and their mother had cautioned them never to interfere.

"What a bloody mess!" Father lifted her chemise and pulled her drawers down, baring her bottom. "Women are so filthy. Ye need the filth beaten out of ye." He turned her over his knee.

Slap! A leather strap came down on her bare bottom.

Sophie cried out. Oh, how it stung, and her belly cramped up with more pain.

Slap! Slap! Slap!

Tears ran down her cheeks as Sophie wailed. "Mama! Mama! Help me, please!"

"Yer mother knows better than to interfere, lass. If she does, I'll be all the harder on her later."

"Father, please stop. You're hurting me. My...my tummy... It's so sore."

"I'm not hittin' ye on yer tummy, am I?"

Slap! Slap!

"Stop it! Stop it! You're hurting her!"

Sophie looked up. Ally had risen from bed and was pushing at their father.

"No, Ally, please," Sophie whispered. "Go back to bed."

"You're nothing but a coward," Ally said. "A coward who picks on people smaller and weaker than you are."

Father pushed Sophie to the floor. She landed, her bones aching. Thankful for being released, she ran to the basin to clean herself, but—

Slap! Slap! Slap!

Sophie turned and swallowed the bile rising to her throat. Ally was now across their father's knees, her bottom bared.

"Ye don't want yer sister to take her punishment? Then ye'll take it for her."

"Smack me all you want. You're still a coward."

"Oh, Ally, please, be quiet. You're just making it worse."

Ally ignored her, continuing to taunt their father.

The door to their small chamber opened quickly. Their mother, Iris, the Countess of Longarry, stood there in her night rail. "Angus, please. Come to bed. Please do not do this to our children."

"I'll deal with you later, ye stupid bitch. Leave us!"

"I will not! You will not hurt my daughters."

Father pushed Ally onto the floor and strode to Mother, cancerous anger in his eyes. "Ye will not talk to me like that again, woman."

He pushed Mother down harshly, and she landed with a thump on the floor. Then he closed the door to the girls' chamber and locked it.

"I'm not done with ye." He grabbed Ally, only eleven she was, pulled her across his knees again, and continued strapping her.

Sophie wept quietly, unable to take her eyes off of the torture befalling her baby sister. Ally's bottom was bright red. It would surely be bruised on the morrow. Sophie stood, wanting to help, but she was paralyzed except for the drops of blood sliding down her legs.

Slap! Slap! Slap!

★ ★ ★ ★

Sophie awoke with a jerk. Her heart pounded rapidly, and freezing tingles prickled her skin all over. Scattered images and smells permeated her mind. Her father—his rotten breath, always so rank—her first courses—the ache—the mess—her mother, tortured yet still so proud and brave.

And Ally.

Always Ally. Her baby sister. Ally always protected Sophie from Father's beatings.

Sophie was the older sister. She was supposed to protect

Ally, not vice versa. But she hadn't had the strength. Ally was strong, always so strong. She still was today.

Ally had taken so many beatings meant for Sophie. And Sophie had never been able to stand up to their father the way Ally had. He beat her to a pulp, yet still she kept fighting... Always fighting...

How was it now that Sophie was enjoying a spanking from Zach? None of this made any sense. The whole idea should repulse her, based on her abusive childhood.

She would have to stop seeing Zach Newland.

Grab every bit of pleasure out of life that you can. Ally's words rang in her head.

How in the world could she consider this pleasure, when the same act had brought her so much pain earlier in life? Not just pain for her, but for Ally and Mother too.

Even if she wanted to stop seeing Zach, which she didn't, she'd already committed to take the role in the musicale. Of course, she could step down. He had another soprano to fill the role—Nanette.

That is what she would do. She would go back to the theatre this afternoon and tell Zach that she could not be his leading lady.

She let out a sigh. If only things could be different. But Sophie was still Sophie.

She was a coward, and she always would be. No amount of courage or faith in herself could change that.

She rose to get ready for luncheon. She took a quick peek in the looking glass and fiddled with her hair a bit, until a frantic knock on the door interrupted her.

"My lady!" Hannah entered without permission. "Come quick! It's Lady Alexandra!"

CHAPTER TEN

Sophie grabbed Hannah by her upper arms. "Ally? What has happened?"

"I don't know, my lady. All I know is they say she's bleeding."

Sophie's heart nearly stopped. Ally was not yet eight months long. If she was bleeding... Sophie couldn't think of it. Ally and Evan wanted that baby so badly! She pushed Hannah aside and ran from her chamber, down the hallway, and down the stairs, nearly tripping over her feet. She stumbled into Graves as she ran down the stairs.

"Lady Alexandra is in the parlor," Graves said. "Bertram has gone for the doctor."

"What happened?" Sophie bit her lip.

"Your sister doubled over in pain. We're not exactly sure what's happening."

"Can't you get her to her chamber?"

"We're not sure if we should move her, my lady."

"Oh, for goodness' sake. Where is Lord Evan? Where are my mother and the earl?"

"They've all gone into town for the day. Bertram will try to find them when he summons the doctor."

Was no one ever here when help was needed? "Isn't there anyone who can help? Surely some of the servants have had experience with childbearing."

"Yes, two maids are with her at the moment."

Sophie burst through the parlor door. Ally was lying on the floor on her back, her eyes squeezed shut. Two maids—Sophie recognized them as Haley, a downstairs maid, and her mother, Elspeth—tended her.

"What is going on? Is my sister all right?"

"I'm afraid her water has broken, my lady," Haley said.

That didn't sound good. "What does that mean exactly?" Sophie asked.

"It means she has begun labor. The baby is coming."

Sophie gasped. "But it's too early! She hasn't yet reached eight months."

"Shh, my lady," Elspeth said. "You don't want to scare your sister."

Sophie clamped her hand over her mouth. No, she certainly didn't want to do that. "All right, then. What are we to do now?"

"Millicent has gone for some linens and toweling, and Cook is boiling water. We need to make her as comfortable as possible until the doctor gets here."

Sophie knelt beside Ally and took her hand. "Ally, dear, are you quite all right?"

Ally opened her eyes. "Oh, Sophie, thank goodness you're here. I...I don't know what's going on. I shouldn't be going into labor for about a month yet, but my bag of waters..."

Sophie braced herself. She had to be brave for Ally. She was not used to such. Ally had always been the brave one. She gritted her teeth and inhaled, letting the air out slowly. "Now, Ally, you're going to be absolutely fine. Bertram has gone for the doctor, and he will also find Evan and Mother and the earl. They will be here for you. Just think... In a little while, you will be a mother. And I will be an auntie."

That got a small smile out of Ally. "If only it didn't hurt so damned much!"

Sophie resisted the urge to admonish her sister for her curse. Now was certainly not the time. "I know, dear. I know. Millicent has gone for some linens, and Haley and Elspeth are here, tending to you. I am right beside you, and I will be the entire time. I promise."

"Thank you, Sophie. I don't think I could get through this without you."

"You won't have to."

"Oh!" Ally gripped Sophie's hand like a vise. "This child is trying to kill me."

"Breathe, Ally. Breathe. This is exactly what mother went through when she brought both of us into the world. Lily and Rose have both been through it, and you will get through it too."

"Lily and Rose were both attended by physicians when they gave birth. Where in the hell is that doctor?"

"I don't know how long ago Bertram left. Do you want me to ask Graves?"

"No, no. Don't leave me."

"Very well." Sophie turned to the older maid, Elspeth. "Would you please go check with Mr. Graves and find out how long ago Mr. Bertram left?"

"Yes, my lady." Elspeth rose and left the parlor.

"Most first babies take a while to come," the younger maid, Haley, said. "I know you're in pain, my lady, but there really is no reason to worry. The doctor will be here in plenty of time. You will be laboring for hours, perhaps even a day or two."

Ally's eyes shot open, wide as dinner plates. "A day or

two?"

"For goodness' sake, Haley, don't frighten her," Sophie admonished. She turned back to Ally. "I promise you, everything will be all right."

How she hoped she spoke the truth.

Before she could ruminate any further, Ally let out a blood-curdling scream.

★ ★ ★ ★

Zach returned to the theatre after a light luncheon. He headed to his office to make some changes to tomorrow's schedule for rehearsals. He had told the actors and actresses to be at the theatre tomorrow at nine o'clock. He wished he'd said eight o'clock. Too late now. He couldn't send word to them in time, so he had to make some adjustments to allow for the extra hour he needed. He entered his office.

And there, seated behind his desk in his leather chair, naked as the day she was born, was Nanette.

Zach let out a sigh. Why had he not been able to get through to her? He'd had his share of women, and most were fine when the end of the relationship came. However, a select few had not been able to accept the fact that he was done with them. Unfortunately, Nanette was proving to be one of the latter.

"Good afternoon, handsome. I trust you had an enjoyable luncheon?" Nanette smiled.

"What are you doing here, Nanette?"

Nanette flicked her gaze down to her exposed breasts. "I should think that's fairly obvious."

"How many times do I have to tell you that what we had

is over?" Zach removed his jacket and hung it on his brass coat rack. "I no longer wish to have a personal relationship with you."

"Well, it just so happens that I don't accept that."

"You have to. We are over. That is final. Now if you'll kindly leave my office."

Nanette stood. "All right, if you insist." She stood, her blond hair cascading over her shoulders, her nipples perky and erect. She walked to his office door and opened it.

Zach gasped. "For the love of God, Nanette, put your damned clothes on!"

Nanette shut the door and turned, smiling. "I'm afraid I don't have any in here, Zach."

Zach looked around. Sure enough, not a shred of female clothing graced his office. "How in the hell did you get in here without any clothes?"

"I sneaked in from the costume room."

"You've been running around my theatre stark naked?"

"Don't be such a ninny. No one saw me."

"You'd better hope to God no one saw you. I swear to you, Nanette, if I get one complaint about your behavior, you will no longer have a place at this theatre. I have a new lead soprano. While I can certainly use you in supporting roles, you are no longer indispensable. Any of the other sopranos can take your place now."

Nanette's eyes blazed with blue fire. "So you're going to dismiss me now, are you?"

"I don't want to dismiss you. I made that clear. I still have use for you here at the theatre. But if you find you cannot accept the fact that our relationship is to be entirely professional from here on, I will have no choice but to throw your arse out of here."

"Oh, Zach," Nanette cooed. "You could never throw my arse out of here. Not when you've had so much fun fucking it."

Zach let out a chuckle. "You're a decent enough fuck. I'll give you that. But your cock sucking leaves much to be desired. I've grown tired of it. I've grown tired of you."

"So your perfect Lady Sophie sucks cock better than I do, then?"

He wouldn't know. But he hoped to find out. "I am interested in Sophie's voice. She has a gift, and she is finally willing to share it with the good people of Bath." He hadn't yet even shown Sophie his cock, but the thought of her rosy lips wrapped around it... Sophie was untried, had never been kissed, let alone sucked anyone's cock. Already, though, he knew having his cock in her mouth would be infinitely better than having it in Nanette's mouth. Lord, he wanted it.

"You will be sorry about this, Zach. I can make your life miserable."

Zach seethed. Who did she think she was, anyway? "That's it. You are dismissed from the theatre. Now get the hell out of here and put some fucking clothes on."

She stomped out, her breasts jiggling, and slammed the door.

Good riddance. But now he had to completely redo all the schedules, substituting one of the lesser sopranos in Nanette's role.

That damned bitch.

★ ★ ★ ★

"Ally, Ally, what is it?"

"She's just having a bad contraction, my lady," Haley said.

"Isn't there anything you can give her for the pain?"

"No, I'm sorry, my lady. I wish there was. Mayhap the doctor will be able to when he gets here. Childbirth is just one of those pains we women have to bear. Oh, here comes Mama."

Elspeth walked briskly back into the parlor. "Mr. Graves said Mr. Bertram left nearly an hour ago in a coach. So the doctor should be along anytime now."

"Thank God," Sophie said under her breath. "Did you hear that, Ally? The doctor should be here soon. Hold tight, and hold on to my hand. I promise you I'm not leaving your side."

Millicent, Ally's maid, arrived with the linens and toweling. "Let's get several layers of these linens underneath her. We don't want her staining this fine Oriental rug."

"Who bloody cares about the rug?" Sophie cried. "My sister is in pain!"

"I'm sorry, my lady. But I'm sure the earl—"

"The earl will only care that my sister is comfortable and well, I assure you," Sophie said.

"Yes, I'm sure he will, my lady," Millicent said. "But it won't hurt to get some linens under her now, will it?"

Sophie sucked in a breath. She was being rude, and she made a point never to be cross with the help. They were people too. "I'm sorry, Millicent. Please forgive me. I'm just so worried about Ally."

"I understand, my lady."

Haley and Elspeth helped Millicent gently move Ally

until the linens were underneath her.

"Can you sit up a minute, my lady?" Millicent asked Ally. "We need to get your gown loosened. You'll be much more comfortable."

"Just get the damned thing off of me, Millicent," Ally said through gritted teeth.

Sophie couldn't help letting out a little laugh. Ally was still Ally, even when in pain.

Sophie continued holding Ally's hand while the three maids gently moved her, loosening and removing her gown. Ally sat only in her chemise and drawers, which were wet from her waters breaking.

"Shouldn't we remove her drawers as well?" Haley asked.

"Yes, we probably should. If she starts to deliver before the doctor gets here, they'll need to be off," Elspeth said.

Sophie's body warmed with embarrassment for her sister. Why couldn't they have gotten her to her chamber? Or at least to a servant's chamber. Anywhere but the main parlor.

Sophie glanced at Elspeth. She had been with the Brighton estate for decades. "Elspeth, have you ever helped with a birth before?"

"Oh, of course, my lady. I attended the countess herself when she birthed both Lady Miranda and Lord Evan."

"But there was a doctor there, yes?"

"No, milady. Only a midwife. I assisted her."

If only a midwife were here. Or a doctor. Or anyone who had delivered a baby, for goodness' sake.

Elspeth gently removed Ally's drawers.

And gasped.

Sophie's heart leaped. "What is it, Elspeth?"

Elspeth's lips trembled. "Lady Alexandra is crowning."

CHAPTER ELEVEN

"Crowning? What the devil is crowning?" Sophie squeezed Ally's hand tighter.

"It means"—Elspeth breathed rapidly—"it means the baby is coming. Now!"

"How is that possible, Mum?" Haley asked. "This is her first child."

"I don't know," Elspeth said. "I've never seen such a thing myself. But as God is my witness, this baby is coming."

"I need to push!" Ally screamed.

"Lord Almighty." Elspeth crossed herself. "Haley, go get Cook and tell him to bring lots of that boiling water he has on the stove. Millie, you come here and help me."

"No," Ally said. "I want...Sophie."

"I'm right here, Ally." Sophie squeezed her sister's hand harder. "And I'm not going anywhere."

"No, I mean...I want you to help Elspeth."

"Ally, Millicent is much better equipped to help."

Ally let out another scream. Sophie shuddered. She had never heard a woman scream at such a high pitch. Ally was in a lot of pain.

"That's good, my lady," Elspeth said. "Now give me another push."

"I want Sophie!"

"I'm right here."

"Please, Sophie, if you ever wanted to do something for

me, do this. I want you to watch the birth of my child so you can tell me everything you see."

Dear Lord. Sophie wasn't sure she wanted to watch. But for Ally, to whom she owed so much, she would do anything. She sucked in a breath. "If you're sure."

"I'm sure—" Then another scream ripped from Ally's throat.

Sophie's pulse raced. "Millicent, please come hold her hand. Once Haley returns, she can assist Elspeth. I will only"— she gulped—"witness the birth."

Sophie reluctantly moved toward Elspeth. She didn't want to look. She squeezed her eyes shut for a moment and then opened them.

God, the blood... Sophie wavered, but got her bearings. Between Ally's legs, a tiny head of black hair appeared.

"Oh my goodness, Ally! I can see your baby! I can see the head!"

"That's it, milady," Elspeth said. "One more push, and I think we'll have ourselves a baby."

Ally screamed, and a tiny person emerged from her womb. Sophie's heart nearly burst. This was her tiny niece or nephew...

A niece! She had a baby niece!

"It's a girl, my lady," Elspeth said.

Ally fell backward. "Oh, a girl... Little Maureen, after Evan's mother."

Haley returned with the water.

"Just in time," Elspeth said, handing her the baby. "Clean up this little one and keep her warm, and then get her to her mother's breast."

"It's over now, Ally," Sophie said. "You have a perfect little girl."

"If it's over, why do I feel so—" Another scream tore from her gut.

"It's just the afterbirth, my lady," Elspeth said. "Not to worry."

Haley's eyebrows shot up. "But Mum, the afterbirth isn't supposed to—"

"Shhh!" Elspeth said to her daughter.

Haley finished cleaning baby Maureen and handed her to Ally, who was propped up by pillows.

"Hold her to your breast, my lady," Haley said. "Keep her warm."

"Yes, of course. Oh, she's so beautiful—" And still another gut-wrenching scream.

"Goodness, what is the matter? Can you help her?" Sophie shuddered, her heart still galloping. Ally had endured so much pain in her short lifetime. If only Sophie could bear this for her.

"I'm trying," Elspeth said. "The afterbirth—it doesn't seem to be coming... Oh!"

"What is it?" Sophie demanded.

"It's... It's... Oh, my lady... It's another baby!"

Another baby? Sophie clasped her hand to her mouth. "Ally, the most amazing thing! It's twins! You and Evan...you're having twins!"

Ally's breath was coming in rapid pants. Haley grabbed baby Maureen from her and wrapped her in warm blankets.

"That's it, my lady... It's coming..."

Sophie watched, mesmerized, as another baby appeared, this one with light-brown hair.

"One more big push," Elspeth said.

Ally let out a deep roar.

Another niece!

"It's another baby girl!" Sophie said.

Ally fell backward, her eyes rolling to the back of her head.

"Oh my goodness, is she all right?" Sophie asked.

"She's most likely fine, my lady," Elspeth said, handing the new baby girl off to Haley for cleaning. "The poor thing's just exhausted."

Sophie hurried to Ally's side and clasped her hand. Ally's eyes were closed and her breathing rapid. Frigid claws of fear crept along the back of Sophie's neck. She had a bad feeling, but Elspeth had assisted many births and probably knew what she was talking about.

Sophie lowered her head and kissed her sister's cheek, whispering, "That was the most amazing thing I've ever seen, Ally. Thank you for making me watch so I could tell you all about it. You have two beautiful daughters, and I have two beautiful nieces. Thank you for this phenomenal gift."

Ally, unconscious, didn't respond.

"Let's get these babies to the nursery right away, Haley," Elspeth said. "Lady Alexandra will not be able to nurse them for a few hours. She needs some rest. Is there a wet nurse available on the premises?"

"I'm not sure, Mum," Haley said. "One of the stablemen's wives had a baby a few months back, but I don't know if she's still giving milk."

"Then go to the kitchen and prepare some bottles with watered-down cow's milk. It will do until her ladyship is able to feed them."

Haley handed the new baby girl to Millicent, who was already holding little Maureen. Millicent cuddled the two babies close to her, keeping them warm.

Elspeth was still cleaning up the mess between Ally's legs. "This afterbirth is messier than any I've seen," she said.

Sophie's nerves skittered. "Is everything all right?"

"I think so," Elspeth said. "There's just an awful lot of blood..."

That did not sound good. Sophie worried her lip. "I do hope the doctor gets here soon."

"As do I, milady," Elspeth said. "The afterbirth has come out, but the bleeding is not stopping."

No! Please, no. Sophie's insides churned. What if Elspeth couldn't stop the bleeding? What if the doctor never got here? Where were Evan and Mother? Why was this happening? These two little girls needed their mother, and selfish though she may be, Sophie needed her little sister.

Sophie continued holding Ally's hand. Beads of perspiration emerged on Ally's forehead, her eyes still closed in what appeared to be a dreamless sleep.

"Oh, Ally, hold on," Sophie said. "You have two baby girls who need you."

The blood still came. Sophie gulped as Elspeth soaked towel after towel with the sticky redness.

The door to the parlor thundered open, and Evan, a true mountain of a man, entered loudly. "Where is my wife?" he demanded and then cast his gaze to the unconscious Ally, Elspeth between her legs trying to staunch the bleeding. "Oh my God! What is happening?"

"Thank God you're here, Evan," Sophie said. "We're still waiting for the doctor, and Ally is bleeding from her womb. But look"—she pointed to the two bundles in Millicent's arms— "you have two baby daughters."

"Two? But my Alexandra... What's going on?" Evan's

face turned pale. His eyes glowed with extreme happiness and extreme fear at the same time. "Where is the goddamned doctor?"

"We don't know, my lord," Millicent said. "Mr. Bertram went to fetch him, and they've not returned yet. You should leave. This is no place for a gentleman."

"You'll have to drag me out of here unconscious then," Evan said. "I will not leave my wife's side."

"Come around to the other side, Evan, and take her other hand," Sophie said. "She needs to feel your presence. We need to give her our will to be strong. Talk to her. Perhaps she'll hear you."

Evan did as Sophie bid and took his place on Ally's other side. He grabbed her hand and clasped it to his cheek. "Oh, my sweet love, please fight for us and our two precious daughters. Where is that fucking doctor?"

Haley returned with two bottles of milk for the babies. She took one child from Millicent. "Let's get these two to the nursery," Haley said.

"I haven't even gotten to hold them," Evan said, his eyes sunken and sad.

"You'll have plenty of time to hold them, Evan," Sophie said. "Haley and Millicent will take good care of them for now. Right now our focus has to be on Ally."

Evan nodded.

Time passed slowly, and Sophie thought the doctor would never arrive until finally, the parlor door burst open, Iris, the earl, and a gentleman who looked to be a doctor entering.

Iris gasped. "What is going on here?"

The doctor took immediate charge. "I need everyone out of here right away. Except for you." He nodded to Elspeth.

Sophie gathered all her strength to release Ally's hand, stand, and leave the room.

Evan was not so quick to leave. "I'll not leave my wife, Doctor. She needs me."

"I'll not deny she needs you, my lord, but I must be able to do my work. You are too emotionally involved and will hinder what I need to do. Please."

Evan must have agreed, because when Sophie turned around, he had let go of Ally's hand and was walking toward the door.

Sophie ran into her mother's embrace. "Mama, I'm so scared. She's bleeding so profusely."

Iris sniffed and wiped away a tear. "She is strong, Sophie, as strong as a woman can be. I've never known anyone stronger than your sister."

Sophie agreed. "Nor have I."

The doctor requested a few more maids and then asked not to be disturbed, that he would have news when some was available.

David Xavier, the Earl of Brighton and Sophie's stepfather, was a rock in this sea of uncertainty and fear. He took his wife's hand and then clapped his son on the back. "There's nothing we can do for Alexandra right now. Be strong and be brave for her, because that's what she needs. Dr. Blake is the best physician in the area, and he will do his best for Ally. Why don't we go see my new grandchildren?"

Iris smiled a weak smile. "Yes, David, I would like that."

"An excellent idea," Sophie agreed. "I'd love to see my new nieces."

"Nice work," the earl said to Evan. "Twins."

"I don't know how to feel right now," Evan said. "Without

Alexandra... I can't even think of it. But two beautiful daughters? I feel like the luckiest man alive."

"Wait until you hold your child. You will feel emotions you never knew you had," the earl said.

"The contradictions in my emotions right now... I'm being twisted apart."

Sophie nodded to her brother-in-law. She knew exactly what he was feeling. The four of them climbed the stairs to the nursery adjacent to Evan and Ally's suite of rooms on the third level.

The new babies were both sleeping, having just finished their first meal. Sophie's heart fell a little. Their first meal should have come at Ally's breast. *But think positive, Sophie. Their second or third will come from their mother.* Swallowing the lump in her throat, Sophie forced a smile and strode forward.

★ ★ ★ ★

Zach finished up the rehearsal schedules and sat at his desk, contemplating his new lead soprano, Lady Sophie MacIntyre. Such a contradiction she was—a regal lady of the peerage, naïve and timid, yet so eager to explore her sensual side, more eager than she even knew or was willing to admit. He never would have guessed she could be such a tigress. He wanted more of her, and not just the sex. He yearned to truly know her, find out what made her tick, help her find her voice. He chuckled softly to himself. He'd never imagined any woman could bring him to his knees, certainly not such a shy and awkward lady of the peerage.

His groin tightened at the mere thought of her pink lips,

her caressing touch, her eyes that glowed with fire when she was aroused.

He'd never courted a woman, had never even considered it. But now?

He withdrew his pocket watch. Nearly teatime. Perhaps a ride out to the Brighton estate was in order, to pay a call on Lady Sophie. He longed to see her face, to hear her sweet voice, to feel her soft lips against his. And maybe another walk about the estate afterward...

★ ★ ★ ★

Sophie gazed down at the dark-blond child she held—adorable baby no-name. Evan held his firstborn daughter, Maureen Iris, the name he and Ally had chosen for a girl—named for both of their mothers.

"And what will your name be, I wonder?" Sophie asked her little niece.

The baby slept. She was so tiny. Millicent had weighed the babies, and neither one of them had made six pounds. Probably normal for twins, and that no doubt explained why they had come so early, Sophie mused.

Evan looked unkempt and worried, yet to see this mountain of a man holding his tiny child... Sophie couldn't help but smile and wonder at the miracle of it all.

But Ally... Her strong, wonderful Ally. How was she faring? No one had come to give them any news, and no one was rushing to leave the nursery. Iris and David were holding hands, Iris's fine features etched with worry.

"You're so beautiful," Evan said to tiny Maureen. He turned Sophie. "May we switch? I'd like to hold...the other one."

Sophie smiled. "Of course." They quickly switched babies so that Sophie was holding Maureen, her shock of black hair slick upon her head. Maureen was slightly bigger than the other baby but still so tiny. "What do you think you and Ally will name the other?" Sophie asked. She purposely said "you and Ally," not just "you." She couldn't accept the thought that Ally might not...

She couldn't even form the words in her mind. Ally would be fine. She had to be.

Maureen started to fuss a bit, and Sophie rocked her gently. "It's all right, baby. Your mama will be with you soon."

Sophie nearly jumped out of her shoes when a knock pounded on the door.

"Yes, come in!" Evan yelled, his tone laced with anger and fear.

The door opened, and Bertram stepped in. "My lords and ladies, the doctor has news."

CHAPTER TWELVE

Sophie's nerves jumped, and she nearly forgot to breathe. Millicent rushed toward her and took baby Maureen. Sophie looked to Evan, who had paled even further than she thought possible.

"Is Alexandra all right?" he asked.

"I'm afraid I don't have that information, my lord," Bertram said. "Mr. Graves sent me up to tell you all to come down with haste. The doctor is waiting for you in the library to discuss her condition."

Sophie didn't know whether to run out of the room and down the stairs or walk slowly. Her mind was such a jumble. How could she be so happy about the babies and so sad and frightened about Ally at the same time? Emotion gripped her like a vise. Fear surged through her veins, cold as ice. She turned to Evan. Ally was his wife now, and he should take the lead.

Evan handed the other baby to Millicent as well. "Very well. Thank you, Bertram."

"We've got you, son," the earl said.

Somberly, they all marched down the stairs into the library.

Dr. Michael Blake stood next to a bookcase, his clothing soiled with Ally's blood. Sophie's heart sank.

"My lord," Dr. Blake said to Evan, "perhaps we should speak alone."

"No," Evan said. "I would like my parents and my sister-in-law with me. They love Alexandra as much as I do."

Thank God. Sophie wasn't sure what she would have done if she had been ushered from the room.

"Very well," the doctor said. "Lady Alexandra has lost a lot of blood."

Evan shot his eyebrows up. "She's all right, then?"

The doctor nodded.

Sophie let out a sigh of relief. "May we see her, Doctor?" she asked.

Dr. Blake shook his head. "Only Lord Evan at this time," he said. "The next few days will be critical. She has lost a lot of blood, but she is a young and healthy woman."

"Whatever you need, Doctor. Whatever you must do, do it," Evan said. "I need my wife, and these babies need their mother."

And I need Ally. But Sophie didn't voice the words. Now was not the time for her to be selfish.

"There is every reason to believe she will recover," the doctor said. "As I said, she is young and strong, and she has a will of steel."

Oh, the doctor had no idea. Sophie couldn't help a small smile.

"However," Blake said, "there is something else."

Evan visibly flinched. "What is it?"

The doctor cleared his throat. "She had lost so much blood by the time I got here, I had to stop it as quickly as I could, and there was only one way to do that."

Sophie's heart pounded against her sternum as if a herd of antelope were trampling inside her.

"Lord, what did you do to her?" Evan massaged his

temples.

"I'm afraid I had to take her womb."

★ ★ ★ ★

Sophie sat in the nursery, rocking baby Maureen. Maureen had just finished a bottle and was dozing. Baby no-name had been fed earlier and was sleeping in her bassinet. Such good babies, not fussy at all. Of course, they were both still exhausted from the birth. Fussiness would come later.

They were both so perfect, and they were the only children Ally would ever have. But at least Ally was alive, although still unconscious. Dr. Blake, Evan, and the earl had managed to move her up to her suite of rooms, where she could rest comfortably in her own bed. The expensive Oriental rug in the parlor had been ruined, but no one cared. All thoughts were on Ally.

A knock on the door startled Sophie. She did not want visitors right now, but it might be news of Ally. "Yes, do come in, please."

Bertram stood in the doorway. "You have a visitor, Lady Sophie. Mr. Zachary Newland has come to call."

Zach. Although Sophie had cleaned up a bit since the birth, she was certainly in no condition to receive callers. "Please give him my regrets, Bertram. I do not wish to see anyone at the moment. I'm sure he will understand."

Bertram nodded. "As you wish, my lady."

Sophie bent back to baby Maureen. How nice for Zach to come by, but he was no doubt looking for another rendezvous in the alcove. Sophie didn't have it in her at the moment.

But perhaps someone to talk to... Yes, she did want to see

Zach after all. She placed Maureen in her bassinet and ran to the door. Bertram was just making his way to the stairwell at the end of the hall.

"Bertram," she called, "I've changed my mind. I would like to see Mr. Newland. Please have him wait for me in the small parlor." The good Lord himself only knew when the main parlor would be presentable again.

Bertram nodded and continued descending the stairs.

Sophie left the babies in Millicent's care. Because Ally had delivered so early, she and Evan had not yet hired a baby nurse. Right now, Haley and Millicent were caring for the babies.

Sophie went to her own chamber to check her appearance. The looking glass did not do her any favors. Her hair was wilted and looked plastered to her head, and her complexion was wan and pale. She bit her lips and pinched her cheeks, but it didn't help much. She couldn't really bring herself to care what she looked like at the moment, even if she was going to see Zach. If he didn't understand what she had been through today, and if he was only interested in her appearance, perhaps he wasn't a man she wanted to be spending time with.

Sophie walked down the hallway and descended the staircase, making her way to the smaller parlor. Zach stood, his back to her, looking as regal as ever in one of his fine tailored suits, his unfashionably long auburn tresses curling around his collar.

She swallowed. "Good afternoon, Mr. Newland."

Zach turned, his expression grave. "Sophie, thank you for seeing me. I came by hoping to take tea with you, but your butler told me what happened with Lady Alexandra."

Sophie nodded and gulped down a lump in her throat. "I don't know what to feel. I have two new beautiful nieces, and that's a wonderful thing. But my sister nearly lost her life and may still, and she'll never have another child."

Zach strode toward her and took her hand, lifting it to his lips and kissing it. "I know. It must be very difficult to know exactly what to feel right now. How is your sister doing?"

Sophie walked to a chair and sat, gesturing for Zach to join her in the chair across from her. "She seems to be stable, according to the doctor, and he is optimistic that she will make it. But she did lose a lot of blood. She's resting in her room now, and Evan is with her."

Zach sat in the chair Sophie motioned to. "Is there anything I can do for you? I know rehearsals are supposed to begin tomorrow, but if you're not feeling up to it, I completely understand."

"Yes, perhaps you should give the part to Miss Lloyd. I'm not sure I could do it justice in my current condition."

"Miss Lloyd is no longer with the company," Zach said. "But if you prefer, I will choose another soprano. Of course, none of them can hold a candle to you."

Sophie sighed. She had made a commitment to Zach and to the theatre. She could do nothing for Ally right now, at least not until she woke up. She let out a small laugh as she imagined what Ally would say to her if she knew Sophie was thinking about giving up the role.

"You know, I think I will be at rehearsal tomorrow after all. If I backed out of this, my sister would haunt me, telling me I should have done this."

Zach smiled. "If you're sure, Sophie. I would truly love to have you in this production, but I don't have to tell you that. You know it already."

Sophie nodded. "Right now, Ally is my first priority. And

what Ally would tell me is to continue with the role, so that is what I will do. For her."

"I am happy to hear that. Truly. Would you care to take a short walk with me? Some fresh air might do you good."

A walk sounded tempting, as long as they didn't end up in the alcove again. She was not ready for that right now. Plus, she wanted to stay close in case Ally woke up. But would Zach be after a rendezvous?

As if reading her mind, he said, "And I am talking solely about a walk, sweet. I know you're not in any condition for... other adventures."

Sophie gazed into Zach's brown eyes. He was a good man, a special man. Not to mention an extremely talented and handsome man. He had shown her some amazing phenomena. She would always hold him close in her esteem for that. Even in her current condition, when she looked at him, her heart jumped. He invaded her thoughts day and night, and even now, with Ally and the babies first and foremost on her mind, she found herself thinking of Zach.

Was it possible she was falling in love with him? She'd never been in love. She'd resigned herself to spinsterhood long ago, but here was a man who didn't see her as a timid lady of the peerage, a wallflower. Zach was interested in her voice and grooming her to be a top-notch performer. And while he may not be in love with her, he certainly seemed to be attracted to her in a way no man had ever been.

Her cheeks were burning as she let out a deep breath. "Thank you for being so understanding, Zach. I think I would enjoy a short walk."

Zach smiled, his white teeth glowing. "I'm glad. We shan't go far. But it's a sunny day, and I would like for you to enjoy it with me."

Zach offered his arm, and Sophie took it. Together they left the parlor, walked through the foyer, and out the front door.

"I don't know much about your sister, Sophie," Zach said, "but from what I can tell, she is an incredibly strong woman. If anyone can get through this, she can."

Sophie nodded. "Yes, she is strong. She is the strongest person I know, except for maybe my mother. They've both been through so much."

"I'm sorry to hear that," Zach said. "Would you like to talk about it?"

Sophie shook her head. "It's not something we talk about."

Zach cleared his throat. "I understand. But if you ever do want to talk about it, please know that I am here and am always willing to lend an ear."

"Thank you." She didn't know what else to say.

"Tell me about your two new nieces. I understand you were present for their birth."

"Yes, it was the most incredible thing I've ever seen. We had no idea Ally was having twins, so it was a complete surprise. She went into labor quickly, and the babies were actually delivered by one of our maids, Elspeth. The first one is named Maureen Iris, after both Evan's mother and Ally's and mine. The second one doesn't have a name yet. Evan is waiting until Ally wakes up to discuss it with her. Right now, she's baby no-name." Sophie sighed. "If only Ally would wake up. She lost so much blood, Zach. I nearly emptied my stomach, watching it happen."

"Well, she has the best doctor money can buy. Dr. Michael Blake is the finest in Bath."

Sophie nodded. Dr. Blake had saved Lily's womb after

a bad fall over a year ago. He hadn't been able to save Ally's, but he probably could have if he'd gotten there sooner. Sophie hoped he had at least saved her life.

She stayed quiet for a while, simply walking, enjoying the green surroundings and Zach's company. When they came to a large boulder, Zach gestured for her to sit.

"There's something I've been thinking about, Sophie." He took one of her hands and held it in his.

She looked up into his beautiful eyes, dazzling in the late-afternoon sunlight. "And what is that?"

"I find that...I'm having feelings for you that I don't think I've ever had for any other woman." He shook his head. "That didn't come out right at all. I am feeling very fond of you, Sophie. I've never actually courted a woman before, but I would like your permission to ask your stepfather if I can formally court you."

Sophie dropped her jaw open. Had she heard him right? All those liberties she had allowed him, and he still wanted to court her? Perhaps Ally'd had the right of it all along. Holding back liberties had gotten her nowhere with Van Arden or anyone else. On the other hand, she was certain many women had allowed Zach many liberties, yet he hadn't asked to court any of them. Was it possible he actually had feelings for her? Feelings that went beyond his love of her voice? His enjoyment of her company?

"Aren't you going to say anything? Surely I haven't offended you, have I?"

"Of course not. I'm flattered. I truly am. I just never thought..." Deep breath. "I mean, you and I have already... And please, please don't think I've ever done that with any other man, because I haven't."

He smiled. "I believe you. I know you haven't been with any other man."

"But you've been with many other women, haven't you?"

He smiled, a glint in his eye. "I will not lie to you, Sophie. I've been with many women in my life. But never have I asked to court any of them."

Sophie let out a sigh. "I just never thought..."

Zach let go of her hand. "I understand. You're not interested."

Sophie shook her head. "No, that's not what I mean. I *am* interested. I just... I'm of an age... And I had pretty much resigned myself to... Oh, this is embarrassing."

Zach took her hand once more, rubbing his thumb lightly over her knuckles, making her shiver.

"You needn't be embarrassed with me, Sophie. I like you very much, and I think these feelings I'm having might blossom into something more. You're a beautiful woman, so much lovelier than you believe. Will you allow me to court you?"

Sophie quivered, her whole body turning to marmalade. Why she was so nervous, she couldn't say. She had already been naked in front of this man, had allowed him to spank her bare bottom. "Yes, Zach, I would be honored to have you court me."

She smiled. Perhaps this would work out. Perhaps babies as angelic as little Maureen and her sister were in Sophie's future after all. Of course, courtship didn't automatically mean marriage. And Sophie had been through so much. Could she be an adequate wife and mother? She didn't have Ally's strength.

But she needn't worry about all that at the moment. A wonderful man wanted to court her, and she would allow it, provided her mother and the earl were amenable.

Zach leaned toward her and pressed his lips softly against hers. "The honor will be mine, Lady Sophie MacIntyre. I will speak to your stepfather as soon as I can."

Zach took Sophie's hand, and they walked back to the estate.

"I shall see you bright and early tomorrow morning at rehearsal, my lady," Zach said, kissing her hand again.

Sophie nodded. "I will be there. I'm actually quite looking forward to it."

And she was.

No sooner had she come in than Graves grabbed her arm.

"Lady Alexandra has awoken, my lady. She's asking for you."

CHAPTER THIRTEEN

Zach, still holding Sophie's hand, looked down at her with grave eyes. "Would you like me to stay?"

How kind of him to ask, but he no doubt had much work to do, with rehearsals beginning on the morrow. She shook her head. "There's no need," she said, her voice shaking a bit. "If Ally is awake, this can only be a good thing." Sophie hoped to God she spoke the truth.

"I shall bid you good day, then," Zach said, giving her hand a chaste kiss. "And I will see you on the morrow for rehearsal."

Sophie nodded and gave him a smile as he left. She then turned to Graves. "How is Lady Ally, Graves?"

"I'm afraid I don't have any information on her condition, my lady," Graves said. "She is in her suite. Lord Evan is with her. All I know is that she wants to see you."

Sophie didn't take the time to thank Graves. Instead, she ran up the two flights of stairs to the third level to Ally's suite of rooms. She knocked loudly on the door.

The door opened, and in front of her stood Evan, his lips a thin line.

"Evan, I came as soon as I heard. How is she?"

"She is weak, but she's awake. We don't know for how long. The poor dear is exhausted. I've summoned Dr. Blake, though she may fall back to sleep before he gets here. But she wants to see you."

Sophie raced through the sitting room and into Ally's

private bedchamber. Her sister lay on the bed, her normally peachy skin pasty, her normally ruby-red lips a light pink. Her golden eyes were sunken. Yet her lips curved up in a small smile. "Sophie," she croaked out.

Sophie glided to her and took her hand. "Oh, Ally, I've been so worried."

"Now goodness, dear, you know there's no need to worry about me. I'm as strong as an ox. And we both know I've been through much worse than this."

Sophie's lips trembled. She knew all too well what Ally had been through, usually by trying to save her, Sophie, from going through it. Of course, that wasn't the case nearly a year ago, when Ally had been beaten badly by Frank Osborne, a clerk at one of Evan's businesses. Ally had recovered then, and with strength and determination, of which Ally had plenty, she would recover now.

Sophie hesitated to say too much. Had Evan told Ally what had happened? That she would never have any more children? Sophie didn't know, and she couldn't very well excuse herself right now to ask Evan.

"Have you been able to see your daughters?" she asked her sister.

"Yes, Mother and Millicent brought them to me a few minutes ago. Two baby girls. Can you even imagine it?"

Sophie smiled. "Yes, I can imagine it. I witnessed the birth. The doctor says that's why you were so big and why you delivered so early."

"They're so tiny."

"Tiny, yes, but with the strength and determination of their mother, they will thrive." Sophie squeezed Ally's hand.

"Sophie, I'm so glad you were with me during the birth. I

asked you to witness it for me so you could tell me what you saw, and I will ask you about it soon, but right now I'm just too tired."

"I certainly understand. But I will tell you now that it was the most miraculous thing I've ever witnessed. Thank you for giving me that gift."

"Thank you for being there," Ally said. "If you hadn't been, I'm not quite sure I would've gotten through it. But knowing you were there..." She let out a small cough.

"Don't tire yourself out, Ally. Just relax and go back to sleep if you need to. The babies are in good hands, and so are you."

"But there's something I need to tell you..."

"It can wait."

"No, I really want you to know. I talked to Evan, and we both agree—we want to name the second baby girl Sophie."

"Sophie?" Her heart did a pitter-patter, and she warmed. "I'm honored, of course, but I thought you hated both our names because they came from our father." She and Ally had both been named after their father—Angus Alexander Sophocles MacIntyre, the Earl of Longarry.

"How can I hate the name of the closest person to me in the world? We've decided to name her after you, after the maid who delivered her, and after Dr. Michael Blake who...saved my life. Sophie Elspeth Michaela."

Sophie's eyes misted. "It's a lovely name, Ally. Beautiful, even."

"Little Sophie is a miracle, a delightful surprise we didn't expect. And that's how I feel about you, Sophie. You taking the role in that production—you're going to find that it leads to many surprises that you never expected. I think it's already led to some."

Sophie couldn't deny what Ally said. She had so much to talk to her sister about, beginning with Zach's offer to court her. Imagine, a man as handsome and talented as Zachary Newland wanted to court her? But Ally's energy was waning. Their sisterly talk would have to wait.

Evan entered from the sitting room. "I think that's enough, my love. You need to rest."

Ally nodded. "Yes, Evan, I am indeed exhausted. Thank you for bringing Sophie to me."

"Anything for you, my Alexandra," Evan said. "Thank you for giving me two precious little daughters."

Sophie became uncomfortable. This was a moment for Ally to be sharing with her husband. She quietly stole out of the bedchamber and out of the suite.

She knew now, in all her heart, that Ally would be all right. She would recover, and though she may feel the loss of her womb, her two little daughters would heal her heart and soul.

She smiled, wandering into the nursery adjoining Evan and Ally's suite. Time to dote on Maureen and little Sophie.

★ ★ ★ ★

Sophie woke early to Hannah's rapping on her door. She had asked the maid to wake her at six in the morning, so she could ready herself for rehearsal.

Goodness, the life of a working girl! Never a life she had imagined for herself, but she found herself strangely rising to the challenge and looking forward to it. With Hannah's help, she bathed, dressed, did her hair, and then descended for a light breakfast.

Only the earl was up at this hour. "Good morning, Sophie," he said jovially. "I understand you will be going to the theatre this morning for rehearsal."

"Yes, I'm a little frightened but looking forward to it. Is there any news on Ally this morning?"

"Blake tells me she's going to be fine. We're glad of that. And I'm thrilled with my two new granddaughters. I hear one is to be your namesake."

Sophie warmed. "Yes, I was quite touched when Ally told me."

"A beautiful name it is, just like the first in the family to carry it." He gave her a wink.

She warmed again, remembering that Zach would be coming sometime soon to talk to the earl about courting her. She still couldn't wrap her mind around that one. Did she even want to be courted? Yes, she did. And God help her, she wanted more...adventures with Zach.

But this morning was all about work. After a scone and some tea, she rose and excused herself.

"A coach is waiting to take you into town to the theatre," the earl said with a smile. "We are all very much looking forward to your debut, Sophie."

Sophie nodded, too nervous to answer. She nearly stumbled walking out the door, so skittish she was. The coachman helped her into the lavish coach, and soon they were off, the horses clopping down the dirt roads, taking her off the estate and toward the city of Bath. Sophie shivered the whole way. It was late April, and she was dressed appropriately, but still she quivered, her nerves not allowing her peace. She hoped she had not made a huge mistake agreeing to take this role.

After what seemed like hours, the coach finally arrived

in front of the Regal Theatre. The coachman helped Sophie down and escorted her in. The doorman welcomed her and showed her where to go. All performers were to head into the theatre itself and sit in the audience chairs, where Zach and the director would tell them what they would be doing today.

Sophie walked nervously toward the theatre when an arm grabbed her from behind and pulled her into a secluded corner. She looked into the blue eyes of Miss Nanette Lloyd.

"You may be Zach's flavor *du jour*, my lady, but I assure you it's only a matter of time until I am back as lead soprano... and as his lead performer in the bedchamber."

Zach had slept with Nanette? Of course, Sophie shouldn't be surprised. She had caught them in that clench.

"What are you doing here, Miss Lloyd?" Sophie asked. "Zach told me you'd been dismissed from the company."

"That was just a silly misunderstanding between Zach and me. I was not dismissed. In fact, I'll be taking over your role later today, when it becomes clear that you can't handle it."

Oh, this woman did have a lot of nerve! Sophie's first inclination was to back down and cower in a corner, but an image of Ally, strong and vibrant, popped into her mind. How would Ally handle the situation? She would fight, just like she had been fighting her whole life for everything that meant anything to her. Sophie had grown a lot in the last few days. She had performed at an audition, been intimate with a man, watched her sister give birth to two babies. Sophie had found strength that she never knew she possessed.

She would use that strength now.

"I assure you I can handle this role, Miss Lloyd. This part is mine and will continue to be mine until the closing of this production. Now, if you'll kindly get out of my way, I'm late for rehearsal."

"Not so fast, you little harlot. I know what you're doing. You're sleeping with Zach. That's how you got this part."

Sophie warmed all over, despite the untruths of what Nanette was saying. She had gotten the part before she and Zach became intimate, and technically they hadn't even slept together yet, at least not done the physical act. "I'm nothing like you, Miss Lloyd. I do not trade my sexual favors for a role. I won this role fair and square on my talent alone."

"Well, goody-goody for you. I can assure you, Zach is not at all interested in you."

Sophie couldn't help herself. "Oh, he's not, is he? Then why did he ask permission to ask my stepfather to court me?"

Nanette's face turned red and her knuckles white as she crunched her hands into fists. "He did what?"

"I'm sure there's nothing wrong with your hearing, dear. You heard me correctly. Zach would like to court me." Sophie struggled to hold her stance. She wasn't nearly as sure of herself as her words indicated.

"That's absolutely preposterous. Zachary Newland doesn't court women. He uses them."

"So are you saying that he used you?"

"Of course not. We had a real relationship. We were in love."

Sophie bit her lip. Surely Zach hadn't loved Nanette, had he? It was unlikely...but what did Sophie really know about Zach?

"Whatever your relationship was, it appears to be over now."

Nanette seethed. "I assure you, whatever you're doing to

get Zach to roll over and beg for you, it will end. He will get sick of you just like he gets sick of every other woman. He has the attention span of a toddler, you know."

Sophie bit her lip again. Nanette's words rang with truth. Did Zach really want to court her? Or was he just conniving to make sure she stayed in the production through its end? Sophie didn't know, but she was damned sure of one thing. She was taking this role, and she was going to handle it to the best of her ability. She enjoyed singing, and if she herself could find joy and also bring joy to others at the same time, she had to do this. She had to come out of her shell and live a little. She had to try to be more like Ally.

"Whether Zach gets sick of me or not is hardly an issue here. I am now the lead soprano, whether Zach is courting me or not. And I will be playing this role, which means you won't be."

Nanette's hand jetted out fast as a whip, and she smacked Sophie across the face.

Sophie jerked backward, stunned. Her cheek was numb for a moment before the pain. Of course, she was used to that. It had always surprised her each time her father hit her—how the pain didn't come instantaneously. No, the numbness came first and then the pain.

Tears misted in Sophie's eyes, but she gulped them back. "If you ever touch me again, Miss Lloyd, I shall summon a constable and have you arrested. Now, I am late to rehearsal." She pushed Nanette out of the way. "Good day."

Sophie walked unsteadily to the theatre. When she opened the door and walked in, Zach waved to her from the stage. "Ah, here's our leading lady now. Lady Sophie MacIntyre, everyone."

The rest of the company seated in the audience applauded. Sophie's cheeks warmed further, and not as a result of Nanette's slap. What was she supposed to do? Take a curtsy? She simply smiled and walked to an empty seat.

"Eugene is distributing your librettos, and our esteemed Lord Thornton is distributing your music."

Cameron smiled at Sophie as he handed her the packet of music. Goodness, it was over an inch thick! How in the world would she learn all of this? It was still late April, and the show opened on Midsummer Eve. That gave her nearly two months to prepare. Still, she shook her head. What had she gotten into?

Nothing you can't handle, Ally's voice said in her head. When the man called Eugene handed her the libretto, she flinched again. Another inch-thick book to memorize. Lord in heaven!

"Today we're simply going to do a read-through of the written part of the musicale," Zach said. "I'd like all of the starring and supporting roles to come join me on stage and take a seat in one of the chairs behind me. Small roles and chorus may stay in the audience for now."

Sophie inhaled a deep breath and stood, making her way to the stage. She chose a chair on the end, so as not to bring too much attention to herself. She looked hurriedly through the libretto and found her character, Lady Eliza Canterbury. Lady Eliza was a woman of the peerage who fell in love with a commoner living on her father's land.

Zach himself played the role of the commoner, Brendan Smith.

Papers rustled as the actors and actresses took their places on stage and opened their librettos. Zach finally took a seat with the rest of them, opposite Sophie.

"All right, ladies and gentlemen. Let's begin our first read-through of *Love on a Midsummer Night* by the Earl of Thornton."

Sophie's voice cracked on her first line, but soon her nerves stopped skittering and she became immersed in the enchanting story unfolding before her. Zach had done an amazing job with these words. Perhaps memorizing her part would not be such a problem. She'd been hoping she would sing on this first day, but the read-through went until noon. Zach dismissed everyone for the day right before lunch, telling them to take their music home and work through it themselves. Tomorrow morning, they would break up into groups and practice the music and then do another read-through in the afternoon, including the music.

Sophie shook her head. She was decent at the pianoforte, but this music was difficult. Still, she could play it note by note and learn it this afternoon. It would keep her busy and keep her mind off of Ally.

Zach cornered her on her way out. "Lady Sophie, could I see you in my office, please?"

She bit her lip worriedly. "Yes, of course...Mr. Newland."

He led her to his office and closed the door. Before she knew it, he had pushed her against the door and clamped his lips onto hers. The kiss was slow and deliberate, loving and caring. But within moments, it became hot and passionate, demanding and searching. Sophie responded in spite of herself, yearning for him, leaning into him, and pressing herself to him.

After several frenzied moments, Zach broke the kiss. He hit his forehead on the wall. "Forgive me. I know you must still be worried and upset about your sister. But ever since I saw you walk into the theatre this morning, I had to have a taste of you."

Sophie's breath came in rapid puffs. She nodded, trying to speak, but no words emerged.

"I'm sorry we haven't had a chance to talk," Zach said. "How is your sister doing?"

"Better," Sophie said. "She woke up last night, and I had a chance to speak with her. She seems better. I just don't know if..."

"Know if what?"

"I don't know if Evan has told her that she'll never have more children."

"She is strong, your sister. She will accept her lot. She has two beautiful babies. She will be fine."

Sophie nodded, hoping Zach spoke the truth. She bit her lip. "Zach, you know I've never performed before..."

"What is it?"

"The music and the libretto—they're so much...more comprehensive than I expected them to be."

"Yes, it is a little daunting at first. But realize that, even with a leading role, only about a quarter of those words and music are yours."

Sophie let out a shaky laugh. "That's still an awful lot to learn."

"It is. But I wouldn't have given you the role if I didn't think you were more than capable of doing it. You're a smart young lady, Sophie, with an incredible talent. We'll be working long and hard on this production, and there will be some late nights for you because I want you to have extra voice instruction."

"But I thought you loved my voice."

"I do. The reason for the extra instruction is to teach you how to sing in a healthy way, so you won't strain your vocal cords. You're going to be singing for hours and hours each day, and if you don't do it correctly, you will lose your voice."

There was so much Sophie didn't know about all of this. "Who will be instructing me?"

"I'll handle some of the instruction myself, but I'm also bringing in a female professional singer—she has an amazing voice—who will be able to teach you nuances that I, as a male, cannot."

"When will these extra voice lessons begin?"

"Probably tomorrow evening, after rehearsal."

Sophie bit her lip again, worried.

"Is something the matter?"

"Oh, no. It's just...I'll be away from the estate so much. And I really did want to keep an eye on Ally."

"I understand." He looked at her, his forehead creasing. "Perhaps we could make arrangements to do the extra instructions at your estate. Dame Helga—she's the soprano you'll be working with—and I could come to the estate three or four evenings a week, if that would be amenable to you and your family."

Dame Helga? The name sounded slightly familiar to Sophie. "If this Dame Helga is as remarkable as you say she is, why isn't she the lead soprano?"

Zach let out a resounding jovial laugh. "She's sixty-six years old, Sophie. I don't think she can accurately portray a twenty-year-old lady of the peerage on stage."

Sophie couldn't help but laugh. In the midst of her mirth, Zach leaned down and kissed her once again. His firm lips made her knees quiver. He reached for the doorknob, and she heard the lock on his door click softly. What about luncheon? And what about rehearsing the music on her own this afternoon?

Well, if Zach wasn't worried about that, why should she be?

He turned her around so she faced the closed door, unbuttoned her dress, and brushed it softly over her shoulders. He loosened her corset and removed it. Sophie throbbed between her legs. Zach turned her back around to face him and pushed her chemise over her shoulders. Soon she stood naked and vulnerable except for her drawers.

"How is it," she asked, chewing on her bottom lip again, "that I always end up naked and you fully clothed?"

He smiled. "We can take care of that if you would like." He removed his jacket and loosened his cravat.

Sophie longed to reach forward and tear off his shirt, but her timidity did not allow it. Instead, Zach unbuttoned his shirt, and Sophie swallowed, her skin heating as each new inch of golden skin was exposed. The mahogany hairs over his nipples and chest drew her gaze. So very glorious.

When his shirt was in a white heap on the floor, Zach began to work on his britches. Sophie's nerves scampered across her skin. She had never seen this part of him, though she had felt it through his trousers. Even now, the large bulge unnerved her. He unbuckled his belt and unbuttoned his trousers. When he brushed them down his thighs, he stood in front of her wearing only his drawers. A small wet spot the size of a pea dampened the fabric. What might that be?

Slowly, Zach brushed his drawers over his hips and down his thighs. Sophie widened her eyes. His...cock—good Lord, the word "cock!"—stood at attention, springing from a bush of auburn curls. She couldn't help staring. It was large—larger than she had ever thought possible. The tip of it wept slightly, explaining the tiny spot of moisture on his drawers. It was majestic and magnificent, with two veins swirling around it like marbling.

She resisted the urge to reach for it.

Zach let out a happy laugh.

Sophie had no idea what was so funny. "What is it?"

"Here I stand, hard as granite and ready to take you, and I forgot one very important detail."

"What might that be?"

Zach looked down. "I forgot to take off my boots first."

Sophie erupted in peals of giggles. She hadn't even considered his boots. In fact, she couldn't even remember how her own shoes had come off during their previous encounters. Zach must have taken care of it like he took care of everything. Even now she stood, her shoes and stockings still on her feet.

Zach pulled off his boots and discarded his stockings and other garments. Then he knelt to Sophie and unlaced her shoes, removing them along with her stockings.

For once, Sophie was less naked than Zach was. She still had her drawers on. She smiled, her gaze still drawn to his cock.

"You can touch it if you want," he said.

She gave him a small smile.

He took her hand and led it to his erection. "Please, touch me, Sophie. I want you to. I need you to. Every night I fall asleep dreaming of your hands on me, pleasuring me, your lips kissing me."

Sophie unclenched her hand and timidly touched his penis. It was warm—so warm and so very hard. Her pussy throbbed. How might it feel inside her? Should she put her lips around it? Ally had told her men like that...*a lot*.

"Yes, yes, sweet. Just like that. Your touch feels so good. Ignite the fire within me."

Zach put his hand over hers, guiding her, showing her how to touch him, how to find his rhythm. She had never imagined that a cock would have a rhythm, but it did, and it matched perfectly the throbbing inside her. Zach moved his other hand toward her breasts and tweaked a nipple. She jerked, sensation traveling like lightning from her skin inward, culminating in the warm spot between her legs.

"God, Sophie." Zach gripped her hand on his shaft more tightly and slowed her down a bit. "This will be over all too soon if you go any faster."

A wave of empowerment settled over Sophie. She had control over him—this large and dominant man. She could bring him to his knees with one thrusting stroke.

She smiled. As much power as he had over her, she held the same power over him. She had never imagined such. And she liked it. Yes, she liked it very much.

But something stopped her. She ceased stroking and looked up into his bronze eyes.

"Zach, are you serious about talking to my stepfather about courting me?"

CHAPTER FOURTEEN

Zach jerked, the loss of Sophie's hand on his shaft tormenting him. What had she said? Something about speaking to her stepfather about courting her? Of course he was serious. How could she think he wasn't?

"Sophie, sweet, of course I want to speak to your stepfather. I just haven't had the chance yet, with getting the new production underway."

Her beautiful cheeks reddened to that radiant raspberry he knew so well. "Of course. I didn't mean to imply that—"

"I understand perfectly, my love. You don't want to go any further until we are officially courting, do you?"

"Well, that's not exactly true. I do want to go further. I mean, we've already gone further than I ever anticipated I would without the sanctity of marriage. I just thought...if you are serious about our courtship...well, we should at least wait..."

Zach smiled. She was just so damned captivating. He wasn't used to waiting for a woman, but he had a feeling Sophie would be worth it.

"I'll tell you what. Why don't I escort you home. You can work on your music as instructed. And I will talk to your stepfather."

"Oh... Well, of course that would be lovely, but I don't actually know if he's at home this afternoon."

"Not to worry. I shall escort you home anyway, and if he is not able to receive me, I'll leave a message with the butler, and the earl can let me know when he is available to receive my call."

"I suppose that will be acceptable," Sophie said. "I do hope he is home."

"As do I." Zach winked at her. "I don't fancy waiting any longer to have you."

Sophie's blush deepened. Clearly she didn't fancy waiting longer either.

★ ★ ★ ★

"Thank you for seeing me, my lord." Zach faced the Earl of Brighton, who sat in a supple leather chair behind a large cherry desk. The walls were papered with velvet-edged burgundy, the molding a darker cherry.

"Not at all, Mr. Newland." Brighton cleared his throat. "Do have a seat."

Zach nodded.

"It's good you stopped by. I've been meaning to thank you for the kindness you've shown my stepdaughter, Lady Sophie. We are all excited about her singing debut in your production come midsummer."

"She is quite a talent. In fact, it is because of Sophie that I need to speak to you."

"I assure you that her mother and I support her performance inclinations. She is a lady of the peerage, but we feel that her talent for singing is paramount, and if she chooses to perform on stage, she should."

Zach cleared his throat. "I'm very glad to hear you say that, my lord. All of us at the theatre are very happy to have Sophie join us."

"Now, what is it that you want to speak with me about?"

"Well...first of all, how is Lady Alexandra doing?"

"It's good of you to ask, Newland. She's recovering nicely, though slowly. She did lose quite a bit of blood, but the doctor assures us at this point that she will make a full recovery as long as she goes slowly and doesn't overexert herself."

Zach nodded. That was good news. It would make Sophie extremely happy, and he wanted Sophie's happiness above anything. "I'm very glad to hear that, my lord."

"As are we all, Newland."

Zach fidgeted a bit with his hands and then spoke. "I would like your permission to court Lady Sophie."

The earl's eyebrows shot skyward. "I say, you wish to court Sophie?"

I thought I just said that. "Yes, my lord. I have grown quite fond of her, and she has indicated that she would be amenable to my suit."

"I see. Mr. Newland, you are a man of the theatre, not a gentleman of the peerage. We had hoped for a titled man for Sophie."

"If I may be so bold, my lord," Zach said. "Sophie's sister, Alexandra, married your own son, and he does not possess a title."

"You make a good point, Newland, but remember, my son is still a gentleman of impeccable lineage."

Impeccable lineage? The man obviously thought highly of himself. Impeccable lineage Zach certainly did not have. A father he never even knew and a mother who died when he was very young... What could he say? "I may not come from the type of lineage you wish for Sophie, but I assure you I care very much for her, and I would be able to support her."

"You no doubt know about her dowry, do you not?"

Zach shook his head. "I did not know she had a dowry. It was my understanding that her father left her, her mother, and her sister penniless."

"Yes, he did. However, I have given Sophie a substantial dowry of twenty-five thousand pounds."

Zach forced himself not to jerk in the chair. Twenty-five thousand pounds? What magnificent things he could do with that amount of money. He had no idea that Sophie came with such an amount.

"That is generous indeed, my lord. I had no idea Sophie even had a dowry."

"You're a smart man, Newland. Surely you don't expect me to believe that you didn't know about the dowry."

"I assure you, I did not know. This is the first I've heard of it."

The earl rose, walked from behind his desk, and stood next to Zach's chair. Lord Brighton was a substantial man and stood a few inches taller than Zach himself did. "I'm afraid I cannot accept your suit for Lady Sophie, Mr. Newland."

Zach's heart fell. He had never imagined that Brighton would say no. "Please, my lord. Sophie and I are quite fond of each other, and I truly would like to get to know her better."

"You'll have ample chance to get to know her while you're working together at the theatre. I know all about you, Newland. I know you have a girl in every port and you've had many mistresses."

"That's absolutely not true!" Zach pounded his hand on the cherry desk. "I'll not deny that I've had my share of women in the past, but what young man hasn't? I've never kept any of them. I promise you that. I am serious about Lady Sophie, and

I will again reiterate that I did not know about the dowry. I am asking only for courtship at this time, my lord, not for her hand in marriage. We must find out whether we suit together."

Brighton shook his head. "I can discuss it with my wife. However, I'm not holding out much hope for you, Newland. We both want a better match for Sophie. Theatre management is by no means a sure thing these days. Your venture is still new, less than a year old at this point. What if we have an economic downturn? The first thing people will do is look for expenses they no longer need to have. Theatre tickets will be at the top of that list."

"My lord, I have been in the theatre since I was nineteen years old. I'm now over thirty, and I not only manage my own theatre, I own it. I'll not deny that I've had benefactors in the past, but at this point, I am making it on my own. I have a good name in the theatre, and that is not going anywhere. We run only top-quality productions, and we have steered clear of the burlesque-type shows, even though they would be an easy way to bring in money to the theatre. I run a fine business, Lord Brighton, and I don't appreciate you alluding otherwise."

Who did this man think he was? Zach was a perfect match for Sophie. He wanted to do this the correct way, but her stepfather wasn't letting him.

"I am making no such allusions, Mr. Newland. I am simply stating facts. Operation of a theatre is by no means a reliable income."

Zach drew in a breath and paused for a few seconds, getting his bearing. "What will it take to get you to agree to let me court Lady Sophie?"

"As I said, I will discuss it with her mother." Brighton held out his hand.

Zach reluctantly shook hands with the earl and then left the room somberly. What could he say to Sophie? She had been relying on him, and he had no doubt that she would refuse to see him after this. She wanted to do everything properly. She was a lady, and he didn't blame her.

Of course, they had done many things already...

He stole down the hall to the conservatory, where Sophie was practicing her music. She was bent over the pianoforte, her lips in a tense line, her forehead beaded with tiny balls of perspiration. She was plunking out notes on the piano and singing them, working through her pieces. Zach hated to disturb her and hated even more to give her bad news.

He gently cleared his throat.

Sophie looked up and smiled. "I didn't realize you were still here."

"I was talking to your stepfather. He says your sister is on the mend."

"Yes, the doctor thinks she will make a full recovery."

"I'm very glad for all of you." Zach fidgeted with his fingers, making a steeple of them and then lacing them together.

"I've been working through this music, Zach, and it's quite difficult. I hope your faith in me is founded."

"I assure you I have complete faith in you, Sophie. You were born to play this role."

"So are we formally courting now?" she asked, her eyes bright.

Zach sighed. "I'm afraid that...your stepfather has refused my suit."

Sophie's lips formed an O. "He what? Why would he do such a thing?"

Because apparently I'm not good enough for you. But

Zach didn't say those words. "He feels we are too...different. That you, a lady of the peerage, would never be satisfied with a working man like myself. He feels the theatre is not a reliable income and that I would not be able to support you."

"But it's what I want."

"It's what I want too, Sophie, more than I ever thought I'd want anything. In fact, I didn't know exactly how much I wanted it until he told me I couldn't have it. You're unlike any woman I've ever known." He'd never known any woman so beautiful who had no idea how beautiful she was. So talented and had no idea how talented she was.

Sophie's cheeks turned rosy, and she bit on her soft pink lips, turning them into a luscious raspberry color.

"I still would like to see you, Sophie, but if you say no, I will understand."

"This doesn't change how I feel about you, Zach. You've shown me such... Oh, I can't even say the words."

Zach lifted his lips into a small smile.

"Honestly, no man has ever paid me a lick of attention. Why my stepfather thinks that some gentleman of the peerage will come by and snatch me up, I couldn't tell you."

"Then no gentleman has bothered to look beneath the surface and find the real you, Sophie. I feel I've scratched the surface, and I want to know you deeper, more intimately. I think I'm... I think we could have something special, beautiful."

Her dazzling mouth dropped into an O shape again.

He could hold back no longer. He took her hands and pulled her up from the piano bench, wrapped his arms around her, held her close, and kissed her sweet pink lips.

Already, he was hurting inside his trousers. This woman affected him like no other ever had. So alluring and so naïve, yet open to exploring her sexuality. Clearly she'd never let another man take liberties with her. For some reason, she had allowed Zach to do so. He had no idea why, but he wasn't going to question it. He needed her. Whether her stepfather agreed or not, he was going to have her.

He dipped his tongue into her soft, warm mouth, drinking of her essence, partaking of her sweet honey goodness. When he needed a breath, he broke the kiss and nibbled across her cheek to her neck, down to the soft skin of her shoulder.

"Zach," she said against his shoulder, "we mustn't do this here. Especially after my stepfather..."

"Please, Sophie," he whispered against her earlobe. "Please say you'll agree to see me, even without your stepfather's approval."

His heart was beating so wildly he felt sure she could feel it against her breast. What would he do if she refused? He couldn't even imagine it. She had become so important to him in so short a time. He still wasn't sure he understood why, but did it matter? She had something that drew him, that spoke to the very innermost chambers of the soul. He couldn't bear the thought of losing her.

"Please, Sophie. Please don't leave me."

CHAPTER FIFTEEN

Sophie pushed backward slowly until her knees hit the piano bench, and she sat down with a plop. "What is it, Zach?"

"Please don't leave me, Sophie."

The need in his voice shattered her defenses. She had every intention of continuing to see him at rehearsal. "Zach, I've made a commitment to the production. I will not leave it."

"Damn it, Sophie, that's not what I meant." Zach let out a heavy sigh. "For the love of God, never mind." He turned and then looked over his shoulder. "I'll see you at rehearsal tomorrow, bright and early." He left the conservatory, his boots thudding on the marble flooring.

Sophie stood, mouth agape. Since when had Zach Newland become so emotional? She didn't want to stop seeing him, but could she go against her stepfather's wishes?

She smiled to herself. Yes. For Zach, she would defy her stepfather. She hated to do it, after all the earl had done for her, Ally, and their mother. He absolutely adored their mother, and he treated Ally and Sophie like his own daughters. Why wouldn't he allow Zach to court her? After all, gentlemen weren't exactly lining up for favors. They never had been.

She had already gone further with Zach than she ever imagined, especially outside the bonds of matrimony. Perhaps she should talk to Ally, or maybe her mother. If she told her mother how much fun she had with Zach, how fond she was of him, perhaps her mother would talk to the earl and get him to change his mind. She truly wanted to be courted by Zach out in the open. This sneaking around was very difficult for her. Sophie obeyed the rules. She was not Ally.

Yes, Ally. Ally would know what to do. Sophie left the conservatory and went up the two back staircases to Ally's suite of rooms on the third level. She knocked lightly. The door opened, and Evan stood there. "Evan, how is Ally doing? I'd like to see her."

Evan shook his head. "I'm sorry, Sophie. Ally is sleeping, and I don't want her disturbed."

Sophie understood. Days or even weeks would pass before Ally was back to her usual energetic self. "All right, Evan. Thank you."

"I'll be happy to come find you if she wakes up."

"Yes, please. I would appreciate that."

Sophie walked quietly to the door of the nursery and peeked in. The new baby nurse, Mrs. Oakes, was feeding baby Sophie. Maureen was asleep in her bassinet.

"Do you mind?" Sophie asked.

Mrs. Oakes smiled and handed her little Sophie. The baby was warm in Sophie's arms, and happiness engulfed her. Only a week ago, Sophie had resigned herself to doting on her cousins' and sister's babies. Now, for the first time, a man was interested in her.

Sophie didn't delude herself that Zach's interest would definitely lead to marriage, but without the courtship, there was no chance of marriage or her own babies. Why had the earl refused Zach's request? Sophie had lived on the earl's estate for a year now, and other than Van Arden, no man had come calling for her.

She knew what Ally would advise her to do—the same

thing Ally would do if she were in her place. Defy authority and continue to see Zach on the sly. They couldn't be seen in public, but that hadn't been a problem so far. They'd taken a few walks around the estate. That was it. The rest of their interactions had taken place behind closed doors.

Sophie handed the baby back to Mrs. Oakes. She would like nothing better than to stay with the babies all afternoon, but she did have music practice. She headed down the stairs.

Graves met her at the bottom of the stairs with a parchment. "This message was just delivered for you, my lady."

"Thank you, Graves." Sophie took the parchment and opened it. Another ominous note in the same handwriting. *You are closer to being mine all the time. I will eliminate all obstacles.*

Sophie's skin chilled. This one was bothersome. It seemed almost...threatening.

If only Ally were awake. Sophie desperately needed to discuss these notes with her. She had been assuming they were from Zach—however, Zach had just left her an hour ago. Would he have sent a note in that short of time? Perhaps he left a note with Graves or left a note for Graves to find. But could Zach have written this one? The tone was...odd. Frightening, even.

Sophie ascended the stairs once again to Ally's room and knocked gently. Evan opened the door.

"I'm so sorry, Evan. I just thought I would check and see if Ally had awakened. I do need to speak to her."

"Actually, you're in luck," Evan said. "She is awake, and she has asked me to go get the babies for her. While I am getting Mrs. Oakes to bring them in to her, you may have a few moments. Just don't upset her or wear her out."

"Thank you. I would never do anything to upset her."

Sophie entered the bedchamber. Ally lay on her bed, her head and shoulders propped up slightly by a pillow. She smiled when Sophie entered.

"Sophie, what a lovely surprise."

"How are you feeling, Ally? You're looking better."

"Oh, please, spare me the untruths. Evan brought me a looking glass, and I look simply ghastly. But I am feeling a bit better."

"I'm so glad to hear that," Sophie hedged a bit. How could she bring this up? "Evan gave me a few minutes to talk to you. I got another note from my secret person." She handed the note to Ally.

Ally read it. "This is a puzzler."

"I was thinking they were from Zach. He actually asked the earl for permission to court me—"

"He what?" Ally's mouth broke into a broad grin.

"Yes, you heard correctly. I was as surprised as you are."

"Oh, Sophie, I didn't mean it that way."

"I know you didn't. And I do want to talk to you about that further. But what do you make of this note?"

"It's probably still from Zach. By 'eliminating all obstacles,' he probably means that he wants to eliminate your insecurities so that you can play the role on stage with confidence."

Sophie nodded. That did make sense. "But what about 'you are closer to being mine all the time?'"

"Well, if he's asked to court you, that part seems self-explanatory. However, it could also mean that you will be his in the sense of him making you into the performer you were destined to be on the stage."

"I suppose... But here's the thing, Ally. The earl refused to allow Zach to court me."

"He did?" Ally opened her eyes wide. "Why would he do that?"

"Apparently he doesn't think Zach is good enough for me, a lady of the peerage. He seems to have forgotten that no other suitors have come calling."

"Do you want to be courted by Zach Newland?"

"Well, of course. We've already been...rather intimate together. It's nice to know that he actually has some feelings for me in other ways as well."

Ally smiled. "Of course he does. He would be silly not to. You're a charming woman, Sophie. You're the only one who doesn't know it."

Sophie's cheeks warmed. Why in the world did everyone think she was more than what she was? She still hadn't reconciled her desire to be spanked by Zach, and she perhaps never would. Maybe the best thing would be to stop seeing him altogether, rather than bring out a side of herself she wasn't sure she wanted to understand.

Sophie opened her mouth to speak, but Mrs. Oakes and Evan strode into the bedroom, each carrying a bundle.

Ally's eyes brightened. "Oh, Evan, let me see them. Please."

Evan handed little Maureen to Ally, and then Mrs. Oakes handed her little Sophie as well. Ally held both babies, one in each arm.

"Are you feeling up to nursing?" Mrs. Oakes asked.

"I'm quite fatigued, but I would like to try."

Sophie squeezed Ally's shoulder. "I'll leave you some time with your husband and children. Thank you for the talk, Ally."

"Anytime, my dear, you know that. Before you leave though, there are some papers in my bureau I'd like you to look at. Top drawer."

Sophie nodded, grabbed the papers, and left.

When she returned to her own chamber, she unclenched the papers in her hand and began to read.

ENTR'ACTE
The Ruby
A House Party at the Estate of Lord and Lady Peacock

"The Marquess and Marchioness of Gutenberg."

Priscilla, known as Prissy, the Countess of Peacock, turned to her husband. "Oh, Percy, it is so good to see Gutenberg and Fannie."

Lord Peacock cleared his throat. "Yes, my dear, I know how you and Fannie enjoy a good frolic. And I am looking forward to spanking both your bums this evening."

Prissy warmed all over. How she loved to have her arse spanked, and not just by her husband but by comely Fannie, the Marchioness of Gutenberg.

"I think our party is all here, Percy. Viscount McHunt and his lady, the Earl of Hardwood and his lovely mistress, Sarah Nora, and of course Baron Beaverhausen and his beautiful baroness."

Peacock cleared his throat. "My esteemed ladies and gentlemen, thank you for attending our house party. If you will all follow, we shall enter the ballroom, which has been handsomely equipped for this evening."

Prissy loved the house parties she and her husband threw. "Ladies," she called, "if you would come with me, I will take you to the ladies' retiring room, where we can prepare for our evening of fun and frolic."

The ladies followed Prissy into the retiring room. "As you

can see," said Prissy, "I have many amenities for you here to prepare for your evening of lust and fun. These adorable maids will help us undress and prepare for our husbands."

Among gossip and giggles, the ladies were stripped of their garments, and the maids hung their clothes and corsets in a wardrobe.

Prissy rested her gaze on her friend Fannie's ample bosom. "Oh, Fannie, your diddeys are always so gorgeous. May I powder them for you?"

"Of course, Prissy. Powder away, my dear. I want them nice and luscious looking. I'm hoping they'll get lots of attention this evening."

"I'm certain they will. Not that your lovelies need any powder, Fannie, but I do adore touching them."

Prissy grabbed a powder puff, dipped it in some fine talcum, and fluffed it over Fannie's ample breasts. "I do think I shall paint your nipples as well. They're a delicious pink already, but with a little rouge, they will be absolutely delectable."

"Oh, yes, please."

Prissy took her brush and turned to Fannie's nipples. She gave each one a quick pinch. "Such gorgeous nipples, Fannie. I think, before I paint them for you, I shall suck on them a bit."

"Do be my guest, dear Prissy."

Prissy bent her head and took one pink bud between her lips. The texture was delicate and soft, but they became hard under her tongue. "Ah"—she sighed against Fannie's breast— "such lovely titties." She sucked one into her mouth, swirling her tongue around it and then giving it the slightest nibble.

"Ooh!" Fannie nearly jumped out of her drawers. "That does feel good, dear Prissy. Do bite the other one."

"As you wish, my dear." Prissy moved to the other hard nipple and took it between her lips, biting it gently.

The stunning Angelica, Lady McHunt, came forward, her ample breasts jiggling. "How gorgeous you are, Fannie," she said. "Might I suck on the other nipple, whilst Prissy feasts on this one?"

"Why, of course, my dear Angelica," Fannie said. "The more the merrier."

Prissy and Angelica sucked on Fannie's nipples for several more moments, slurping and biting. Prissy's own pussy grew wet. If only one of these ravishing ladies would suck her cunny.

When she could take it no longer, Prissy let Fannie's nipple drop from her lips. It was magnificent now, a pleasing burnished red. "My dear Fannie," she said, "I don't believe you need the rouge now."

Angelica dropped the other nipple from her mouth as well, nodding. "No, dear, your nipples are a glorious scarlet."

Fannie turned around and dropped her drawers to the ground. "Then perhaps one of you good ladies would dust my bum for me. I want it to be exquisite for the gentlemen to spank this evening."

Angelica grabbed the powder puff from the jar of powder. "Please do allow me, Fannie."

Prissy smiled and left her two friends to the fun. She turned to her other two lady guests—Poppea, Baroness Beaverhausen, and Sarah Nora, the mistress of the earl of Hardwood. They were engaged in a luscious openmouthed kiss, and the sight of their tongues twirling over each other made Prissy's quim quiver.

Clearly, these ladies were good with their tongues. Why not ask for a favor? After all, she was the hostess of this enchanting soirée.

"I do so hate to interrupt you, ladies, but I was wondering if one of you would do me the honor of sucking my cunt?"

The lovely Sarah Nora, her almond-shaped brown eyes lashed in ebony and her long brown hair hanging loosely around her milky shoulders, broke the kiss and turned to Prissy. "Why, my lady, I would love to taste your sweet cunny."

Sarah Nora was a beauty. Her lips were colored with red and so full that Prissy could not wait to feel them against her wet folds. But she didn't want to leave the adorable blond Poppea out of the fun. "If you ladies would both remove your drawers, I think we could arrange ourselves in a triangle and each of us could have her pussy licked."

"But aren't the gentlemen waiting for us in the ballroom?" Poppea asked.

Sarah Nora scoffed. "Oh, let them wait. Let us have some fun without them. They will all want their cocks sucked, and while I enjoy a good cock sucking, I've found that no one eats pussy like another woman." She winked.

"When you put it that way..." Poppea winked back. "Sarah Nora, you take Prissy's pretty little quim, I shall take yours, and Prissy, that leaves you me."

Prissy smiled. She had tasted Poppea's sweet quim on several occasions. It was a tasty delight, and she was happy for the opportunity to eat her this evening. The ladies arranged themselves on the soft Oriental rug, each lying on her side.

Sarah Nora spread Prissy's legs. "What a pulchritudinous little pussy you have, Prissy."

"Yours is lovely as well, Sarah Nora," Poppea said.

Prissy didn't answer. She was too busy diving into Poppea's sweet cream. Poppea had a splendid pussy with swollen red lips and a flavor of pears and vodka. Prissy lapped at her, tonguing her clitoris, eating at her soft folds, probing her tongue inside her entrance.

Poppea groaned and moaned, her words muffled by her face in Sarah Nora's pussy. Sarah Nora, meanwhile, was sucking on Prissy's hardened nub.

Prissy's skin tightened, and little sparks skated across her. Oh, this woman could suck pussy. Prissy began moving her hips, undulating them, wanting so much for a hard cock to slide between them. As if reading her mind, Sarah Nora inserted first one and then two fingers into her. Prissy groaned against Poppea's cunt, eating more voraciously as Sarah Nora finger-fucked her.

"Yes, Prissy, such a dazzling pussy, so hungry for me." Sarah Nora inserted one more finger. "Can you take my fist, my darling?"

Prissy moaned into Poppea's pussy. *Yes*, she screamed in her mind, but her hips answered for her, bearing down and taking what Sarah Nora was giving her.

Though Sarah Nora was petite, the sensation was much like a cock in her pussy. Suddenly, soft lips claimed her clitoris, and Prissy shattered around Sarah Nora's fist.

Her climax fueling her, she reached into Poppea's pussy and fingered her, bringing about the lady's climax. And then Sarah Nora herself, her voice cutting through their moans and groans.

"Yes, Poppea darling. I'm coming, I'm coming."

The three women, sated, sat up slowly, each smiling. Prissy looked toward the other end of the room and found Fannie and Angelica eating each other's pussies, Angelica sitting on Fannie's face. Soon they, too, climaxed together, gyrating and wailing.

Prissy stood. "Well, I can see now that all of our cunnies are red and swollen. We've all had our first climax of the evening, ladies. I'm so thrilled that we could share them together."

"I suppose we cannot hog all the fun," Angelica said. "We should join the gentlemen in the ballroom now. I, for one, could use a good cock."

"And I," Fannie said, "would love to have my arse spanked until it's red as a beet."

Prissy warmed all over. She looked down. Her own red lips were visible beneath her black bush. Oh, the gentlemen would be thrilled. They all loved a swollen cunt.

The ladies were all naked now, and Prissy grabbed several feather boas that were hanging in the wardrobe. She gave one to each of the ladies, saving the red one for herself. "If you will follow me, ladies, we shall join the gentleman." Prissy led the ladies back to the ballroom.

Her husband, Percy, was already spanking Baron Beaverhausen's arse. Beaverhausen was leaned over a table with his fists bound to posts. The Earl of Gutenberg was sucking on the Earl of Hardwood's cock. The man befit his name. Viscount McHunt, known as the voyeur in their circles, was watching and licking his lips lasciviously.

Prissy cleared her throat gently. "Well, I can see you have already started without us."

Percy looked up from the leather paddle he was using on Baron Beaverhausen. "From the looks of your cunnies, I'd say you've started without us as well."

The ladies all giggled.

"Really, Percy, did you think we wouldn't? You know how much I love a woman to suck on my pussy."

Prissy climbed on the table where Baron Beaverhausen was bound. "In fact, I don't think I've had my fill of pussy licking yet. Would you mind, Beaverhausen, sucking on my cunny while my husband whips you?"

"Not at all, my lady. Bring your sweet quim to me."

Prissy scooted forward and braced herself with her arms on the table. She spread her legs. Baron Beaverhausen began lapping at her cunny. Each time Percy landed another smack on his arse, Beaverhausen ate her pussy more greedily. Prissy climaxed again, and then again.

"I say, your arse is nice and rattled, chap. Why not give my wife's cunt a rest? I think she needs her arse spanked now."

Prissy tingled all over. She did love a good spanking. And though she'd been spanked by many, her own husband was the best and knew exactly how she liked it.

"Oh, Percy, I would truly love that."

"Then come on down, my dear, and grab the posts. Beaverhausen, do go ahead and bind her. Let's get my wife's arse nice and red."

Before she grabbed the post, Prissy looked around. She was the hostess, after all, and she needed to make sure her guests were enjoying themselves. All were occupied. Viscount McHunt was now licking Fannie's pussy, and Angelica and Sarah Nora were both sucking on Gutenberg's cock. Poppea was pleasuring herself with a glass phallus from one of the shelves, while Hardwood hovered above her, fucking her mouth. Prissy smiled. Her guests were having fun.

She grasped the posts, and Beaverhausen secured her wrists with a silk binding.

Percy began by stroking a feather over her arse. She loved this part—the softness, the sweetness, yet she never knew when the first smack would—

"Oh!" A leather strap came down on her arse.

"You like that, don't you, my sweet Prissy?"

Priscilla bit her lip. "Oh, Percy, you know I do." The lovely sting melted over her arse, permeating through to her innermost center, slowly turning into pleasure. Sparkling tingles surged through her. Then the feather again, the softness such a grand contrast to the sting of the slap. And just when she was getting used to the contrast—

Smack! Another came down on her arse.

"Such a stunning arse you have, my dear," Percy said. "These ladies here are all lovely, but not one arse can hold a candle to yours."

"Oh, you do say the sweetest things, my love," Prissy said, biting her lip again.

Four more swats, and Prissy was near orgasm. "Percy, my love, you must fuck me now. I need a hard cock in my quim."

"Would you like to do the honors, Beaverhausen?" Percy said.

"I would be obliged," Beaverhausen said.

Seconds later, the head of a cock nudged Prissy's lips. Beaverhausen was large, the largest man here tonight, and oh, such a sweet burn would he give her.

"Yes, Beaverhausen," she said. "Fuck me good. I need a good fucking. Have at me, Beaverhausen. Hammer me."

He thrust his cock into her wet cunt. "Dear Lady Peacock," he said, "you do have the tightest little quim. It's a pleasure to fuck you."

"I'm going to spank your bottom while you fuck my wife, Beaverhausen," Peacock said.

Smack! As Percy's strap came down upon Beaverhausen's

arse, he plunged harder into Prissy's cunt.

"Nice, Peacock," Beaverhausen said, his breath hot against Prissy's neck. "Each time you smack my arse, I can thrust even farther into your wife's tight pussy."

Beaverhausen continued to fuck her into oblivion. Prissy longed to slide her fingers downward and diddle her clitoris, but she was still bound. But the stretch, the exquisite stretch of Beaverhausen pounding her, the vibrations tingled her nub— soon she was on the verge of climax.

"Wait, wait! I'm going to come!"

"As am I, my lady. One more good swat, Peacock, and I'm going to shoot my load."

Smack!

The sting bubbled through Prissy as if it had come down on her own arse. Her orgasm started in her clitoris, slid through her pussy lips, and up into her cunt through her whole body, emanating into her arms and legs, tingling. One last thrust, and Beaverhausen pulled out, spurting his cream onto Prissy's back. Its warmth drizzled over her.

"Good God, Peacock, your wife's pussy is the tightest in here."

"Yes, 'tis a lucky man am I," Percy agreed.

Beaverhausen strode to a shelf, brought back a moist rag, and cleaned Prissy's back. "Thank you for a most wonderful fuck, Lady Peacock."

"It was my pleasure, Baron Beaverhausen." Prissy smiled.

Prissy's arse was not yet sated, and she wanted another spanking—this time from one of the ladies. She looked around to see who might be available. She preferred Fannie, but her friend was being fucked by her husband, Gutenberg, and Hardwood was fucking Angelica's arse. McHunt the voyeur was watching. That left the adorable Poppea available. Currently, she was pleasuring herself with a glass phallus in her arsehole.

Prissy strode toward Poppea, who was lying on a leather chaise longue, her thighs pulled upward, plunging the phallus in and out of her tightness.

"You look so beautiful, Poppea," Prissy said.

"Prissy," Poppea panted. "If you would suck on my clitoris for just a moment... I am so near climax..."

"You know how much I love your pussy, Poppea." Prissy knelt down and flicked her tongue over Poppea's hardened bud. A couple swipes, and Poppea was convulsing.

"Oh, yes, yes! That's it, that's it!"

When Poppea came down from her climax, she removed the toy and sat up. "I'll be sore for a few days, but it was worth it. I do love fucking myself in the arse."

"It was quite delightful to watch, Poppea," Prissy said. "And now, might I ask you a favor?"

"Of course, my dear. Anything."

"Would you spank my bottom? Percy already gave me a flogging, but I want a woman's touch."

"Well of course, my dear Prissy. Would you like me to use an implement, or is my hand what you are requiring?"

"Actually, I would like you to sit right here on the chaise longue. I will lie over your lap, and I would like you to spank me with your bare hand."

Poppea patted her lap. "As you wish, my dear."

Prissy's nipples hardened and her cunt throbbed as she lay across Poppea's firm thighs.

Poppea gently stroked her arse cheeks. "Has my Prissy been a bad girl today? Has she been naughty?"

Smack! Poppea's palm came down on Prissy's arse.

"Oh, Poppea, just like that. I fear I've been a naughty, naughty girl."

"Then you shall be punished."

The sting permeated through Prissy's body, changing into pleasure that tingled from the tips of her fingers to the tips of her toes.

"More, more, Poppea!"

Five more smacks, and Prissy was near another climax. She maneuvered her fingers underneath her, found her clitoris, and began rubbing the moist bud.

"Touching yourself?" Poppea smirked. "That is a no-no, my dear. You need more punishment."

Oh, yes, more punishment. Just what she needed. She smiled into the chaise longue. "Yes, yes, I've been a very bad girl, Poppea."

"Then you need to be spanked."

One more smack, and Prissy shattered against Poppea's thighs.

"Yes, yes, dear Prissy, come for me." Poppea smacked her again. "Come all over me."

When Prissy had recovered from her climax, she sat up, her bum sore. "Thank you, Poppea dear. I needed that badly. Such a superb spanking." She leaned forward and pressed her lips to Poppea's.

Poppea returned the kiss, their tongues tangling and dueling. Such lovely lips Poppea had. They eased back, giving each other soft pecks.

Poppea was splendid to kiss, and Prissy's pussy began moistening once more.

When they finally broke the kiss, Prissy looked into

Poppea's radiant blue eyes. "Well, my dear, I see our frolic has only just begun." Prissy leaned back on the chaise longue and spread her legs. "And now, Poppea, if you don't mind, there's nothing I like better after a spanking than a good gamahuching."

ACT II
CHAPTER SIXTEEN

Sophie splashed cold water over her face from the basin in the ladies' dressing room at the theatre. She had just ended her third day of grueling rehearsal, along with two evening voice lessons with Dame Helga. Tonight, after a quick supper here at the theatre that Cook had packed her this morning, she was to have her first private instruction with Zach.

Yet another reason existed for the cold splashing of water. Sophie couldn't get the erotic story of Lord and Lady Peacock and their house party out of her mind. Clearly, the reason Ally had given it to her was to show her that some people enjoyed spanking play as part of their sexual experience. Perhaps Ally wanted her to think it was normal. But was it also normal to frolic and have relations with people other than one's own spouse? If it was all done with each other's consent, perhaps it *was* normal. What was normal, anyway? Normal for one person might be completely abnormal for another. Lord, the philosophy alone was enough to boggle one's mind.

Sophie's own bum ached for a good spanking. Of course, right now was not the time. She toweled her face dry and looked around the dressing room.

The other ladies were getting ready to leave for the

evening. They hadn't made an effort to be overly friendly with Sophie. She wasn't sure why. Maybe because she was a lady of the peerage and they were all common folk. Or perhaps it was Sophie's imagination. As timid as she was, she didn't go out of her way to be friendly to them either. Perhaps she should try.

She walked toward two of the girls in the chorus. "I was just wondering... Are you ladies hungry? Cook prepared me a delicious dinner in this basket, but he always gives me way too much. I would be...most happy to share it with you."

One of the women, Mary, rolled her eyes. "Really, my lady, we can see to our own meals."

Sophie's heart fell. She truly was just trying to be friendly.

"Oh, Mary," the other girl, Elizabeth, said, "she is kind to offer to share her repast with us. I, for one, appreciate the thought, Lady Sophie."

Sophie smiled. "Not at all. And please, call me Sophie." She opened the basket. Inside was a feast of cold fried chicken, fresh fruit, a French baguette, and a canteen of watered-down wine. "Do help yourself."

Elizabeth grabbed a chicken drumstick and took a bite. "Delicious! Do you eat this well all the time?"

"The Brighton chef is quite a talent. We are very well fed."

"Well, it must be nice to be fed so well all the time," Mary said, raising her eyebrows.

"Mary, really..." Elizabeth said. "You ought to try the chicken. It's scrumptious."

Sophie fumed. Here she was, trying to be nice, but Mary would not let her. And unbeknownst to Mary, Sophie knew well the torture of hunger. "You are both welcome to as much food out of my basket as you care to eat. I am happy to share what I now have in abundance. It may interest you to know, however, that my father squandered what little money his estate had on gambling and the drink. My mother, sister, and I lived in near poverty until his death. So I know what it is like not to eat so well on a regular basis."

Sophie turned, leaving her basket open. She was no longer hungry. She headed to Zach's office for her private voice instruction. She was early since she hadn't finished the dinner hour. She would wait until Zach got there.

She was surprised when she saw Zach sitting at his desk. "I'm so sorry I didn't knock. I just assumed you would be out at dinner since I was so early."

"No, no. I find myself not very hungry these days. Since you're here, we may as well begin."

Zach seemed distant, same as he had been since he left Sophie's home the afternoon when the earl had refused his suit for Sophie. He rose from behind his desk, walked to the pianoforte in the corner, and sat down on the bench. He opened his score to one of Sophie's songs. "Let's start at the beginning of this one and see what you've learned from Dame Helga this week."

Zach started to play, and on cue, Sophie began singing.

After a couple of lines, Zach stopped her. "Your jaw is tight. I can see how tense you are. You need to keep your facial muscles relaxed. Too much tension in your throat will affect your voice."

Dame Helga had told her much the same. However, right now, Sophie was a little tense after her altercation with Mary and Elizabeth. She said only, "Thank you, Zach. I will try."

Zach began playing at the beginning, and Sophie came in on her cue. She tried to be aware of her facial muscles and consciously relax them. After a few more bars, Zach stopped.

"You're still tense, Sophie. You've untightened your jaw a bit, but now your shoulders are tense. I can see it in how you're standing." He rose from the bench and stood, facing her. He placed both hands on her cheeks and began massaging her jaw. "Relax. This will help. I promise. When *you* are relaxed, your vocal cords will be relaxed, and they will be able to work better and produce finer sound. Just as you must tune a pianoforte or any other instrument, so must you care for your voice. Your voice is your instrument, Sophie. You must take great care with it."

His fingers on her face felt heavenly. Sophie found her eyes closing as he massaged down the tight corded muscle of her neck and onto her shoulders.

"So tense. You need to relax, sweet." He continued manipulating her upper arms and then back up to her shoulders and neck. "My God, you're so lovely. I want so much to kiss you right now."

Sophie popped open her eyes. "Please."

Zach's lips came down on hers gently. The kiss was slow and deliberate at first, so different from their previous raw and passionate kisses. It held a bit of sadness. Perhaps Zach truly wanted to court her and was just as disappointed as she that the earl said no. They continued the kiss, devouring each other gently, their desire building.

Sophie brazenly probed her tongue into Zach's mouth and touched his. They dueled and swirled together, the kiss gaining momentum, passion. Yes, this was the kiss she had been waiting for, the kiss that would help her relax.

When Zach finally broke the kiss and drew in a deep breath, he moved Sophie to the divan on the far wall of his office and gently laid her down, her neck and shoulders propped up on the arm of the divan. Slowly, he stroked one finger from her temple down her cheek to her chin. Sophie's skin tingled in the wake of his touch. Zach sat on the edge of the couch and leaned toward her, raining tiny wet kisses on her cheek and neck. He brushed a strand of fallen hair behind her ear and then kissed her jaw, trailing his tongue along her outer ear and gently plunging it inside. With his other hand, he slid his fingers from her forehead down the bridge of her nose, tracing every line of her face, down to her lips. Instinctively, she puckered her lips and kissed his fingers as they traced the contours of her chin. He followed the trail down to her chest and over the swells of her breasts still tight within her corset, her nipples hard as pebbles.

"So very beautiful, Sophie." He pulled her upward and unfastened the back of her dress, slid it over her shoulders and her waist, discarding it. While she was still sitting forward, he gently unlaced her corset. He traveled down her body and removed her shoes and stockings. He pushed her back down gently, and his fingers continued their quest. She was clothed only in her lacy chemise and her drawers. He glided over the gentle swell of her breasts and circled one nipple. It beaded beneath his touch. He flicked and tugged at it through the flimsy fabric. He then meandered downward to her navel and swirled a finger softly around it, delving in and out of the sensitive area.

Sophie squirmed under his gentle ministrations, her core vibrating. She worried her feet together and clenched her hands into fists. God, what he did to her!

Without probing into her drawers, Zach followed the lines of her legs down to her feet, where he caressed her toes, his touch a whisper against the sensitive skin. Slowly, he drew back upward, unlacing her drawers when he got to the apex between her thighs. He slid her drawers over her hips, discarding them, and then he pushed her chemise upward, baring her breasts.

"Sophie, how I've missed you." He leaned down and took a nipple between his lips.

Sophie gasped, her body blazing. She had missed him too.

Yes, she wanted the conventional courtship, but barring that, this was not something she could leave behind. She wanted to experience everything with Zach—the things she thought she would never get to experience. Perhaps it wouldn't lead to marriage, but she couldn't make herself regret any of it.

Zach sucked on one nipple and toyed with the other with his fingers, gently pulling and tugging, making Sophie squirm. Moisture trickled between her legs, and soon her thighs were damp with her own essence.

Zach let the nipple drop from his mouth with a soft pop. He inhaled. "God, Sophie, I can smell you. You're so ready for me, so wet for me." He traced his finger over the mound of her breast and down her abdomen to the thick blond bush in between her legs. "Yes. So wet."

"Put your finger in me, Zach. Like you did that first time. I need to feel part of you inside me."

Without further urging, Zach breached her, gently massaging the inside of her walls. Sophie sighed, her hips moving involuntarily, matching the rhythm of Zach's finger. In a moment, he added another, stretching her. The slow tempo of his fingers combined with the exquisite stretch hurled Sophie toward the precipice.

"Oh, Zach, it feels so good." She writhed. She knew what she wanted, but she didn't have a clue how to ask for it.

He continued his assault inside her pussy, finding a spot

that drove her not just toward but over the precipice. Her climax came with a jolt, shattering her, leaving her spent but still wanting more.

She longed to turn over, to have Zach's hand come down on her buttocks as it had before. But how could she tell him?

"Zach..."

"Yes, sweet?"

"I want... I need..."

"Anything, sweet."

She turned over, lying stomach down on the soft divan. "Your fingers, back inside me..."

He obliged, inserting one and then two fingers back into her wetness. "Like this, my love?"

"Oh, yes," Sophie purred into the pillow. "And now..."

Smack! His palm came down on her bare bottom, catapulting her into another mind-bending climax.

"Sophie, your bum is so flawless. Especially when it's this beautiful shade of red."

Pleasure-pain. Sophie couldn't get enough of it. Still, she wondered why she craved such. She would figure it out someday, but for now, all she wanted was the blissful torment that consumed her.

His palm came down on her arse again, and then again. As the sting metamorphosed into pleasure, she shattered again, all the time his fingers pumping in and out of her wet channel.

"My God," she said. "I can't even believe...how much I..."

Zach didn't pressure her to finish her thought. Instead, he smacked her once more, slightly harder this time, and drove into her pussy with his fingers so forcefully that he unearthed her most explosive climax yet. She melted into the hunter-green brocade divan, the physical, emotional, and spiritual kaleidoscoping together into one euphoric and satisfying thrill.

Still fully clothed, Zach leaned down and slid over her back, the tweed of his jacket scratching her. "You're so exquisite. I must have you this night, Sophie. Please."

He meant the act, of course. Sophie had known it would come to this if she continued down this path, and she was not sorry that it had. She wanted to experience what Ally had experienced, and she wanted it with Zach, whether he was officially courting her or not.

"Come sit on my lap," Zach said.

Sophie did as he bid, rising, taking her place upon him, the wool of his trousers scratching her sore bottom in a delicious way. She placed her hand on his cheek and then moved to the back of his neck, toying with his auburn waves. Brazenly, she lowered her mouth to his and gave him a soft kiss on the lips, still cupping his cheeks.

"Loosen my cravat, Sophie," Zach said.

She did so and then drew her hand down, the linen of his shirt soft against her fingers. And underneath the linen, his hard chest beckoned. Still, she continued downward until she grasped the bulge in his trousers.

"Oh my God," he groaned.

She brought her hands back up to his face to kiss him again. After a few moments of feverish kisses, he ripped his mouth from hers and kissed her neck, her shoulders, the tops of her breasts, squeezing them.

"Now my shirt, Sophie. Please."

With longing and desire, Sophie kissed him again and began unbuttoning his shirt. Zach threaded his fingers through her hair, unfastening it from its tight coiffure. Sophie parted the two sides of Zach's shirt, exposing his manly chest. Again she kissed him, their lips sliding together, their tongues touching. She caressed his hard shoulders, his skin warm beneath her fingertips. She pressed her chest to his and her mouth to his neck, raining tiny kisses over the corded muscle, and then she slid down, kissing his chest, his abdomen, the muscle hard and warm under her lips.

She smiled against his groin. She knew what he wanted. She was frightened, to be sure, but she wanted to give him everything. She crept back up again and kissed him.

Their lips mashed together, and they both gave in to their frenzied passion. Sophie was on fire, her nipples so hard she knew she must be poking him. She gathered all her courage, broke the kiss, and licked down his abdomen again. Slowly, she unbuckled his belt and unfastened his trousers. His bulge beckoned to her. She lowered her mouth and kissed his erection through his drawers.

He jerked. "Yes, sweet. God."

His trousers and drawers still around his hips, she gathered her bravery and pulled out his cock. He grabbed the wrist of her other hand and brought her fingers to his mouth, sucking on them gently. The sweet suction of his mouth made her pussy throb.

Sophie pulled off his boots and his trousers and then slid up his body again and gave him a kiss on the mouth.

"My God, Sophie. What you do to me," Zach rasped.

Such power! She returned to his cock. She had seen it before, but that did not make it any less magnificent. She started with tiny kisses to his bollocks, and then she slid her tongue up the entire length. She twirled around the head of his cock, licking off the drop of fluid emerging. Mmm, salty, musky.

Zach threaded his fingers in her hair and used his other

hand to clutch hers. Sophie, gaining more courage, wrapped one fist around his cock and continued sucking. She withdrew her mouth from his cock for a moment and used her hand to find his rhythm as she kissed up his abdomen to his lips again.

Then back to his cock. She sucked it until he stopped her, gripping her shoulders and bringing her to his mouth for a kiss.

"You have to stop, love. If you don't, I won't get inside you this night. And God, I need to be inside you."

Zach helped her to her feet. He was still sitting on the divan, and he kissed the side of her waist, the area right below her breasts, sending shivers across her body. He nipped at a nipple, and her skin blazed further.

"You're so beautiful," he said. He pulled to his feet and switched positions with her, setting her down on the divan. He crouched between her legs and took another turgid nipple into his mouth. He sucked, nibbled, and then bit down hard.

Sophie gasped. Pleasure-pain, like the spanking—but different.

Her tummy churned, her pulse racing. The pain in her nipple traveled to her pussy and made her gush.

He kissed down her abdomen to the moist spot between her legs. He buried his face in her bush of curls and inhaled. Then he moved down farther, licking her thigh, kissing her knee, her calf. He ran his tongue along the instep of her foot to her toes and sucked on them, massaging the ball of her foot with his fingers.

"I want to worship every part of you," he said. "You're an angel to be exalted. So perfect."

He licked her heel, her ankle, her instep, and again took each toe into his mouth. Red heat ribboned through her with each new inch of skin he tortured with his tongue.

He progressed up her calf to her knee again, dotting kisses everywhere he stopped. Gripping her thigh, he kissed upward, massaging her.

Her pussy was hot with fire. She needed his tongue, his fingers...but still he kissed her thighs, skillfully avoiding her wet heat.

"Zach, please!"

He sucked at the juncture between her pussy and her thigh, and she nearly imploded on the spot. Would he never get to her pussy?

"Zach... Ah!"

He sucked her wet folds into his mouth and pulled. Sophie cried out, emotion boiling within her. He continued to drink of her. Sophie moved her hips in rhythm with him, and then, wanting to taste herself, she pulled him upward into a kiss.

Spicy, tart...mmm. Her pussy juice mingled with the robust flavor of Zach. Perfect. Sophie trailed her hands down Zach's sides and gripped his taut buttocks. He jolted and groaned. A smile curved her lips.

Again, the power.

She captured his cock once more and worked it with her hand.

"Please, sweet. Your mouth." He stood, and his hardness bobbed before her.

She thrust her mouth down upon his length. She took her free hand and ran it over the swells of her own breast, pinching her nipple. Such a jolt! God, the pleasure-pain. It all felt so good.

"Are you ready for me, my love?" Zach asked.

Terror rushed through her, but in a good way. She wanted him inside her. Still holding his cock, she stood and rubbed it against the lips of her pussy. Then she lay down upon the divan and spread her legs.

"Let me make sure." Zach leaned down and swiped his tongue across her wet folds.

She nearly unraveled.

"Yes, ready. Such an angel." Then he hovered over her and placed his cock at her entrance.

Anxiety filled her, but need won out. "Do it quickly, Zach."

He pierced her.

She cried out, but he clamped his lips upon hers to deafen her noise. As they kissed, the pain—such good pain—turned into a burning, igniting a bonfire in her core. He pulled out and then thrust back in. God, the exquisite burn, and then... pleasure mounted. She started moaning. Zach broke the kiss and took a nipple between his lips as he continued to fuck her.

Oh my God. Had anything ever felt so good? When he broke away from her lips, she looked into his burning cognac eyes.

"Need a taste of you," Zach ground out. He pulled out of her, slid down, and crushed his mouth to her pussy. He sucked her clitoris between his lips.

Sophie nearly shattered. But she wanted to come with him inside her.

"Please, Zach, please. Come back inside me."

He smiled against her folds and then moved upward and pushed back inside her. He fucked her slowly, all the way in and all the way out.

Sophie burned, her skin rippling. Dear God, this was what she had been missing. This was what Ally wrote about in her erotica, what she did with the man she loved. No wonder young women needed chaperones. If any of them knew what they were missing...why, they'd sell their souls to the devil himself for this ecstasy.

Finally, Sophie understood.

And she didn't ever want to stop.

Zach grunted, gripping her shoulders. With every thrust, she became more and more his, more and more taken. She gave him a part of herself, one she could never get back.

She didn't want it back.

Zach's thrusts became more and more powerful. This exchange of power between them, this joining—heaven itself couldn't be any better than this.

When her climax hit, she splintered into a million pieces, each a fiery spark sending energy straight to her core. Above her, Zach continued to plunge into her, her pussy blazing with each lunge. She cried out, grasping his arse and pulling him into her, so deep she could feel him against her womb. Deeper, deeper...

"I can't hold off any longer, Sophie." He closed his eyes, thrust into her one last time, and pulled out, squirting his essence onto her belly.

Then he leaned down and kissed her.

She returned his kiss with all the emotion bubbling inside her, all the love and devotion she felt at that moment. For this must be love, yes? She had never felt anything like it—an all-consuming longing for another person.

She had no delusions that he could grow to love her, especially since her stepfather wouldn't allow him to court her. But this might be her only chance to experience this wonder, and she was going to take advantage of it.

"My God, Sophie," Zach said when he broke the kiss. "That was unbelievable. I've never..." He moved away from her, helped her up, and then sat next to her on the divan, his legs splayed apart, his cock now soft against his auburn bush of curls. He looked completely and beautifully spent.

"You've never what?" Sophie asked.

"It's just never...been so *intense* before. You're something else, Sophie."

Something else. That was a good thing, right? All she knew was that she had just experienced the most precious thing she could remember in her life.

She was in love. It hit her like a brick to her head. And she knew, in her heart and soul, that if she hadn't been in love with Zach Newland, she never would have given him her virginity. He had shown her so much pleasure, had given her such an amazing gift—she would love him forever, whether or not he ever returned her feelings.

She began gathering her garments.

"Let me help you, love."

"I need to...wash first."

"Of course. Forgive me. I should be taking care of you. Unfortunately, I don't have a basin in here. Wait here, and I will get one."

Sophie warmed all over. How kind of him to take such good care of her.

Had she bled? She looked down at her thighs and saw a couple of rust-colored smudges. Not too much.

When she heard the door open, she smiled, ready to see Zach's face.

But then she dropped her jaw toward the ground.

CHAPTER SEVENTEEN

"Well, well. I see now why Zachary made you his leading lady." Nanette Lloyd pursed her lips and stared at Sophie's naked form on the divan. "Quite a tight little body you have. Just his type."

Sophie shuddered in embarrassment. "I assure you that this is not what it appears to be." What rubbish. It was exactly as it appeared, but what else could she say?

"Really? Because what it appears to be is you trading your sexual favors for the leading soprano role in Zach's production."

"This has nothing to do with my role," Sophie said. "Now if you would kindly leave—"

Nanette let out a laugh. "Are you kidding me? I'm not going anywhere. Wait until I have a little chat with Zach about this new development."

"Whatever is going on between Zach and me is not any of your business." Sophie tried to stop the redness she knew was coloring her cheeks...and the rest of her.

"Actually, it *is* my business, because Zach Newland is mine. I've told you before to stay away from him."

Anger rose within Sophie. Who did this woman think she was? Zach had chosen to make Sophie the lead soprano before they had begun any type of relationship. And now that she had found something heavenly with Zach, Sophie intended to keep it for as long as he'd have her. Neither Nanette Lloyd nor anyone else would stop that. She stood, her nudity be damned, and faced Nanette. "You don't scare me, Miss Lloyd. I intend to see Zach as often as I want."

"We shall see about that." Nanette landed a punch to Sophie's nose.

Sophie cried out, landing back on the divan, blood trickling from her nose. Oh, how it hurt! Like a chisel going through her nostrils into her brain. Tears rolled down her cheeks. Her father had punched her in the nose once. It was the worst pain she could remember, worse than the caning, worse than the kicking. Blood trickled into her mouth, the metal tang hitting her tongue.

A few minutes later, Zach returned with a basin of water and some cloths. "Oh my God! Sophie, what happened? Are you all right?"

Sophie sniffed. "Nanette... She came in here... Is she gone?"

Zach knelt at Sophie's feet. "What in the hell was she doing here? I'm so sorry, Sophie. What did she say to you?"

"Same thing she always does. Warned me to stay away from you. And this time, she punched me in the nose."

"My poor sweet love. I'll take care of you. I'm so sorry."

"Believe me, I've been through worse."

"So you've said. I'm afraid that doesn't make me feel any better."

Sophie didn't respond. What was there to say? She didn't feel like rehashing the abuse she had taken at her father's hand. She flinched as Zach wiped the blood from her face.

"I'm sorry, love."

"It's sensitive right now. It will heal."

"Still doesn't make me feel any better. Here"—he held the

rag to her nose—"hold this until the bleeding stops. I need to tend to...other things."

Zach gently spread her legs and placed a warm cloth against her swollen folds. "Not a lot of blood. That's good. Are you sore, my love?"

"A bit. But it's...a *good* sore." And it was. Sophie didn't know how to explain it any better than that. All she knew was that she welcomed the pain that had come with giving Zach this most precious of gifts.

"Hold this against you," he said, placing her hand on the rag between her legs. "I would do it myself, but I want to take care of your nose."

Sophie smiled.

He was such a gentleman. Somehow, she had to get her stepfather to change his mind about their courtship.

"Zach?"

"Yes?"

"Would you...call on me tomorrow evening after dinner? I would like to speak to my stepfather *with* you. If you're still interested in courting me, that is."

"Of course I am. You are very special, Sophie. I... I believe I could..."

"Could what?"

He gingerly cleaned the blood from Sophie's nose and lips. "Still the same perfect shape. Thank God she didn't break your nose."

"Could what?" Sophie said again.

"Never mind. I'm so thankful you're all right. I'll have Nanette banned from the theatre. I'm so sorry."

"I was rather embarrassed. I mean, here I was, sitting on your divan, naked as a bird."

Zach smiled. "You have no need to be embarrassed about that, sweet. You are quite exquisite naked."

Sophie warmed all over, tingles shooting through her.

"And I will be happy to call on you tomorrow evening. At what hour?"

"Perhaps nine o'clock. We should be done with dinner, and the men will be smoking their cigars. I will try to speak to my mother and stepfather before then, and then perhaps all of us can talk together."

"I will be there." Zach smiled.

★ ★ ★ ★

The next day, when Sophie returned home from rehearsal, she found her mother taking tea alone in the smaller parlor.

"Hello, Mother. I wonder if we might speak."

Iris took a sip of her tea. "Of course, my dear. What is on your mind?"

"Did the earl tell you that Mr. Zachary Newland requested permission to court me?"

Iris nodded, setting her tea on its saucer. "He did, Sophie."

"Then you know that he did not allow it."

Iris nodded again. "Is this Mr. Newland a man who interests you?"

Sophie drew in a breath, gathering strength. Zach was worth fighting for. "Yes, Mama. He is a very fine man, a self-made man. I respect him very much, and I also respect his talent."

"I understand. However, David would like more for you."

"Mother, this is the first man who has ever asked to court me. I'm nearly five-and-twenty years old, an old maid by today's standards. I am interested in Mr. Newland. I like him. I think he likes me. I would like for him to court me."

"Very well, dear, I will speak to David about it." Her mother smiled. "I am sure we can come to some agreement."

Sophie leaned forward and hugged her mother. "Oh, thank you, Mama. I just know it will work out. Mr. Newland is coming to call on me tonight at nine o'clock. I was hoping that you and the earl might be able to speak to him then."

Iris shook her head. "I'm afraid not, Sophie. David is in London today and will not be returning until the morrow."

"Oh, drat. I suppose I should send word to Zach not to come."

"Nonsense. He is certainly welcome to call on you, whether you are courting or not. You may entertain him in here this evening. It will be a few weeks before the main parlor is ready."

Sophie smiled. Her mother understood, and she would no doubt make her husband understand. She *could* tell her mother she was already in love with Mr. Newland. Given how quickly her mother and the earl had fallen in love all those many years ago, when Ally and Sophie were mere babes, they ought to understand attraction that defies logic. She smiled to herself. No, she'd keep quiet. Her love for Zach was a delicious secret she could savor by herself a little longer.

Sophie kissed her mother on the cheek and bid her good afternoon. She would spend what was left of the afternoon doting on her new nieces and resting before the dinner hour.

★ ★ ★ ★

Sophie sat alone in the smaller parlor, waiting for Zach to call after dinner. She watched the clock—nine o'clock, and then quarter past. Where was he? Half past. When the clock struck ten, she decided to retire for the evening. Surely Zach had a good reason for not coming.

Still, disappointment flowed through her veins. She had been looking forward to seeing him, even though the earl wasn't present to discuss their courtship. The tender spot between her legs reminded her of their wonderful afternoon together.

Her mother, Iris, came in. "Sophie, dear, I did not know you were still in here."

Sophie frowned. "He didn't come, Mother."

"I'm sorry. I'm sure something came up that required attention, probably at the theatre."

Sophie nodded. "Yes, I am certain that is what happened." Too bad she didn't believe the words that came out of her mouth.

A rap on the door brought Graves. "My ladies, Lady Sophie has a caller. Mr. Zachary Newland."

"Tell him I'm unable to receive him at this late hour, Graves," Sophie said.

"No, Graves. My daughter will see him." Iris smiled and took her hand. "Listen to what he has to say. You need do nothing else."

"Thank you, Mama."

Iris smiled gently. "I will be in my sitting room, reading, if you need me." She turned to Graves. "Show Mr. Newland in."

Graves bowed and left, returning shortly with Zach.

Sophie sat demurely on the divan, refusing at first to make eye contact. However, that was rude, and Sophie was not a rude person. She looked up, saying nothing.

Zach's eyes were bloodshot and sad. "I do hope you can forgive my tardiness, Sophie. There was a...scene at the theatre this evening."

Sophie widened her eyes. "What happened?"

"It's a long story. Nanette came in, having one of her tantrums. Two of my sopranos, who were working late rehearsing, actually quit the show because of her antics. Now I have to find two more performers as soon as I can."

"I'm so sorry. Why didn't you send word that you couldn't make it? I would've understood."

"I wanted to see you. And I kept thinking that I could get here at least at a reasonable hour. Yet time was ticking by, and now I'm later than I ever thought I would be. Can you forgive me?"

Sophie was well aware of what Nanette was capable of. She believed Zach without question. "I hope Nanette will no longer be a problem."

"No, she will not be. I had her escorted out of the theatre by a constable, and he made it clear to her that she would risk arrest for trespassing if she came back."

Sophie breathed a sigh of relief. No more Nanette. That was a blessing to be sure. "Unfortunately, my stepfather is not at home to speak to you tonight anyway. He is in London until the morrow. Perhaps you can come back then?"

"I'm afraid I can't come tomorrow, sweet. I'm dining with a few benefactors, and I'm hoping to get their backing for the show. In fact, I would like you to join me. The benefactors love to meet the new performers."

"I'm not sure if that would be appropriate if we're not officially courting."

"Honestly, I don't know the rules of the peerage, but I think it would be entirely appropriate for you to attend as one of my performers. Several of the other performers, both men and women, will be in attendance. I should like very much for you to be there."

"Then I shall be there." Sophie wanted nothing more than to make Zach happy and proud of her.

Zach smiled and sat down next to her on the divan. He leaned toward her and placed a soft kiss on her lips. "You are wonderful, did you know that?"

Sophie warmed from the tips of her toes all the way up to her hair. The sweet words from his husky timbre never failed to arouse her. He kissed her again and then stood, holding out his hand to her. "Would you dance with me, Lady Sophie?"

"Why...there's no music."

"I don't care. The sweet memory of your voice is all the music I need."

Sophie stood and floated into his arms. He was so much taller than she, her head came to his chest slightly below his shoulders. He leaned down and kissed her lips softly, gently.

Zach trailed his hands around her face to her shoulders and down her upper arms.

Something in Sophie snapped—something animal. The need to touch him warred with the fact that she was in the parlor where anyone could walk in. She loosened his cravat and began unbuttoning his shirt. His beautiful chest beckoned. Sophie gripped his muscular torso and pressed her lips to his chest.

Zach shuddered. He cupped her cheeks and brought her

up to his mouth where he kissed her, forcing her lips open. They kissed passionately, their tongues tangling, as Sophie continued to trail her fingertips over Zach's hard chest. When they broke the kiss for a much-needed breath, Sophie kissed his neck, his shoulders, his upper arms.

"You're driving me mad." He leaned down and licked her neck, gliding up to her earlobe and sucking on it. He pulled one of her legs up against him so her pussy met the bulge in his britches.

She nearly shattered then and there, gasping against his shoulder. He pulled the other leg up, lifting her off the ground so he was holding her, her dress still draped around her, her swollen bud now tight against his erection. She sighed into him, moving her hips slightly to increase the friction. So good...

But they were in the parlor. Anyone could walk in. Of course, Ally was still bedridden, and Evan wouldn't leave her side. Iris probably wouldn't bother them, and the earl was gone. A servant wouldn't dare come in. Would he?

She couldn't take the chance. "Zach," she said.

"Yes, sweet?" He nipped the outer edge of her ear.

"If we sneak out of here and go to the servants' stairwell, we can go to my bedchamber. I'm on the second level. My mother and the earl and Ally and Evan are on the third level. No one would hear us."

"Are you sure? Are you actually suggesting..."

Sophie amazed even herself. "Yes, that is exactly what I'm suggesting. I want you to take me to my bed."

CHAPTER EIGHTEEN

Safely ensconced in her bedchamber behind a locked door, Sophie turned to Zach. "Undress me."

A sound left his throat, kind of like a growl. Within minutes, Sophie's gown, petticoats, corset, chemise, and drawers all lay in a pile on her leather reading chair. Zach's shirt was still open from when she'd unbuttoned it in the parlor. She leaned into his chest and inhaled. His scent—tobacco, cinnamon, male musk—nothing like it. She inhaled again. "Zach, you smell so good."

"As do you, my love. I can smell that honey from your pussy. Are you wet for me?"

Brazenly, she lifted one of her legs, spearing it around his hip. "Why don't you see for yourself?"

He slid one hand down her arm, over her waist and buttocks, and between her legs. "Yes. Your sweet essence." He slid his fingers through her folds, brought them up to his mouth, and sucked on them. "You're delicious, Sophie. I'll never tire of your flavor."

Still standing, they moved slowly, as they had in the parlor, dancing. Sophie finished unbuttoning Zach's shirt and removed his cravat. She brushed his jacket over his shoulders, and then his shirt and cravat, leaving them in a pile of wool and linen on the floor.

She kissed his chest again, twirling her tongue around one of his nipples, and then she tilted her head up for a sweet kiss from her lover. Zach threaded his fingers into her hair and removed her hairpins, letting her blond tresses cascade down her back in a soft curtain. He lifted one of her legs around his hip again, grasping her buttocks. Sophie continued trailing her fingers over his hard chest, kissing his muscular torso.

Zach licked her neck, her shoulders. "God, you smell good. Like vanilla and sex." He again pulled her up in his arms, holding her as she straddled him. "You're so small, Sophie, so light. It's like holding feathers." He put her down and turned her around so her back was against his front. He kissed the side of her neck as he toyed with her breasts. Then he slithered down her back and kissed the crease between the cheeks of her bottom.

So good. She closed her eyes, reveling in his moist assault.

He turned her around again and kissed her navel, kneeling before her as though worshiping her. He rose a bit and took a nipple into his mouth. The hard nub throbbed for his touch. With his other hand, he toyed with the folds of her wet pussy.

Eyes still closed, she quivered, the sensations arrowing to her core.

Up again he glided to her mouth, continuing to torture her pussy with his fingers. A raw kiss, a kiss of two animals branding each other, frantic and hurried. He brushed his fingers over her nipples, and her pussy creamed. She began working the belt to his trousers as he tugged and twisted her nipple. Though it pained her to escape the nipple and pussy torment, she needed his cock. She knelt down before him and put her mouth over the bulge in his trousers.

"God, Sophie. You drive me insane."

She smiled against his erection, pulling the belt off his trousers. He grabbed it from her and, quick as a jackrabbit, scampered around her and tied the leather strap around her wrists, capturing them behind her back.

"Oh!" she gasped.

"Is this okay, Sophie? I promise I will not harm you."

Sophie trusted him. Trusted him with her life. Somehow she knew he would never hurt her and that his only quest was pleasure.

She nodded.

He moved back in front of her, brushed his trousers and drawers over his hips, and held out his hard cock to her. "Suck me."

Sophie never considered disobeying. She took his arousal between her lips and sucked hard. She pulled back and licked the tip, longing to touch its warmth with her fingers. The fact that she couldn't was oddly arousing.

Zach grabbed her hair and helped her find his rhythm, pushing her upon him until she nearly gagged and then seeming to know instinctively when to pull back. "Yes, sweet, fuck me with your mouth."

Sophie swirled her tongue around the head of his cock and then took him to the back of her throat again.

She again fought the urge to gag but soon got used to the sensation.

"God, love, that's wonderful." Zach pulled his cock away from her and leaned down to kiss her lips.

They kissed with passion and desire, Sophie's hands still bound behind her back. Zach stood, and Sophie slid up his body, kissing his taut abdomen and chest and then finding his lips again. Nectar trickled down her thighs. Something about being bound, about being completely vulnerable to him—she was hotter than an inferno.

Zach broke the kiss, turned her around, and prodded her toward the bed, bending her over it, her hands still shackled. He leaned down, his chest warm against her back, the fine hairs tickling her. He whispered in her ear, "I'm going to spank you now, Sophie. Tell me that you understand. Tell me that you understand why I need to spank you."

And suddenly the truth came to Sophie in a sparkling vision. Zach needed to spank Sophie for the same reason that she need to be spanked. It was as integral to his psyche as it was to hers. He enjoyed it as much as she did, and it was part of his sexual experience. Who knew why they were both wired this way? Did it really matter, if it brought them both pleasure?

No, it did not.

"I understand," Sophie said. "I understand perfectly. Tell me that you understand why I want you to spank me."

"Oh, I do," he said, nibbling on her earlobe. "I understand, Sophie."

"Then spank me, Zach. Please. Spank me hard."

He rose and...*swat*! His palm came down on her bare behind.

Sophie jolted, her pussy throbbing. Oh, God, how she wanted this—the pleasure-pain. She ached to feel nothing but his hand coming down upon her, longed to sink toward the depths of hell until—*snap!*—the agony transformed into nirvana, and instead of plummeting, she was floating to the heavens, each cell in her body bursting into a joy so thorough, so profound, that every horrible event in her past ceased to exist and only she was left.

A pure Sophie. An unbroken Sophie. A whole Sophie.

Unadulterated.

Real.

Only Sophie.

He spanked her again, and then again. "Such a beautiful bum you have. I love how it becomes a luscious cherry when I spank it." His palm came down on her once more.

The sting, the pain, the amazing pleasure. Sparks shot through her, radiating to every nerve in her body and then spiraling inward again to her pussy. Her nipples were so hard they were poking into her mattress. She needed more. So much more.

Her wrists were still bound, so she couldn't grip the covers. Her body slid on the silk comforter as Zach continued to spank her.

"I have a wooden paddle at home," he said. "But on you, my love, I prefer to use my hand. I like to gauge how much force I'm using. I like the feel of your smooth skin against my palm. When I strike you... God, it's so arousing. You cry out, and then you drip from your pussy. So bewitching... So erotic... Sophie, I'm... I'm..."

You're what? she wanted to ask, but she was biting into the comforter as he struck her again. The sting flowed through every fiber of her body and again melded into her core.

And then...the softest sensation against her bottom. Zach was kissing her, licking her, blowing on the places where he had struck her.

"So beautiful, Sophie. So lovely."

She gasped when he licked a quite forbidden place, circling his tongue around her tight rim.

"This is paradise, Sophie"—his breath was scorching against her sensitive skin—"for both of us. Will you let me take you there?"

She shuddered. She hadn't talked to Ally about this

particular act. No, she couldn't. She wasn't ready, though the soft swipes of his tongue made her tremble, shooting flaming arrows to her center.

He continued to lick her puckered hole, at the same time inserting two fingers into her pussy. "So beautiful," he said against her skin.

She whimpered when he moved away from her pussy and brought his face to hers on the bed. "May I? May I take your arse?"

She turned her head so she could speak. "I'm sorry. I'm just not ready for that yet." Someday. Someday soon. Right now, she wanted his cock jammed inside her wet pussy.

"I understand. I was just thinking... Because you're probably sore from yesterday... Maybe it would be better to try..."

"Zach, I'm not that sore. I need you inside me. I think I might die an untimely death if you don't get inside me."

"My love..." He rose and pulled her off the bed, unbinding her wrists. He crushed her against him, bending his legs, lifting her, and forcing his cock inside her heat.

Sophie cried out, the pleasure was so intense. She cupped his cheeks and kissed him as he lifted her on and off his cock. When they broke the kiss to breathe, Sophie looked down. Her breasts jiggled as he pounded into her. A few minutes later, he knelt down, still within her, and laid her on the floor. Positioning her legs upon his shoulders, he continued to fuck her, thrusting hard and fast. She slid her hands up his arms, caressing his taut muscles.

Sophie whimpered, the feeling so deep and intense. A great sense of loss enveloped her when Zach removed his cock and pulled her onto his knees, forcing her mouth upon him.

But, oh, the taste of him, salty with the appley tang of her own juices. She slid all the way to his bollocks, licked his shaft, and kissed his sac. Zach slowly lowered himself to the floor, and Sophie still hovered above him, her mouth upon his cock.

"Come here, my love." He gently maneuvered her so that she was sitting on his face, his lips tormenting her wet folds as she continued to suck on him. God, his mouth on her pussy... She exploded.

After her climax subsided, she rolled off of him. He pulled her onto the bed, laying her so her hips graced the edge. He stuffed her pussy full of his cock again, pounding, thrusting, plunging, deeper and deeper. He pinched one of her nipples, and she shattered again, coming around his cock. He continued fucking her hard.

Tension built within her, and she was ready to shatter again.

And still he fucked her. "I want to see how much you can take, Sophie. How much of my cock can you take tonight?" He looked into her eyes, piercing her with his glowing glaze.

She climaxed once, twice, thrice more, her body melting into the silk of the bed, her energy drained. "Zach, please. Enough. I...can't..."

Finally, he pulled out and spewed onto her stomach and breasts.

He leaned down and kissed her lips—one soft, sweet, wet kiss. And with that kiss, Sophie said to him the words she couldn't say aloud.

I love you, Zach.

★ ★ ★ ★

Zach rolled off Sophie, completely sated. He had never had such an intense experience with a woman. To think, a day earlier he had taken her virginity, and still she had opened so completely for him this evening in her own bed. She, a lady of the peerage, had invited him to her bedchamber to make love to her. This had been the most erotic, intense, and loving experience of his life.

Loving? Had he truly thought the word? The words had been on the tip of his tongue as he was making love to her. He had wanted to tell her he was in love with her, but it was too soon.

Was it? Zach had never been in love before. He had never even thought he had been in love. Now, these intense feelings, this desire to be with her, the need for her to understand his dominance... Never before had he asked a woman to understand why he was striking her. Sophie was different. He needed to know that she understood, even though he wasn't sure he understood himself.

And she did. Her own need was as great as his. Perhaps one day they would figure out why they both shared this need. Perhaps they could figure it out together.

"I should leave you now, love."

"No, Zach. Please, stay. It's late, and I would love to sleep in your arms."

Zach would love nothing more. Sophie was a grown woman, and if she wanted this, why should he not oblige?

He kissed her lips softly. "I would love to spend the night here with you."

★ ★ ★ ★

Zach awoke before dawn and smiled. Sophie was nestled against him. The moon shone in through her window, casting its glow on the curves of her face. Her blond hair was fanned out on her pillow in a soft curtain. Her lips were still swollen and red from his kisses, parted slightly in sleep.

He hated to wake her, but he didn't want to her to awaken and find him gone. He rose from the bed to find his jacket. He pulled his timepiece out of the pocket and looked at it in the moonlight. Four o'clock. He had to leave before daylight. If he were found on the grounds, Sophie could be in for a world of hurt. He dressed quickly.

He sat down on the bed gently and nudged her shoulder. "Sophie?" he said in a low voice. "Sophie, wake up, love."

She stirred slightly and then stretched her arms above her head, her breasts peeking out from the covers. So beautiful, she was. He had to fight the urge to reach for and make love to her again. Already his cock was stirring.

He nudged her again. "Sophie?"

Her eyes fluttered open, big and bright, even though they were clouded with sleep. "Yes? Is everything all right, Zach?"

Zach smiled. "Everything is perfect. However, I must leave you now."

She reached for him. "No. Don't leave..."

Oh, the temptation. If only he could stay... Forever if she'd have him.

"I must. I must leave before anyone is awake and I can sneak out quietly. If I were caught here, in your bedchamber, or even on the premises at this hour, your reputation would be ruined."

"I don't care about my reputation."

Zach chuckled quietly. "That's sleep talking, sweet. Trust me, it's for the best if I leave now. Besides, I have to get home and prepare for today's rehearsal. I'm usually up two hours from now anyway."

She smiled. "If you insist."

Zach leaned down and kissed her lips. "I do. And you will be due at rehearsal at nine o'clock this morning. My leading lady must not be late."

"Just one more kiss..." She reached for him.

He was not made of steel. He descended to her. His shirt was still open, and his chest pressed against her stunning breasts. She parted her lips for him, and he delved inside, tasting of her sweetness. Far from wanting to, he broke the kiss.

"Sleep now, my sweet. I'll see you soon at the theatre."

With all the strength he possessed, Zach rose from the bed, leaving his sleeping beauty there. Quickly, he adjusted his cravat and headed out.

★ ★ ★ ★

Upon returning home, Zach lay down in his own bed for a bit, thinking of the previous evening. Sophie was a prize. How had some young gentleman not snatched her off the market yet? Her shy nature, most likely. It certainly wasn't her lack of beauty. The only lack of beauty was in her own mind. He checked his timepiece again and rose. Time to get to the theatre. He washed quickly at his basin, dressed, and was descending to the first level when a rap sounded at his door.

At this hour? He opened the door and was surprised to see two peelers standing there, one of whom he recognized, the brother of one of his actresses. "Harkins, what is it? What are you doing here?"

"Are you Mr. Zachary Newland?" the other peeler, sporting a moustache so orange it looked painted on, asked.

Zach nodded. "I am, as Harkins here can tell you."

"I must ask you to turn around, sir," Moustache said.

What in the world was going on? "Turn around? I don't understand." Then he spied the handcuffs.

"I'm truly sorry about this, Newland," Harkins said. "But you do need to turn around."

Moustache cuffed him. "Mr. Newland, we're taking you in on suspicion of murder."

CHAPTER NINETEEN

Sophie awoke a couple of hours later, feeling more rested than she had in...well, her entire life. She welcomed the soreness between her legs and on her bum. She felt deliciously used. And used was a good thing, if she consented to it. It made her feel good, gave her immense pleasure. What could be wrong with that?

She summoned Hannah to help her with a bath and then clothed herself quickly in one of her weekday dresses, a light-green calico. She was a working girl now, and silk morning dresses would not do. She would save them for Saturday and Sunday mornings.

She strode to the stairs to descend for breakfast but instead decided to rise to the third level to check on Ally first. She rapped gently, so as not to wake Ally if she was still sleeping.

Ally's maid, Millicent, answered the door. "Lady Sophie, how nice to see you. Lady Ally is awake. Lord Evan has already left on business for the day. I know Lady Ally would like to see you."

Sophie smiled. Thank goodness! Ally was the one person she could speak to about her amazing night.

Ally sat upright in her bed, baby Sophie at her breast. "Sophie! How lovely to see you this morning. I was hoping you hadn't left for the theatre yet."

"I don't have to be there until nine o'clock. It's so good to see you awake, Ally. How are you feeling?"

"Sore. But that is to be expected. Honestly, I'm dying to get out of this bed, but Evan won't hear of it. I'm only allowed out to use the convenience, and quite frankly, it's becoming tedious."

"Evan is right. You must take care of yourself." Sophie gazed down at the baby, her heart warming. "And how is my little namesake doing today?"

"She is quite ravenous, as you can well see. I'm told by Mrs. Oakes that both babies are thriving. I could not be happier. Well, I could. If I were up and around and taking care of them as I should be."

"The babies are in good hands. Mrs. Oakes is a treasure, and Mother and I dote on them whenever we can. You know that."

Ally sighed. "Yes, I know. It's just... Well, can't be helped..."

"What?"

"I suppose you know that these are the only two babies I will ever have. I don't want to miss one moment of their lives."

Sophie took Ally's hand. "So Evan told you."

Ally nodded, a tear emerging in her right eye. "Last night. We both cried a lot. But then we both admitted to each other how happy we were that we had two perfect daughters and that fate had spared their mother." The tear trailed down Ally's cheek as she smiled.

Sophie swallowed the lump forming in her throat. She summoned a smile for her brave sister. "I truly am sorry for that loss, Ally. But there's really nothing to mourn. You have your life, and you have two beautiful children. That is more than a lot can say. After all, Mother only had two children."

"Yes, but Evan's father and mother had three, and Auntie

Flora and Uncle Crispin had three. And the good Lord only knows how many Lily and Rose will have. I just always imagined myself having three children, possibly more. And I'll never be able to give Evan a son. He says it doesn't matter. And perhaps it doesn't. He doesn't have a title to pass on. But doesn't every man yearn for a son?"

"Ally"—Sophie patted her sister's arm—"not every man is our father. We may have paid a price for not being boys, but these two little darlings never will. Evan will be a doting and loving father to them. Why, he'll be so overprotective, he will probably never let them out of his sight, especially once they come of age."

Ally sniffed and nodded, cuddling baby Sophie. "You're right, of course. That husband of mine is a true treasure. I am pretty much the luckiest woman on earth."

Sophie smiled. Happiness for her sister welled up in her heart. Ally was indeed a lucky woman. Would Sophie ever be as lucky?

Only time would tell. Though Sophie desperately wanted to speak to Ally about her previous evening, she couldn't bear to at this moment, while Ally was mourning her loss. She stroked her sister's hand. "I must go down and have a light breakfast. I'm due at the theatre soon. I hope you're awake when I return this evening. I would love to have one of our long talks."

"And I would love that as well, dear. I have missed you so much, Sophie."

★ ★ ★ ★

"Murder?" Zach looked over his shoulder at the peeler cuffing him. "Have you lost your mind? Who in God's name was murdered?"

"From the evidence," Moustache said, "you know very well who was murdered."

"I'm telling you I don't!" Zach resisted against the handcuffs, his heart thundering. "I'm not a common criminal, damn it. Harkins, tell him!"

"Newland,"—Harkins cleared his throat—"you may want to cease speaking until you see a barrister or solicitor."

"I don't need a fucking solicitor. I need to be let go. I have a theatre to run, gentlemen. I have not murdered anyone."

"Your theatre has been barred from entrance pending a criminal investigation," Moustache said.

"My theatre? What exactly are you saying?"

"I am saying what you already know, Mr. Newland. Someone was found murdered in your theatre. Your cleaning personnel found the body this morning and called us."

Zach widened his eyes. Someone had been murdered at the theatre? And now they had penned it off? How would they have rehearsals? How would they get the show ready? He reached to rake his fingers through his hair but of course could not move his hands. Here he was, under arrest. Perhaps he should be more worried about that than the fate of his production.

"May I ask who was murdered?"

Harkins cleared his throat again. "Your lead soprano, Nanette Lloyd."

★ ★ ★ ★

Sophie descended to the small dining room for a quick breakfast. Her mother was seated alone in the room, a plate of fruit and scones in front of her.

"Good morning, Mother."

"Sophie, good morning. I trust you slept well?"

Sophie's cheeks warmed. She hoped her mother didn't notice the redness she was sure was present. "Better than I have in weeks, actually. You'll be happy to know that I just saw Ally. She was awake and feeding baby Sophie."

"That's excellent news. I shall go see her before she falls asleep again."

Sophie nodded and sat down, and a footman brought her a plate of breakfast and poured her a cup of tea. She murmured her thanks and was about to take a sip of tea when Bertram entered.

"Pardon my intrusion, my lady, but a new message has been delivered for you."

"Another? At this hour in the morning?"

Bertram nodded, handed her the parchment, bowed politely, and left.

Sophie opened the parchment and read.

That bitch will no longer be a thorn in your side. You will be mine soon.

Icy tentacles gripped Sophie's neck. The penmanship was the same as the previous notes, which she had assumed were from Zach. Goodness, why had she not just asked him? This one could not be from Zach. She had no idea what it was even referring to.

Whoever was sending these notes had become a danger. She, timid Lady Sophie? An object of someone's obsession? How could this have happened?

The time had come to speak to her mother and the earl about this. Graves, as well. He could at least tell her who had been delivering the notes. She stood, no longer hungry, and headed to the foyer. When she found Bertram, she asked, "I beg your pardon, Bertram, but where is Mr. Graves this morning?"

"I'm sorry, my lady, but I do not know. He asked me last night to take his morning shift. As he is getting closer and closer to retirement, I am taking over more and more of his duties."

Sophie nodded. "Thank you, Bertram. Did you happen to see who delivered this parchment this morning?"

"Just one of the young lads from Bath. I've seen him before, but he's one of several. A lad of about thirteen years, blond hair, blue eyes."

No help at all. "Thank you, Bertram. It's time for me to leave for the theatre."

★ ★ ★ ★

"I demand you take me to my theatre now. I need to see what kind of evidence you have against me."

"Sorry, sir, but we have to handle this by the book." Moustache wrinkled his nose.

"Damn it! We have to go by the theatre to get to your offices. I only wish to see what's going on. Nanette Lloyd left the theatre last night before nine thirty, at which time I left the theatre. And I assure you that when she left, she was very much alive. Angry, but very much alive."

"I insist you stop speaking, Newland," Harkins said. "You'll have a chance to talk to your solicitor."

"For God's sake, I'm innocent of any wrongdoing here. You know me, Harkins. I'm no killer. I have no need of any solicitor. Now take me to my theatre."

Harkins looked to Moustache. "You know, Benny, it *is* on our way. The fellow has a right to see why he's being charged."

Moustache—Benny—furrowed his brow. "You always love to make your own rules, don't you, Harkins?"

"He's a good chap, Benny. He gave my sister an audition and a job. We've been to dinner at his home, for God's sake. He just wants a quick look at the scene."

"The boss won't like it."

"Please," Zach said again. He had to find out what was going on. His heart was nearly beating out of his chest.

"Fine," Benny relented, looking to Harkins. "But you owe me one."

Zach breathed out a sigh. He would get to the bottom of this ridiculousness. Nanette couldn't possibly be dead. The bitch was too mean to die. This was one of her cruel hoaxes. She was trying to get him back. Well, it wasn't going to work.

Within a few minutes, they stopped at the theatre. It had already been roped off. Damn, what was he going to do about the production? He had put much of his benefactors' money and some of his own into the production. It was to be Sophie's debut. It had to go on.

"Could you unbind me please? There are people here that can't see me like this. I'm the owner and the manager, for God's sake."

"I assure you," Benny said, "the only people here are law enforcement. Everyone else was told to leave. This is a crime scene, and it is currently under investigation."

"Oh, for the love of..." Zach huffed.

Harkins escorted him across the barrier and into his own damned theatre. The nerve of all of them. Several constables and inspectors milled about.

"I see nothing out of the ordinary, so far, except my doorman and my night shift are not here. I usually relieve them when I come in at six bells."

"What you are looking for is not out in the open. One of your night persons is the one who called us at about four this morning."

Zach knew where he had been at four in the morning. Of course, he couldn't tell the constables that. Sophie's reputation was at stake.

"I assure you I was not here at four in the morning, gentlemen."

"Four in the morning was just the time when your worker found the body. We're not sure when the crime took place yet."

The peelers escorted Zach through the hallway toward his office. His office door was open, and several inspectors and constables hovered around inside.

"Move out of the way, gentlemen," Harkins said. "The suspect here wants to see the scene."

"Laddie, he has no right. The boss won't like it," one of the men said.

"Yeah, well, I'm not telling the boss, Jonesy, and neither are you. You owe me for bending the rules for you enough times. It don't hurt to let him have a look. I know him. He's a good bloke. Then we'll take him in."

Jonesy relented, and the group of people parted.

Zach widened his eyes, his heart soaring to his throat, his stomach churning with nausea.

Nanette lay naked and prone, a pool of blood surrounding her. Next to her hand, on the wood floor adjacent to his Oriental rug, written in presumably her own blood, were three letters.

Z–A–C.

CHAPTER TWENTY

Zach swallowed, his nerves jumping. No wonder they were looking to him to answer for this.

"So you see, Mr. Newland?" Benny said.

Zach said nothing in response. What could he say? The evidence literally pointed straight to him. He had last seen Nanette alive and well after their argument the previous evening. He had left around nine thirty and arrived at Sophie's estate around ten. He had stayed there until four in the morning. Clearly he had an alibi, but he was unable to tell the constables. At least not without talking to Sophie first.

"What have you got, lads?" Harkins asked.

"We haven't been able to ascertain the exact time of death," Jonesy said. "However, when the employee of the theatre found her at four, he said the body was still warm. Rigor still hadn't set in when our first men arrived. Rigor set in around six. Since rigor can set in anywhere from two to six hours after, we estimate that death occurred between midnight and three thirty, before the employee arrived."

Zach's heart jumped. Yes! He did have an alibi. Sophie's mother had witnessed him arrive at the estate at ten o'clock. But of course, she didn't know he was still there at three thirty.

But Sophie did.

"Gentlemen," Zach said, "I assure you I had nothing to do with this."

"The same employee who found Miss Lloyd said he

witnessed you and her arguing last evening. Is that not correct?"

"Yes, that's correct, but she left here alive and well shortly after nine o'clock, after which I also left the theatre and did not return until now."

"Mr. Newland," Benny warned, "you may want to stop talking until your solicitor gets here."

"I'm telling you I need no solicitor. I am innocent."

"Is there anyone who could testify to your whereabouts between nine o'clock last night and three thirty in the morning?"

Zach forced back a nod. Yes, there was. Sophie. But he could not say anything without speaking to her first. He couldn't be responsible for the demise of her reputation. He also could not name his servants. They would not be able to testify because he had indeed not been home. He hadn't gotten home until after four in the morning.

None of this made him look good.

He needed to call his solicitor. And he also needed to speak to Sophie.

"No, I'm afraid not."

"Well, if you were at home," Harkins said, "surely you have house staff who could testify to that fact."

"I...er... I wasn't at home."

Harkins let out a chuckle. "So you were with a lady friend, then? Not a problem. We just need to speak with her."

Zach shook his head. "Afraid it's not that simple, gentlemen." He cleared his throat. "I would like to send word to my solicitor."

★ ★ ★ ★

The coach arrived at the theatre, and the coachman helped Sophie alight. Sophie swallowed. What in the world? The theatre had been roped off. Several of the actors and actresses stood, milling around, talking in hushed tones.

Sophie spied Elizabeth, the young actress who had been kind to her. She approached the young lady. "Do excuse me, Elizabeth, but what is going on?"

"Oh, Lady Sophie, it is the most horrible thing. Evidently a murder was committed at the theatre last night."

Sophie jolted. "A murder? Who was killed?"

"Nanette Lloyd, the former lead soprano of the company. But that's not the worst part."

Goodness, what could be worse than someone getting killed? Even if it was that horrible Nanette. Sophie did not wish death on anyone. She said a quick prayer for Nanette's soul.

"What could be worse than someone being murdered, Elizabeth?"

"The inspectors have closed down the theatre. And they're holding... Oh my goodness, it's too terrible to even speak the words."

"What? What is it?" Sophie's nerves were on edge, and she resisted the urge to shake the information out of Elizabeth.

Elizabeth visibly shivered. "They're holding Mr. Newland as their prime suspect in the murder."

Sophie gulped. It could not possibly be true. But then... the notes she had received... Had they truly been from Zach after all?

She shook her head, banishing those unwanted thoughts.

Zach was not a killer. The tenderness he had shown her, taking her virginity... But again, he liked to smack her. Did that mean he had a violent streak? But that didn't make him a murderer, did it?

Still, he had said that he and Nanette had argued last night, and that was why he was late getting to the estate...

No! Zach had been with her in her bed for nearly the entire night.

"That's impossible."

Elizabeth nodded. "We all think so too. But for now, we must pray that the inspectors find the truth so Mr. Newland can be let go."

"Did they know what time the alleged murder took place?"

"From what I hear, sometime after midnight."

Perfect. Sophie could give Zach an alibi. Of course, it would mean exposing the fact that he had been with her all night. But Zach's innocence was more important than her reputation. She had to see the constables right away.

"Do excuse me, Elizabeth, but I have an errand I need to run. It's of the utmost importance."

"All right, Lady Sophie. Keep Mr. Newland in your prayers."

"You can be certain that I will."

Sophie spoke to the coachman quickly and told him where to take her. A few moments later, they arrived at the law enforcement headquarters.

As the coachman helped her down, Sophie said, "I'm afraid I don't know how long I'll be. I need to speak to someone in charge."

"Not a worry, my lady. I'll wait for you."

"Many thanks." Sophie curtsied and hurried in. It was a small building of red bricks, nothing like Scotland Yard in London. A uniformed officer sat behind a clerk's desk, a frown on his face. Several other peelers milled about.

Sophie's timidity set in, and her skin turned to ice. Now what? Was she truly ready to destroy her own reputation to save the man she loved?

Love. Zach might never love her back, but she could save him. Was it worth her reputation to do so? Yes, it was. She slowly approached the clerk's desk and softly cleared her throat.

The young clerk looked up. "Yes, madam, may I help you?"

Sophie inhaled and let her breath out slowly. "It's my lady, if you please. I am Lady Sophie MacIntyre, and I wish to speak to...whomever is in charge of arresting Mr. Zachary Newland."

"Yep, Mr. Newland was just brought in. Got him in a holding cell at the moment."

Sophie shivered. The thought of Zach being stuck in a tiny cell... Oh, she could not bear it. "You have made a terrible mistake."

"I'm afraid the evidence we have against Mr. Newland is overwhelming."

"I don't care how overwhelming your evidence might be. Mr. Newland is innocent, and I can prove it."

"And who exactly are you, my lady?"

"I just told you. I am Lady Sophie MacIntyre. I am the lead soprano in his new production. We've been working together for the last couple of weeks."

"A lady of the peerage rehearsing for a musicale?"

Sophie's cheeks warmed. "Yes. I, a lady of the peerage,

227

am now the lead soprano in Zachary Newland's company at the Regal Theatre. I am proud and honored to be a part of his company."

The clerk's cheeks reddened. "Of course, my lady. I meant no disrespect. But I'm afraid that unless you were with Mr. Newland at midnight last night, you cannot offer any proof of his innocence."

Sophie opened her mouth to speak, but her lips trembled.

The clerk narrowed his eyes. "Oh...I see. My lady, are you sure you want to do this?"

Sophie nodded. She was sure. More sure than she'd ever been about anything.

"I assure you, telling lies to save your employer is not a wise decision."

Sophie stood on her tiptoes to appear taller. "Who says I'm going to be telling lies?"

"I see." The clerk shuffled some papers on his desk. "Mr. Newland is conferring with a solicitor at the moment. I will let them know you're here. Please do have a seat." He pointed to some uncomfortable-looking wooden benches.

Sophie nodded, walked away from the desk, and sat on one of the benches. Yes, they were indeed uncomfortable, especially on her sore bum.

In a few moments, a constable appeared and escorted her to a room where Zach sat with a man she didn't know. "Gentlemen," the constable said, "here's Lady Sophie MacIntyre."

He shut the door behind him, leaving the room.

"Sophie"—Zach stood—"what are you doing here?"

"I've come to prove your innocence."

"I can't let you do that."

"Newland," the other gentleman said, "if the lady is willing—"

"No." Zach pounded his fist on the table. "I won't let her ruin herself."

The other man stood. "My name is Declan Tate. I'm Mr. Newland's solicitor. I will be preparing his case for one of the barristers."

Sophie curtsied politely. "Would you please tell him to let me help him?"

"Believe me, I want nothing more than for you to help him. My client is innocent, as we both know. And unfortunately, you're the only one who can prove that."

"I'm willing."

"Sophie," Zach said, "have you thought this through?"

"What is there to think through? I cannot let an innocent man go to the gallows when what I know can save him. Especially not you. You're...too important to me."

Zach's lips trembled. "But your reputation..."

"My reputation?" Sophie shook her head. "Do you really think my reputation is more important than your life?"

Mr. Tate nodded. "The lady is quite right, Newland."

"You'll be ruined."

"I'm ruined anyway, Zach. I have been since the first time you laid a hand on me. And you know what? I didn't care then, and I don't care now. I care about you. I will not let you hang for something you didn't do when I can stop it. Now bring in the constable, and I will make my statement."

Zach shook his head. "No one has ever been willing to do something like this for me. You're putting my needs above your own. I don't know how I can ever repay you."

"I'm not doing it in any expectation of repayment. I'm

doing it because it's the right thing to do. You know as well as I do that it is, and I would like to think you would do the same thing for me if our positions were reversed."

"Of course I would, only I wouldn't be the one ruined. You would be."

"Well, as Ally would say, that is just the way of the world. We women don't get a fair shot. Perhaps in the future we will, but for now I have to accept life for what it is. I'm sure I will be the fodder of much gossip. But Ally, who I respect more than anyone in the world, never cared about that. Why should I? Now"—she nodded to Tate—"could you please find a constable and bring him in?"

Tate nodded and left the room.

Zach took Sophie's hands in his own. "Are you sure you want to do this, my sweet?"

Sophie wiped a tear rivering down her cheek. "I can't bear the thought of you locked up in here when you didn't do anything wrong. Besides, I know who did this."

"You do?"

Sophie shook her head. "Well, I don't know actually, but someone has been sending me notes. I had assumed they were from you."

"No, I haven't sent you any notes. What kind of notes?"

"They seemed innocuous at first, but then I got one this morning. It said that Nanette would no longer be a thorn in my side."

Zach caressed her cheek. "You could be in danger, sweet, and I can't bear the thought of that. Tell the constable about the notes, Sophie. Perhaps they will lead to the real killer, and you will be safe."

"I will tell him. And believe me, I don't regret what I'm

about to do. I don't regret any of the time I've spent with you."

"Nor do I. And Sophie, for what it's worth...thank you. For saving me. And I don't just mean today."

Sophie smiled. She truly didn't know what he was referring to, but if he could remember their times with pleasure, she would be all right, no matter what their future held.

★ ★ ★ ★

After Sophie's statement, Zach was released. However, the theatre would be closed for a few days while the inspectors continued to gather evidence. It would open again next week, and rehearsals would continue. Zach had high hopes that the production could still go on schedule. It would just require some long days and a lot of work. He had to cancel the dinner with his benefactors as well.

Something niggled at the back of his neck. Who had been writing Sophie those notes? Whoever it was had probably murdered Nanette. Nanette had been unkind to Sophie on more than one occasion and had assaulted her.

Worry nagged at him. Sophie was not safe. Whoever was writing those notes was a threat to her and had tried to frame him for Nanette's murder. That much was clear, for the killer had used her lifeless fingers to form the letters Z-A-C in her blood.

He had to protect Sophie. As for Nanette, he'd let the inspectors do their job. He was exonerated, and though it pained him to know what Sophie would go through because of it, he couldn't be sorry. To know that there was a person in the world who would do something like that for him...

He had never imagined being that special to anyone.

And the truth was, Sophie was also that special to him. He had to find out who had been writing those notes. Zach Newland was not a killer, but if he got his hands around the neck of whomever was threatening Sophie, he might turn into one. Her safety was paramount.

Once all of this died down, he would go to Sophie, confess his love, and ask for her hand—that is, if Brighton didn't come to him and demand he do so first. Her stepfather may not think he was good enough for her, but he had compromised her now, and soon everyone would know. If the earl forced Sophie to marry Zach, he would have what he wanted most in the world.

Zach hoped with all his heart that she wanted him, too.

★ ★ ★ ★

A few days later, gossip and innuendo started to spread. Sophie's mother and the earl called her into Brighton's office for the talk that Sophie had been dreading.

"Please, sit down, Sophie," the earl said, nodding to one of the chairs in front of his desk. He sat down behind his desk.

Iris sat next to the desk, in another leather chair.

Sophie sat, her skin tingling all over. The time of reckoning had come.

"I suppose you can guess why your mother and I have called you in here to speak to us."

Sophie nodded.

"We want you to know that we don't blame you for this, Sophie," Iris said, her eyes kind.

Sophie furrowed her brow. They didn't blame her? Well... that was good. And confusing.

Brighton cleared his throat. "We're very sorry that you

had to go through this. I assure you that the man has been in my employ since he was a lad, and I never thought him capable of such things."

Confusion muddled Sophie's brain. What were they talking about?

CHAPTER TWENTY-ONE

"He is gone, and he will never bother you again."

Should she go along? Evidently they hadn't heard any gossip regarding her and Zach. Maybe she was imagining that it was flowing like the wind through the city of Bath and its outlying areas. Perhaps Zach and the solicitor had found a way to keep it quiet.

"I'm so sorry, my lord, but I am sure I do not know what you are talking about."

Iris stood, walked to Sophie, and sat down in the chair next to her, taking her hand. "My dear, we're talking about Bertram, of course."

"Bertram?"

"Yes. But now I'm confounded. You indicated that you knew what we were talking about."

Sophie warmed. "I'm sorry, Mother. I was confused. My mind has been so cluttered, with the theatre closing and all. I've...not quite known what to do with myself. Thank goodness it's reopening tomorrow and I can get back to rehearsal."

Iris nodded. "Of course, dear."

"What's going on with Bertram, Mother?"

"Bertram has been dismissed from the estate," the earl said. "Graves found out that he had been writing secret notes to you. Why did you not inform your mother and me that you were getting notes?"

Bertram? Young and awkward Bertram? Then again,

Sophie was also awkward. Perhaps he felt they were kindred spirits. "They seemed harmless, at least until the last one. I guess I never really thought about who might be sending them."

"We've spoken to your sister, and she said that you thought Mr. Newland might be sending them."

Caught in a lie. That wasn't good. Since when had she started lying? "At first, yes. Up until the last one, that is. The last one was quite...creepy. I know Zach—er, Mr. Newland—would never have sent it."

Brighton cleared his throat. "I've spoken to the inspector in charge of Miss Lloyd's murder investigation. Newland has been exonerated, though the inspector wouldn't tell me how. They seem to think whoever sent the notes might be responsible for the murder, so Mr. Bertram is being held for questioning."

Sophie's skin froze. "He seemed like such a nice man."

"Yes, he did," the earl said. "He has been on this estate for near twenty years now, since he was a small lad. But Graves says he has been shirking his duties, and then, when Graves discovered that he was the one sending in the notes, your mother and I felt we had no choice but to dismiss him. When I talked to the inspectors and told them that he was the one sending you the notes, things all fell into place."

Sophie sighed. "Well, at least they have the right suspect now."

"Was this Miss Lloyd a problem for you?" the earl asked.

"She had no love for me. I took her position in the company, so who can really blame her? She became such a problem that Zach—er, Mr. Newland—had to let her go from the company."

The earl nodded. "I see. Well, at least her attacker will be brought to justice."

"Yes," Sophie said. "Though I had no real use for her, she did not deserve to be killed." She fidgeted. "Is there anything else you wish to speak to me about?"

Brighton shook his head. "No, my dear. You may go."

Sophie forced a smile, stood, and left the office. Her reputation, as far as her parents knew, was still intact. Whether that was a good thing, she couldn't say. If only she could escape the chill on her skin.

Mr. Bertram.

Who would have thought?

★ ★ ★ ★

Zach tried to keep the evidence that exonerated him under wraps, but gossip was beginning to reach his ears. Meanwhile, the constables had arrested Thelonius Bertram, a servant on the Brighton estate. He was supposedly the one who had been sending Sophie those notes, and he was now the prime suspect in Nanette's murder. Mr. Tate said Bertram was maintaining his innocence and denied ever writing notes to Sophie.

Zach didn't honestly know what to believe. Nanette had been a true pain in his arse, but he would never have wished death upon her. That said, it was nice not to have her around anymore causing turmoil.

May Day fast approached, and even though he desperately needed the extra time to make up for the days the theatre had been shut down, he was closing so they could all enjoy the festival. He hoped he could escort Sophie. The earl would probably not allow it, but he would ask anyway.

He looked around his office, which had been cleaned, the rug replaced—no evidence that a murder had taken place there. He was glad to have his theatre back, but he had a strange feeling that Nanette's killer was still out there. The young man Bertram hardly seemed the obsessive murdering type. And Zach wasn't sure why, but sometimes he felt like invisible eyes were watching him, burning holes in his skin—invisible bodies lurking around every corner, like shadows in the darkness.

Probably just his imagination.

★ ★ ★ ★

The next day, Zach sat in the earl's lush office, waiting for Brighton to receive him. Graves had shown him in and told him the master would be in shortly.

Zach wiped his sweaty palm on his trousers. Why so nervous? He only wanted to escort Sophie to the May Day festival on the morrow. Of course, Brighton had refused him once...

The door opened, and Brighton strode in, his brow furrowed. Zach stood.

"Sit down, Newland," Brighton said, taking his place behind the mammoth desk.

Zach dropped his bottom back into the leather chair and waited for the earl to speak.

Brighton shuffled some papers on his desk, clearing his throat. His lips were pursed in a thin line. This didn't look good.

"I suppose you know why I've called you here," Brighton finally said.

Called him here? He'd come of his own accord. "I'm afraid

I don't understand, my lord."

"Nonsense. I asked Graves to send word to you yesterday. That is why you're here, is it not?"

"I beg pardon, but I received no message from Graves. I've been keeping long hours at the theatre to make up for the days we lost, so it's possible I missed it in my post."

"What brings you here, then?"

"I'm here to ask permission to escort Lady Sophie to the May Day festival."

Brighton pounded his fist on the desk, shaking the giant structure. A granite paperweight fell to the floor perilously close to Zach's toes. "You sit there and tell me you have no idea why I wished to see you? And you have the nerve to ask to escort my stepdaughter to a festival when I told you in no uncertain terms you could not court her?"

Zach's heart quickened. "That is exactly what I'm saying, my lord."

Brighton shook his head. "The truth is, Newland, my wife spoke to me about your possible courtship of Sophie. It seems Sophie is quite fond of you and wanted the courtship. I was ready to allow it, until..."

"Until what?" Zach's stomach plummeted. This could only be heading in one direction.

"Did you really think I wouldn't find out that you compromised my stepdaughter, Newland?"

Zach let out a cough. "No, my lord. I didn't think you wouldn't find out. But please understand that—"

"Be silent!" The earl's fist came down on the desk again. "I shall do the talking here."

Zach's temper ignited. He was a good man, damn it, and he didn't deserve to be treated so disrespectfully. "If you do all the talking, this won't be a conversation."

"It doesn't have to be. You'll listen and do as I say. You've compromised Sophie, so you must do right by her."

"Marry her, you mean?" Zach's heart sped.

"Yes."

"That is hardly a hardship to me, my lord. I love Sophie." The cannonball that had been weighing on him lifted. How freeing to say the words!

The earl cleared his throat again. "Love is neither here nor there. You will marry her regardless."

Zach couldn't help a smile. "It will be my honor to make her my wife. I shall propose to her soon."

"Not so fast. I still don't think you're good enough for her. If Sophie weren't so fond of you, I'd beat you to a pulp with my bare hands for what you've done."

Zach let the hypocrisy slide. He knew well the story of the earl and countess. They had met some twenty years ago, both married to others, and fallen in love and consummated their adulterous union. Sophie had told him. She'd also told him of the earl's own son, Evan, and her sister, Ally. He'd ruined her as well. Zach glued his lips shut. No good would come of voicing these ironies.

"I guess I should be happy the lady is fond of me, then," Zach said. "I assure you I'm more than fond of her. You're wrong about me, my lord. I'm a good man with a good business. I will take care of Sophie."

"Just see that you do." Brighton returned to a document on his desk.

Was that his cue to leave? Zach stood. "Please know, my lord, that I didn't plan to compromise your daughter. We're drawn together, she and I. We have something...special."

Brighton grunted, his gaze not leaving the document.

Why not continue? "Since Lady Sophie and I are now betrothed in your eyes, may I assume you will have no issue with me escorting her to the festival?"

Again, a grunt.

Zach smiled. He took that as a "yes."

★ ★ ★ ★

Sophie rose early on May Day to walk about the estate and gather flowers to take to the festival. She smiled happily as she sat on the veranda, filling May baskets and then fashioning the white, yellow, and pink blooms into a crown for her head. She made one for Ally as well, even though her sister couldn't attend the festival. The wreath would bring some brightness into Ally's bedchamber. With more posies left, she couldn't resist. She made tiny garlands for Maureen and little Sophie.

"Sophie, how grand! You've brought in the May!" Ally gushed when Sophie presented her with the crown. "You do look stunning in that white morning dress. I suppose you bathed your face in the morning dew as well?"

Sophie smiled. Bathing one's face in the morning dew on May Day was an old wives' tale, said to preserve one's beauty. "You know there's never enough dew for that."

"When is Mr. Newland calling for you?"

"Soon. I'm so glad the earl is letting him escort me. In fact, I should go. He could be here any second."

"Do have a sensational time, Sophie."

★ ★ ★ ★

Zach arrived promptly, and the two delivered Sophie's May baskets to tenants on the Brighton estate. Iris and Sophie had placed loaves of Cook's delicious white bread in the baskets under the flowers.

"Don't be seen," Zach teased. "I'll not let anyone claim a kiss from you but me."

They laughed together as they rode the rest of the way to the celebration outside of Bath, arriving in time to see the parade led by the May Queen. She was none other than Lady Patricia Price-Adams, Cameron's sixteen-year-old sister. Her coal-black hair was a striking contrast to the white peasant dress and flowers she wore, and her sapphire-blue eyes gleamed as she laughed, tossing petals to the children, including her adorable brown-haired sister, Lady Katrina.

"Tricia looks absolutely stunning," Sophie said, clasping Zach's hand.

"She does," he agreed. "It's quite an honor to be chosen as May Queen."

"I admit I don't know much about these traditions," Sophie said. "My father never allowed us to celebrate, and when he died and we moved to Mayfair, my Uncle Crispin wouldn't allow it either, being a devout Christian."

"The May Queen represents the Roman goddess Flora, who personifies spring." Zach smiled. "Are you hungry? There's a feast to be had here, my lady."

"You know, I am, actually. I got up with the birds to gather flowers for the baskets, and I had not but a scone with lemon curd to break my fast."

"Then let's get you some beef on a stick and a Beltane

cake." Zach took her arm.

"A Beltane cake? What is that?"

"Beltane is the English pagan name for May Day, and it's a celebration of fertility and renewal. Perfect for spring, of course. A Beltane cake is a rich eggy confection with scalloped edges. But," he warned, his eyes grave, "if you get the piece that has been darkened with charcoal on the bottom, you might be pelted with eggshells."

Sophie jerked back. "What?"

Zach laughed. "Old folklore, love. That won't happen today, I promise you. The only people who get the blackened pieces at this festival are jesters who are paid to be in on the fun."

The cake was indeed rich and delicious, though Sophie sneaked a peek at the bottom. No black charcoal mark, thank goodness.

Next, they took part in the Maypole dance. Zach led her in the patterns of the dance, and they each held an end of ribbon, weaving it around the pole.

They watched groups of men dressed in green-and-white do a rhythmic dance with swords to folk music. Morris dancing, Zach called it. By then, midafternoon had set in, and the party was becoming raucous. Alcohol was flowing freely, and a group of pagan Druids were starting the spiral dance. Sophie had seen the dance last summer, at the Midsummer celebration, but this time, the Druids began stripping off their clothing.

Sophie shuddered, looking away.

"Sorry, sweet. Things tend to get a little rowdy at this festival. It's the celebration of fertility and all."

"I don't particularly want to see anyone create life here

out in the open," Sophie said. Clearly, the Druids were headed that way. The air was thick with lust.

"I understand. I'll take you home." Zach kissed her cheek chastely and took her arm.

But Sophie didn't want to go home. The mood of the festival had aroused her. She felt free. Alive and free. Sexually free. And bold.

"It strikes me, Zach, that I've never been to your home. Might we go there?"

★ ★ ★ ★

"Spectacular!" Sophie gazed with widened eyes.

Zach's townhome in Bath was lush with the finest furniture in the parlor and dining room. Decorated in hunter green and burgundy, the entire home screamed of masculinity. It was perfect for Zach.

Of course, what she really wanted to see was his bedchamber.

As they ascended the stairway, Zach said, "Sophie, I don't think you know what you've done for me. I still can't believe someone could stick her neck out for me like that."

"My parents found out," Sophie said demurely. Iris had spoken to her quietly the previous night. She'd left the earl out of the conversation, thank goodness.

"Yes, I know. Brighton spoke to me."

"Oh!" Sophie cringed. "I hope he wasn't too hard on you."

"No. I got to escort you to the festival, didn't I?" He winked.

Sophie smiled, her body tingling. "You don't have to thank me anymore. I did what was right. But I do have to thank you for the lovely day at the festival."

At the top of the stairwell, she grabbed Zach and kissed him. She was not in the mood for formalities. She wanted Zach, and she would have him. Now. And she had a surprise for him.

She bit on his lower lip, its lushness filling her senses. So soft and full, like silk against her tongue. As they kissed ferociously, Zach toyed with the buttons on the back of her dress. Soon the white silk was in a heap on the wood floor at the top of the stairs.

He ripped his mouth from hers. "God, love, you're not wearing a corset." His breath was ragged.

She smiled, her body blazing. Her surprise. "I didn't have a peasant dress to wear to the festival, but I wanted to be authentic in some small way. Peasant girls often don't wear corsets."

"Your figure is so exquisite I didn't even notice." He thumbed her nipples through her gossamer chemise. "It's a crime to bind these breasts, Sophie. You should never wear a corset again." He lowered his head and sucked a nipple right through the fabric.

She groaned. Oh, she could climax from his stimulation of her nipples alone! Soon her chemise and drawers joined the dress in the white puddle on the floor.

"Zach, your servants..."

"Shh, love. I gave them the day off for the festival. They won't bother us."

He kissed back up her chest to her earlobe and sucked on it. She pulled the billowy pirate shirt he'd worn to the festival out of his britches, reached underneath it, and traced her fingers up his abdomen to his exquisitely golden neck.

"Oh!"

With a whoosh, Zach had lifted her and carried her to a doorway like a pirate's prize. He walked her through a sitting room into a decadent bedchamber. The furniture was dark oak, and a burgundy-and-black Oriental rug covered the wood floors. The bed—oh, the bed—was covered in black silk.

Zach set Sophie gently upon the soft duvet, the silk smooth and cool against her skin. Then he stood, removing his shirt over his head. His chest beckoned her, those copper nipples begging for her touch. She drew him forward and began working on his britches. They were old-style peasant britches, laced with leather cord rather than buttons and a belt. Her hands shaking, she unlaced them and pushed them over his muscular thighs. His erection was apparent underneath his drawers. He fluidly removed his boots, stockings, and drawers and then knelt beside the bed, spreading her legs.

Soon his tongue was probing her pussy as he feasted on her. Sophie moaned, reaching down and threading her fingers through his silky locks, pushing him farther into her heat.

When the convulsions started deep within her, she released one hand from Zach's hair and clenched her fist in the silk comforter. Higher and higher she soared, crying out, and when she hit the pinnacle and began her descent, she found her other hand pinching her nipple.

Touching herself—how could anyone think it was bad?

Zach climbed up to her and kissed her, letting her taste their delicate mélange of flavors. Her pussy still throbbing from her climax, she sighed as he lay down beside her and pulled her on top of him.

"Ride me, my love." He thrust up into her, filling her.

Sweet joining. Sophie again cupped her own breasts, fingered her nipples, tugging at them and pinching them.

"So beautiful when you touch yourself," Zach rasped. "God, Sophie."

He reached forward and touched her clitoris. *Pop!* A climax hit her so hard and so fast she nearly fell on top of Zach. He held her, still thrusting, nursing her through the euphoria. When she calmed, Zach pulled her off of him.

"I'm not ready for it to be over yet, Sophie." He sat up, pulled her over his knee, and smacked her bottom gently. "Have you been a bad girl, my Sophie, my love?"

Sophie wasn't sure what he meant. She said nothing.

"Your reputation has been ruined by saving me from the hangman's noose." He smacked her again. "Was it worth it, my Sophie?" *Smack!*

"Yes, it was worth— Oh!" She began climaxing against his hand. Placing his fingers inside her, he urged her on, milking her climax until he'd squeezed every drop of pleasure out of her.

When she was coming down—*smack!*—he slapped her again. "Your bottom is so dazzling, Sophie. How I adore it." He rained some tiny kisses on the cheeks of her buttocks, and then— *Smack!* One, two, three more times he spanked her.

The sting permeated through her, metamorphosing into pleasure as usual, but then—

Smack!

And again, harder—*Smack! Smack! Smack!*

Sophie bit her lip. The pain...it was no longer transforming...

Smack!

She gnawed furiously at her lip, drawing blood, tears forming in her eyes. Should she tell him to stop?

Smack! Smack! Smack!

No, let him. He needs this. He needs you to understand...
But she could no longer bear it. "Zach! Stop it! Please!"

Strong fingers massaged her buttocks. "What have I done? My love, I'm so sorry."

"It's...all right..." She sniffed.

"No, Sophie, it is not all right. Your bottom is way too red. Why didn't you stop me?"

Tears rivered down her cheeks onto the black silk of the bed. "I...I wanted to understand. You...seemed to need it."

Zach turned her over and pulled her into his arms, caressing her shoulders, her arms. He cupped her cheeks and forced her to meet his brown gaze. Tears misted in his eyes. "My God, you're a treasure. But Sophie, I never need to hurt you. You must always tell me what your limits are. When you say stop, I will stop, no questions asked." He wiped away an errant tear. "God, I've become a beast. My worst nightmare."

"I...I'm sorry, Zach. I should've said something."

"Yes, you should have. But you have no reason to be sorry. I am not the one who is hurt here. You are." He buried his head in her shoulder. "Sophie, please don't leave me."

Sophie squirmed, escaping his grasp, and sat on the bed next to Zach. She gasped. No doubt about it—her bum was sore.

Zach covered his face with his hands, sobbing softly. "Don't leave me. Please, don't leave me."

Sophie took both his hands in hers, unmasking his face. His smoky eyes were sunken and sad. "I'm not going anywhere. What is this about?"

Zach stood. "I want to run you a warm bath, Sophie. It will ease the pain."

"You didn't answer my question—"

"I have to do this. Please, let me take care of you." He walked to a door and opened it, entering what was presumably his bath chamber. A while later, he called Sophie in.

Sophie couldn't help staring. The bath chamber was luxurious, even nicer than those at the Brighton estate. A claw foot tub stood with real running water. While her mother and the earl's bath chamber had running water, the rest of the chambers at the estate did not. She still depended on Hannah to prepare her baths.

Zach had regained his composure somewhat. He lifted her and gently placed her in the tub.

"Zach," she hedged. "I... I won't deny that I enjoy your spankings. But we've never talked about this. We've never talked about why you enjoy giving them so much and why I enjoy receiving them."

"I honestly haven't thought about it much," Zach said. "I've always liked to take a dominant role in the bedchamber. Some women like it. Some don't. If they don't, I don't do it. You... You were something special from the beginning. Somehow, I knew without asking that you would enjoy a spanking. It's like...your body told me what to do."

"I was quite surprised that I do enjoy it. I've always been rather conventional, as you probably guessed. I had no sexual experience—not even a kiss—before I met you. But something about you..."

"I understand perfectly. Something about you too..."

"I've been thinking," Sophie said. "I... Well, I've told you before that my childhood was less than happy."

"Yes, you have." The sadness in his eyes flickered again.

"The truth of the matter is, my father was a tyrant. He beat and raped my mother. And he also beat Ally and me."

Zach widened his eyes, the anguish on his handsome features increasing. "Oh, no. Don't tell me he—"

Sophie shook her head. "No. He never touched either of us in...that way, thank God. My mother saw to that. But Ally was so strong. Even though she was two years my younger sister, she would provoke our father, make him come after her to spare me. I don't know why she did it. I've never talked to her about it at length. But she protected me, Zach. She protected me when I should've been protecting her as the older sister."

Zach sniffed. "I'm so sorry that you went through all of that. But if I know your sister, she did what she wanted to do."

"Yes, she wanted to protect me. She always considered me so fragile. And I was a timid child. I'm still a timid woman."

"You don't seem so timid to me." Zach managed a slight smile.

Sophie closed her eyes, inhaling the fragrant steam of the bath. "My actions have shocked me, truth be told. I can't seem to control myself with you."

"Nor I with you, my sweet. Today seems testimony to that effect."

She opened her eyes. Again his face was etched with grief.

"Please," she said, cupping his cheek and drawing him to her. "I promise you I'm all right."

"That will never happen again. Never." He closed his eyes. "Go ahead, love. Tell me what you're thinking."

Sophie cleared her throat. "The spankings... They unnerved me at first, mostly because I enjoyed them so much. And I couldn't figure out why, coming from my childhood. Something that was such a heinous part of my life—why would I enjoy it now?"

"It seems pretty clear to me," Zach said. "You're taking the punishment for your sister now. You feel a lot of guilt that she took your punishment when you were children, and now you crave it."

Sophie widened her eyes and let her jaw drop. Was that truly what she was doing? "But why would I...?"

"Sophie, it's just a theory. You may just enjoy spankings. A lot of women do. But coming from your background, psychologically speaking, it seems to make sense."

"Oh, but that makes me so...crazy."

Zach let out a tiny laugh. "Crazy? You're about as far from insane as any woman I know. You're kind and sweet and good. Not to mention achingly beautiful and sensual. If you enjoy the spankings, what does the reason matter? Perhaps you *are* seeking the punishment your sister took for you. Or perhaps you just like being spanked. If it gives us both pleasure, why should we not do it?" His face fell into anguish again. "Of course, I can't risk hurting you again."

Sophie pressed a soft kiss to his lips. "You won't. I won't allow you to."

He swallowed visibly, nodding.

"And what you said about the spanking giving us both pleasure—you sound like Ally. She's a firm believer in pleasure. But as far as I know, she's never been spanked."

"Yes, as far as you know..." Zach gave another small smile.

"If you have a theory as to why I enjoy the spankings," Sophie said, "do you have a theory why you enjoy giving them?"

Zach wrinkled his forehead. "I never really thought about it. My childhood wasn't great either. My father left when I was a babe and my mother died when I was seven. I begged her not to leave me, but she was ill and so weak, Sophie. We had no relations that I knew of, so I had to beg in the streets until I was old enough to find work."

Sophie's heart nearly broke. "Oh, Zach, I'm so sorry. Is that why you ask me not to leave you? Because of your mother?"

Zach arched his eyebrows. "I don't know. I've never thought about that either."

"I can't bear the thought of you begging, being hungry."

"I've long gotten past it. I found work in the stables at the home of one of the gentry in London. It was there I realized my love of performing. The young ladies in the household got drama lessons, and I would sneak in and watch them. One time, the instructor, a young man, made them bend over and he smacked their bottoms. I'm not sure why he did, whether it was part of the lesson or whether they had done something bad. But I was aroused by the sight of it. When I lost my virginity to a servant girl years later, when I was fifteen, she asked me to spank her. I did, and she seemed to enjoy it. None of this explains why I enjoy it, however."

Sophie smiled. "Actually, Zach, it explains perfectly. You had so little control of your own life. It makes perfect sense that you would want to exert control in the one place that you could—the bedchamber."

"That makes a little bit of sense, but now I own my own theatre. I have complete control over everything in my life."

"But you didn't always. You were dependent on others for your very existence for much of your life. That is when our psyches are formed. I no longer have Ally taking beatings for me, but somehow I seem to feel guilty for all that she took all those years ago, and it makes me crave them now."

"Well, as I said, that's just a theory."

"And while you have a lot of control now, you still don't have total control. When you were framed for Nanette's murder, you didn't have control, even though you knew you were innocent. Perhaps that is why you went so far today."

Zach furrowed his brow. Was this making sense to him?

"Perhaps," he said finally. "But again, just a theory."

"Yes." She smiled. "They are just theories."

"I suppose what is important, Sophie, is that we both have something the other person needs." He ran a soft cloth between her breasts. "The truth is...I have very intense feelings for you."

Sophie shivered. Was the water getting cold? No, it was still nice and warm. The shivering came from the inside. "I have feelings for you too. You must know that I would not have been intimate with you if I hadn't sensed something special in you."

"I do know that. And the fact of the matter is..." He drew in a breath. "I have fallen in love with you, Sophie MacIntyre."

Sophie's heart raced, and sunshine exploded within her. She rose from the tub, dripping, and jumped into Zach's arms.

Zach laughed. "Does that mean you're happy about my revelation?"

"Happy? I'm ecstatic. And I love you too, Zach. Completely."

"Well, since your father has demanded that I do right by you, he shouldn't balk at us marrying."

"I love my stepfather, and I appreciate everything he's done for me, Ally, and our mother. But I am of age, Zach. He can't force me to marry anyone. I choose you of my own accord."

"Then you'll marry me?" he asked.

"Of course I will." Sophie smiled.

Zach twirled her around, splattering water all over the

bath chamber. He squeezed one globe of her bottom and then jerked backward, nearly dropping her. "I'm so sorry. You're probably still sore."

"Really, do you think I care? I, timid Sophie MacIntyre, just received an offer of marriage from an amazing, handsome, wonderful man. Zach, I truly thought I was destined for spinsterhood."

"Not if I have anything to say about it." He smiled. "I'll take care of you, my love. Your stepfather may not believe I'm worthy, but the theatre is a good business."

"Of course it is, and I'll be happy to perform for you as often as you like."

"Would you still? After marriage?"

"Of course. Why would I give something up that has brought so much joy to my life? I want to be part of the theatre, Zach. It's a huge part of your life, and now it will be a huge part of mine."

"Then we'll run it together, my charming soon-to-be Mrs. Newland. I can't think of anything I'd like more."

She winked. "Not anything?"

He laughed. "Perhaps a few things." He carried her to the bed, placed a pillow under her bum, spread her legs, and kissed her in her most private area. "I'm going to feast on you, Sophie, my lovely wife-to-be. I'm going to eat you until you come and come again and are begging for me to stop."

Sophie spread her legs eagerly, and Zach dived between them, sucking on her clitoris, sliding his tongue through her slick folds.

"You taste so delicious. I will never tire of eating you."

Eating her... Words she'd considered vulgar a mere few weeks ago. Now they aroused her. She wanted him to eat her.

She would gladly spread her legs for him whenever he asked.

He pushed her thighs forward and slid his tongue across that most private place. "One day, my love."

Sophie nodded against the comforter. She had read of the act in the story of Lord and Lady Peacock. Angelica got taken in the arse, and Poppea did it to herself with a... Well, in the story, it was called a glass phallus. Perhaps another name existed for it. She would ask Ally.

"Such a bewitching little puckered hole, my Sophie. It's a tight heaven, I tell you." He slid his tongue over it again.

She shivered—such an intense feeling. Who knew such a forbidden place could create so much pleasure?

She felt his tongue probing and even entering it. Then he moved back to her pussy and then up farther, meeting her gaze, his chin glistening. "My love, may I show you the hidden joys of this little gem?"

Sophie nodded. She could not deny him anything now. She had already given him so much more than she'd ever given anyone, had ever even thought of giving anyone.

He smiled. "You won't regret this, sweet."

He glided his tongue along her anus again and again, and just when she was getting used to the amazing sensation, his fingertip slid inside the tight hole.

She jerked, the burning pain invading her senses.

"Breathe, Sophie. You will adjust. Give it a few seconds."

She let out the breath she only then realized she'd been holding.

"Trust me," he said soothingly. "Trust me."

She did trust him. With her life, in fact. She let out the breath again and forced herself to relax. Soon the pain was gone, and he was slipping his finger slowly in and out of her anal opening. He leaned down and took her pussy in his mouth while still finger-fucking her arsehole.

Oh, the pleasure—such that she never imagined. A few more seconds of his tongue tantalizing her, and she shattered into a euphoric climax.

When she had come back to earth, she opened her eyes and found his head between her legs, his gaze meeting hers.

"Again," he said.

CHAPTER TWENTY-TWO

Six Weeks Later

Sophie took her second, third, and then an unprecedented fourth curtain call after the finale of *Love on a Midsummer Night*. A total of four dozen red roses were handed to her, from Zach, from the director, and from two of the theatre's benefactors.

Life had been good these past several weeks. The ominous notes had stopped, despite the fact that Mr. Bertram, still incarcerated, maintained his innocence. Though she and Zach hadn't been able to spend a lot of alone time together due to their unrelenting schedules, they constantly stole looks at one another during rehearsals, reminding each other of their love. Ally had recovered, and babies Maureen and Sophie were thriving.

Yes, life was good.

Breathless and exhausted, Sophie left the stage for the dressing room. She was waylaid by Ally and Evan, her mother and the earl, Lily and the duke, and Rose, who had accompanied Lily and the duke because Cameron was working the performance.

Ally looked radiant, her chestnut hair pulled up and tumbling over her neck in ringlets. Her golden eyes were dancing. She pulled Sophie into a fierce hug. "Oh, my darling, you were absolutely spectacular. Your voice never sounded sweeter. You will be the toast of the town in no time."

Sophie couldn't speak. She just smiled.

"My dear Sophie," her mother said, "you are positively glowing."

Sophie didn't doubt it. She was warm and clammy and on top of the world.

Everyone wanted a hug, and everyone wanted to congratulate her. She appreciated it, she truly did, but she really wanted to see Zach. He had disappeared after the curtain calls, no doubt to his office.

She finally forced herself to speak. "Thank you all for coming. I do so appreciate your support. And I'm so glad you enjoyed the show. Rose, Cam is a genius. His music and Zach's words were a joy to sing. They made me look good."

"Don't be silly," Rose said. "Cam and Mr. Newland are both geniuses, but so are you."

The others all agreed, hugging Sophie again. She was blessed to have such a loving and supportive family. Most of all, she was betrothed to the most wonderful man in the world. Sophie missed him. They had sneaked in some kisses when they could, but Sophie was looking forward to spending some quality time with her husband-to-be.

Tomorrow was Sunday, and Zach had promised the cast a day off—the first since May Day. Sophie planned to surprise Zach at his townhome and spend the day in his bed.

She finally broke away from her family, and instead of going straight to the ladies' dressing room, she made a detour to Zach's office. She was surprised to find it dark. She opened the door, but still blackness greeted her. Zach was nowhere in sight. Perhaps he was in the men's dressing room, removing his stage makeup and changing into street clothes.

Sophie made her way to the ladies' dressing room to

do the same. The ladies applauded when she entered, and Sophie's heart melted. They had finally opened up to her and accepted her. She had proved her worth during the grueling six weeks of rehearsal, working as hard or harder than they all did. She would not be seen as a pampered lady of the peerage. And truth be told, she was *not* a pampered lady of the peerage. She had probably grown up in worse circumstances than they had.

After removing her stage makeup as best she could, she changed back into her street clothes with the help of one of the dressers.

She quickly ran past Zach's office. Still dark. So she strode to the men's dressing room and waited outside. When one of the male cast members came out, she said, "Barrington, have you seen Mr. Newland?"

"I'm sorry, Lady Sophie. I didn't see him the entire time I was in the dressing room."

Sophie wrinkled her forehead. "That is odd. He's not in his office either."

"Perhaps he had business to attend to with benefactors. I'm sure he'll turn up. Have a pleasing day off on the morrow."

"Yes, thank you. You do the same."

The man disappeared down the hallway.

Well, Sophie couldn't stick around waiting for Zach. Mother and the earl were holding their coach for her, and she didn't want to keep them waiting any longer. She let out a sigh and headed for the lobby.

On second thought, she went back to the dressing room. She wanted to take some of her roses home to grace the estate. She grabbed one of the bouquets, and a small envelope dropped out of it and onto the floor.

"Curious," she said aloud. She picked up the small

parchment and opened it. Her heart nearly stopped.

Only one more obstacle to go... You will be mine.

★ ★ ★ ★

Zach awoke on the floor of his bedchamber. He opened his eyes. Where was he? And how had he gotten here? Through his blurry vision, he saw his hand lying next to him, soaked in something red and sticky. Blood. He lifted his hand and balled up the blood between his fingers. He lifted his head—Augh! Big mistake. His skull throbbed, as if someone were hammering inside his brain. Where was the blood coming from? He touched his forehead lightly, his hair stiff and sticky.

Fractured images came back to him. He'd been waylaid after the performance by a gentleman who was asking questions about donating to the theatre. He had walked the man out to his coach...

That's the last he remembered. Had the man hit him in the head? Slipped something in a drink? Yes, they'd had a drink. Here at his home? *Think, Zach. Think.* What had happened?

It was still dark. What time must it be? He was alive, so perhaps he hadn't been hurt that badly. The wound on his head seemed to have stopped bleeding. He should get up and take a look in the looking glass, but he couldn't seem to move.

Sophie. Where was Sophie? His heart started thundering. She would have gone home with her parents. Of course. *God, please let her be all right.*

His lips were parched and his tongue dry. If only he could get up for a dipper of water... He could feel his legs but couldn't seem to move them. He gathered all his strength... His legs moved slightly, twitching, but he couldn't focus enough to sit up.

Objects began to blur. His hound dog, Rufus, entered the room, sniffing. He licked Zach's face. It felt kind of like a mini massage... His consciousness wavered, and he fell back into oblivion.

★ ★ ★ ★

"Thank you," Sophie said to the coachman as he helped her down. "Please be back for me in a couple of hours. On second thought, stay for a few moments. If Mr. Newland is not at home, I will be back out."

"Yes, my lady."

It was a glorious morning in Bath. The sun shone over the city. Sophie knew better than to inhale. City air was not nearly as fresh as the country air at the estate. Still, the town was pretty, and Zach's townhome sat in a nice little neighborhood.

If only Sophie could enjoy it. Worry bubbled in her gut. She hadn't told anyone about the note. She wanted to speak to Zach about it first. Perhaps Mr. Bertram was innocent after all.

She rapped on the front door.

No answer.

Hmm, strange. She rapped again. Finally, Zach's butler answered the door. "Lady Sophie, I thought you would be at the hospital."

She widened her eyes, her heart hammering. "Hospital? What do you mean?"

"Mr. Newland is at the hospital. His valet found him this morning in his bedroom, unconscious with a wound to the head."

Sophie gulped. Dear God... The note... The obstacle...

Forgetting niceties, she turned and ran from the butler and back down to the coach. "Take me to the hospital," she yelled to the driver.

"Yes, my lady."

Sophie bit her lip and fidgeted with her hands during the entire drive. She tried to assuage herself with the knowledge that hospitals were no longer places where people went to die. The one in Bath possessed the most up-to-date equipment and the most knowledgeable staff. Last year, Cameron's little sister, Katrina, had spent some time there when she was stricken with an infectious illness. She came home good as new.

So would Zach.

Sophie had to believe that.

She could not lose Zach. A tear fell down her cheek. She just could not.

The hospital smelled of alcohol and ether. Nurses floated around in long black gowns with white pinafores across their chests and white hats on their heads. Sophie ran up to the desk clerk. "I need to see Mr. Zachary Newland."

"Are you a family member of Mr. Newland?"

"Well, we are going to be married."

"I'm afraid there is no next of kin listed on Mr. Newland's paperwork," the clerk said. "Therefore, you will not be allowed to see him, but I can check with his doctor and get a report for you."

Sophie bit her lip. That would have to do. "Thank you. I would appreciate it."

The clerk left her station and returned a few moments later with a man Sophie recognized.

"Dr. Blake," she said, "are you Zach's doctor?"

Blake nodded. "Lady Sophie, I hear you're asking about

Mr. Newland."

"Yes, anything you can tell me?"

"He was apparently drugged with something in a beverage. We don't know exactly what, but his vital signs are good and we expect him to recover."

"What about the head wound?"

"It was superficial. Luckily, the bleeding stopped on its own. He has a mild concussion, but he will recover."

"When will he be released? We're in the middle of the production."

"I understand that, my lady. He will probably be released in a few days. His understudy may have to take the role for a couple performances."

Sophie's heart fell. Zach never missed a performance. But his health and well-being were more important. She thanked God he was all right.

"Thank you so much, Doctor. I'm so very relieved."

"Not at all, my lady. If you will excuse me." He nodded, turned, and walked down the corridor.

Sophie breathed a sigh of relief. At least Zach was safe. But who had sent that ominous note to her last evening? She had been on top of the world and hadn't let it sink in as much as it should have.

She rode home in the carriage. The time had come to tell her mother and stepfather about the new note. She wasn't looking forward to that conversation.

She found her stepfather and mother in the main parlor, which had been completely redecorated after the birth of Ally's twins. "Mother, my lord, I need to speak to you both."

"Of course." Iris looked up. "What is it, Sophie?"

"I...I received another one of those notes last night after

the show."

The earl stood upright from the divan. "What?"

"I received another note. It was in one of the bouquets of roses." She pulled the note out of her pocket and handed it to him.

Brighton cleared his throat. "I'm no expert, but the penmanship does seem to be similar to the others. However, there is a suspect in custody—Mr. Bertram—and our own Graves found him writing the notes."

"He has maintained his innocence this whole time," Iris reminded her husband.

Brighton nodded. "It is curious... Sophie, I'm afraid you won't be able to do any more performing until—"

Sophie stomped her foot. "No! I will not allow this man to control me. I was controlled by a man my whole life until Father died. So were you, Mother. I was a sensation last night. I will continue being in the show."

"Sophie!" Iris shook her head. "What has gotten into you? You cannot speak to David like that. This is so unlike you."

"Maybe I've changed, Mother. Maybe I'm not timid little Sophie who never causes any trouble anymore. I will perform. It's bad enough that the leading man will have to miss a few shows."

"Mr. Newland? What are you talking about?" Iris asked.

"Zach was attacked in his home last night. He is in the hospital recovering from poisoning and a head wound."

"Goodness, is he all right?"

"Dr. Blake is attending him. He expects him to recover."

"My God..." Brighton said, raking his fingers through his silvery hair. "Is it possible that Bertram is innocent as he claims?"

"I'm afraid at this point anything is possible, my dear," Iris said.

"Mother... F-Father..." The word stumbled off her tongue. "I need you both to know something."

"What is it, Sophie?"

"I know that you refused Mr. Newland's request to court me, and I know neither of you were happy with my choice to become...intimate with him."

The earl grunted. Iris simply sighed.

"Mother, you wanted me to find love. I have found it. Zach is perfectly well-off and will be able to support me just fine. And he will let me continue to perform. We will run the theatre together. We've talked about it."

Iris gasped. "This is never what I wanted for you, Sophie."

"Did you want me to be a spinster forever? I have found a worthy man who loves me and whom I love."

"But the working..."

"I enjoy the working. And...I'm *good* at it. I'm good at something!" Sophie smiled, lifting her skirts and twirling around. "I can bring joy to other people by singing. Is that not the greatest gift someone can have? To make others happy?"

Brighton grunted again. "If the girl insists on working, Iris, there is not much we can do. And she is talented. There's no denying that."

Iris smiled. "I want only what's best for you, Sophie. I admit, I've never seen you happier since you've been with the theatre."

Sophie smiled again, but worry for Zach stripped it from her quickly. "Thank you both."

"But don't you want children, Sophie?" Iris said.

"Of course I do. You know how much I love Maureen and

little Sophie, and little Morgan and little Joy."

"But if you're working, how would you care for children?"

"There is no law that says I have to have children right away, is there?"

"Well, children have a way of coming into the world whether you are ready for them or not," Iris said.

"Zach and I will figure it out together. I promise you. You *will* have more grandchildren." Sophie fidgeted with her handkerchief. "Right now, Zach is the most important thing. Once he recovers, maybe he'll remember some details about who attacked him."

"Yes." Brighton cleared his throat. "And for the time being, we need to alert the constables that you received another note and find out if there's any way Bertram could've sent it from his cell."

"I don't see how that could be the case," Iris said.

"You'd be surprised, my love," the earl said. "Criminal minds have a way of getting things done."

Sophie shivered. The man was behind bars, and still she and Zach were not safe from him.

A knock on the door startled all three of them.

"Yes," the earl called.

Graves entered, his demeanor solemn. "I beg pardon, my lord, my ladies. Another parchment has arrived for Lady Sophie."

CHAPTER TWENTY-THREE

Sophie froze, ice penetrating her heart. Not another one... How was he writing them while he was incarcerated? How was he getting them delivered?

"I'll take that, Graves," the earl said, standing. "Who delivered it?"

"One of the messenger boys in town."

"The same one who has delivered the rest of the notes?"

"I cannot say, my lord. It's been weeks since we received one of the notes, and Mr. Bertram took possession of some of those, so they may not have been delivered at all."

"All right, then. Thank you, Graves."

Graves bowed politely and left.

"What does it say, David?" Iris asked.

Brighton read the note, and his face went white. He folded the parchment.

"David?" Iris nudged.

"Nothing you two need to concern yourselves with."

Sophie whipped her hands to her hips. "I certainly do need to concern myself with it. A woman was murdered because of this person's obsession with me, and now Zach has been attacked. Please, my lord, you must tell me what it says."

He nodded. "If it's all right with you, Iris."

Iris's lips trembled. "Go ahead."

Brighton cleared his throat. "It says, 'You will be mine now.'"

Sophie shook her head. "I don't understand. Everyone knows I am betrothed to Zach. Does Bertram not know that Zach will recover?"

"Probably not," the earl said. "After all, Mr. Bertram is being held. Clearly he must've had someone else attack Mr. Newland, and he doesn't realize that whoever did the attacking left before he finished the job."

Sophie's heart dropped to her stomach. *Left before he finished the job...* Someone had truly meant to kill Zach.

Why it hadn't happened, she didn't know. Perhaps a servant had been near to discovering them, or perhaps whoever it was had lost his nerve.

The truth hit her more forcefully, knocking the air out of her lungs.

Zach could be dead right now.

Whoever was obsessed with her wanted Zach dead.

Dear God...

"Mother, my lord, I'm not sure Zach is safe in the hospital. Bertram will send someone else after him."

"Sophie," the earl said, "I think we need to face the fact that perhaps Mr. Bertram is innocent as he claims. It would be too difficult for him to send notes and facilitate an attack on Mr. Newland from inside a prison cell."

Confusion muddled Sophie's mind. If it wasn't Bertram, whoever was responsible for this was still out there. And an innocent man was being held captive. None of this made any sense.

"I don't understand any of this. Why would someone be obsessed with me of all people? I'm a nobody."

Iris took her hand. "Sophie, my dear girl, you've never been a nobody. And after last night... Well, you're going to be the toast of Bath."

That didn't make Sophie feel any better. She had loved working on the show, and opening night had been more than she'd ever imagined, but being a public figure would only put her and Zach in more danger.

"Mother, we have to find out who's doing this. If it's not Mr. Bertram, who could it be?"

"I don't know, my dear. David?"

"Graves had good evidence implicating Bertram. They found parchments matching the notes to Sophie in his personal belongings, along with a pen and quill, all hidden in his chamber. In addition, Graves said he questioned the messenger boys, and none of them remembered delivering a message to Bertram. Yet Bertram intercepted several and brought them to Sophie. Circumstantial, yes, but it was enough for me to dismiss the man and have him arrested."

"But what if they're holding an innocent man?" Sophie said. "That isn't fair."

"You're right," the earl said. "But I think, at this point, it is best to keep Mr. Bertram incarcerated until we find the real culprit."

Sophie gulped but nodded. She hated the idea of Mr. Bertram being locked up if he was indeed innocent, but the last thing they needed was one more potential suspect running around. "I just don't have any idea who it could be."

"Perhaps one of the cast members of the show?" Iris said.

"I don't think so. None of them would ever hurt Zach. He's their meal ticket, after all."

Brighton nodded. "Sophie makes a good point."

"In the meantime, I need to go visit Zach at the hospital," Sophie said. "I'm frightfully worried for him."

"I'm afraid not, Sophie," the earl said. "I don't want you leaving the estate until we find out who is behind this."

"But...my rehearsals! You cannot keep me here."

"Oh, I can, and I will. Your safety is paramount."

"I'm afraid I agree with David," Iris said. "I couldn't bear it if anything happened to you."

"Nothing's going to happen to me," Sophie said. "This person is presumably in love with me. He's trying to make my life better in his twisted way, not hurt me."

"Perhaps that is so, but what I said stands. You are not to leave the estate."

"What if I have some servants escort me?"

"No." Brighton shook his head. "You are safest here. For all we know, it is one of our own servants who is doing this to you. After all, we all thought it was Bertram. And it still might be. For now, Sophie, consider yourself under house arrest."

★ ★ ★ ★

Zach trudged through a murky black river, his muscles aching, his mind fraught with exhaustion. All around him was darkness, except for a small sliver of light in the distance. So far away...but it drew him like a magnetic force. He had to keep going... Had to get back...

Back to Sophie...

As he trudged, unintelligible voices murmured above him. He couldn't make out any words, but they seemed to be urging him toward something, asking him for something...

He lifted his right leg out of the quicksand and stepped forward, drowning it in the murk again. Now the left leg...

The sliver of light started to fade away...

Must keep going... Must make it back to Sophie...

★ ★ ★ ★

"Mr. Newland?"

Zach's eyes fluttered open, his brain a mass of gibberish. A vaguely familiar face hovered above him, shining a light in his eye.

"Mr. Newland?" A light reflected off the man's forehead.

Yes, the doctor's head mirror. Was it...sunlight from the window reflecting off of it?

His thoughts were muddled.

The doctor held Zach's eyes open with his finger, and again the head mirror reflected light into them. Zach tried to close them.

"Mr. Newland? Can you understand me?"

Yes, he understood. He tried to speak, but only a croak came out.

"It's okay. Don't try to talk. You'll be talking in no time."

The doctor placed his hands on both sides of Zach's neck and palpated. "Any headache, Mr. Newland?"

Zach shook his head. At least he thought he shook his head. No headache but...fuzzy brain. His thoughts were jumbled.

"You've been unconscious for about twenty-four hours. You have a concussion. You also were poisoned—we think through a beverage. Luckily you didn't get enough of it to harm you."

Where am I?

But, of course, the words had not come out. Zach willed his lips to part and tried to force the words out. Again, all that came out was a grunt.

"Your voice will be back soon enough. I'm Dr. Michael Blake, your physician."

Zach grunted again. *What happened to me?*

"We aren't sure who is responsible for this, Mr. Newland. But the constables and inspectors are looking into it. We expect to have you out of here in a few days."

But the production. What about the production?

The stage director and manager would have to take care of things. His understudy was decent. If he had to do a few of the performances, so be it.

Sophie? Where is Sophie? And then he remembered. Trudging through the dark murk... The sliver of light leading him out. It was Sophie.

He opened his lips again. "Sophie."

Dr. Blake turned back toward him. "What was that?"

"Sophie." He exhaled.

"Lady Sophie MacIntyre. Of course. She has been here to ask about you. I'll make sure she's informed of your progress."

Zach's eyes fluttered shut. Everything was all right now. Sophie...

★ ★ ★ ★

This must be what Ally felt like.

Sophie couldn't help smiling at the recollection of all of Ally's adventures after Mother and the earl had first gotten married. Evan had been left in charge of them, but Ally was determined to go to London to see her then paramour, Mr. Landon. She kept sneaking off the estate, paying off servants to get her to London. Evan had been mad as a bull, but the two ended up falling into deep love.

Now, here Sophie was, a good girl, paying off a couple of servants to get her to Zach's house. She had heard from Dr. Blake that he had been released the day before. She intended to go see him and take care of him. He needed her.

She walked quickly to the livery, her reticule filled with sovereigns to pay the servants for their silence. She smiled.

Until strong hands grabbed her from behind. Before she could cry out, a damp handkerchief was clamped over her face.

Not again. She had been through this before, nearly a year ago. How could it be happening again?

Don't breathe, Sophie. Don't breathe. Don't breathe in the chemical on the handkerchief.

Don't...

Breathe...

★ ★ ★ ★

Zach felt better than he had in days as his coach made its way to the Brighton estate. Defying his doctor's orders, he had left his home. His head was feeling fine, and he had his energy back. He needed to see Sophie and make sure she was all right. She had not been allowed to visit him in the hospital, and he would not have wanted her to see him that way anyway. But now all was right with the world, and he was coming to see the woman he loved. He pushed his feet against the floor of the coach, willing it to move faster. When they finally arrived at the manor, he alighted quickly and nearly ran to the door and knocked.

Graves answered, his lips in a stern line.

"Mr. Graves," Zach said, a smile on his face, "I have come to see Lady Sophie."

"Of course," Graves said. "I will see if she is able to receive you."

Zach stood in the foyer, waiting for Sophie. His feet wanted to dance a jig, so elated was he to be able to see the woman he loved.

A few moments later, Graves returned. "I'm afraid Lady Sophie is not receiving visitors today."

"Did you tell her it was me?" Surely Sophie would want to see him.

"I did indeed. She said to please forgive her, but she is not feeling up to visitors today."

"How very odd. I was sure she would want to see me."

"I don't know what to tell you, Mr. Newland. Perhaps tomorrow."

Very odd. Zach's neck chilled. Something wasn't right. "What about Lord and Lady Brighton. Are they here?"

"I'm afraid no one is receiving today, sir."

Zach left, sadness embracing him. He had so looked forward to seeing his lady.

Well, she would be at rehearsal tomorrow. Although his understudy would be performing the next two shows, Zach would still oversee the rehearsal, and he would see Sophie then. As he rode out, the summer sun was setting over the horizon in radiant rainbows of pink, violet, and orange.

He returned home, ate a small supper prepared by his chef, and retired to his chamber, his head hurting a bit. The doctor said he would have headaches for a few weeks. He took a headache powder, lay down, and fell into slumber. He would see Sophie on the morrow at rehearsal.

★ ★ ★ ★

Sophie awoke in darkness, trembling with icy fear. She had been abducted once before, when a group of zealots against obscene literature had mistaken her for Ally and had taken her because they thought she was writing erotica. In truth, Ally had been the one writing the erotica. Evan and Ally had rescued her, but not without Evan getting shot. He recovered fully, thank God, but here she was in the same peril again. Someone had taken her.

She searched her mind. Yes, she had been on her way to the livery to have a coach take her to Zach's house. She desperately needed to see the man she loved. She waited while her eyes got used to the darkness. Soon, a window drew her gaze, moonlight streaming in. So it was nighttime. She had no idea what time it was or even if it was the same day.

Footsteps shuffled in the other part of the house. For this was a house, wasn't it? She was lying on a bed. Her hands were bound together, as were her feet. She couldn't move.

Her mouth was dry and parched. Perhaps they would give her some water?

"Hallo? Is anyone here?"

The shuffling came nearer.

"I...I am quite thirsty. May I have a drink of water?"

"We should have blindfolded her," a voice said.

"He didn't say to. He told us to bind her hands and feet, which we did," another voice said.

Who were these people? And whom were they talking about?

Someone entered the room. Sophie couldn't make out his facial features but he was large. He might have been wearing a mask. He pulled her arms up.

"Sit up, my lady."

The stranger held out a dipper of water, and she drank from it. The lukewarm liquid soothed her parched throat but didn't really quench her thirst. Her hairs stood on end as fear coursed through her veins.

When she had finished drinking, she looked up at the man holding the dipper. He was indeed wearing a black mask. "Who are you? Why am I here?"

"Those questions will be answered in the morning, my lady. For now, go ahead and rest."

"But...I need to use...a chamber pot."

"Oh, for corn's sake. Jake, she needs a chamber pot," the man yelled.

Jake? Sophie didn't know anyone named Jake.

The other man brought in a chamber pot. "I don't know what to tell you. I guess unbind her and then we'll bind her back up. One of us will have to watch her."

Sophie couldn't bear the thought of it. "For goodness' sake, where would I go? Please, just a little privacy."

"It couldn't hurt," Jake said. "I don't really want to watch her piss anyway, Harry."

"Well, I wouldn't mind." Harry unbound her hands and then her feet, chuckling. "I'll watch her. Make it quick like."

"Please. I can't have you..." She looked away. No privacy. Just like during her childhood...

"God a'mighty, fine," Harry said. "You have two minutes."

The men left, closing the door.

Sophie took care of her necessities quickly. And then she looked down at the ceramic pot. Was the window open? She walked toward it. No. The pot would make quite a handsome weapon. If only she hadn't filled it. The last time she was abducted, she had been too scared to do anything except what her abductors told her. She had not caused any trouble.

She was no longer that timid and shy creature. Holding her nose, she held the pot and stood at the door. She'd just have to use the pot with the urine in it.

"I'm finished now," she called.

The door rattled, and in came Harry. Sophie heaved the pot over her head and brought it crashing down on his skull. The centrifugal force kept the urine safely in the pot. Not that she would have minded soaking him with it.

"What the...?" Jake rushed in. "So you thought you'd get a little brave, did you?" He pushed Sophie down on the bed.

Within a few minutes, she was bound again. Jake dragged Harry's body out of the room.

He returned a few minutes later. "You just lost any privileges I might have given you," he said. "You'll stay here until the boss gets here in the morning."

Sophie buried her head in the ragged quilt on the bed and cried. No one even knew she was gone yet. No one would notice if she didn't come down early for breakfast to get to rehearsal, because she was under house arrest. Her stepfather had notified the director that she would be missing a few rehearsals, so no one at the theatre would notice she was gone. No one at home would be looking for her until luncheon at the earliest.

When would this "boss" get here? And what did he want with her?

The boss—he had to be the person who had sent the notes. Harry was out cold, and Jake wouldn't tell her anything. But they knew who he was. She was sure of it.

How was this happening again? She had never hurt a fly in her life, and she didn't intend to. What woman of the peerage was kidnapped not once but twice?

She hated being bound, despite the fact that Zach had bound her hands once. That was different. Zach would never hurt her and would unbind her as soon as she asked him to. She knew nothing about these men. They were clearly hired by someone to take her. Whoever this boss was, she wasn't looking forward to meeting him.

She tried stifling her tears. She didn't need her nose to run, because she couldn't empty it. Nothing to do now but wait.

Please, Zach, find me. Find me before he does.

CHAPTER TWENTY-FOUR

When the director told Zach that Sophie would not be at rehearsal, he made his apologies to the cast and rushed out of the theatre. A bad feeling niggled at him. He should have pushed his way into the manor yesterday and demanded to see Sophie.

He arrived and rapped loudly at the door. Where in the hell was that damned butler? He always came to the door right away.

Finally, the door opened. A young maid he didn't recognize stood there. "Yes, sir, may I help you?"

"I need to see Lady Sophie. Right away."

"Why, Lady Sophie is still abed."

"Wake her, then. I came to see her last night and was told she was not available to see me. I will see her now, God damn it."

"Goodness, sir, no need to use such language. Let me find Mr. Graves."

"I'm not interested in seeing Mr. Graves. I want to see Lady Sophie right now."

The maid curtsied and scurried away, looking petrified.

★ ★ ★ ★

The sun had risen, and Sophie still lay on the bed. She still didn't know where she was—only in a shack that apparently had at least one other room.

In a few moments, Jake, still masked, came in, carrying a tray containing some bread, porridge, and a glass of water. He unbound Sophie and urged her to eat.

She sucked down the water quickly but couldn't force down the bread and porridge. She just wasn't hungry. The meal reminded her of some of the sparse meals she had been forced to eat when she, Ally, and their mother lived in poverty when their father was still alive. He would be gone for weeks on end, leaving them with no money and no food. They had made do the best they could. Sophie was used to going to bed hungry. After a while, hunger didn't really exist.

Still, no one would realize she was gone yet.

If she were Ally, she would be looking for ways to escape. The window? It was high and narrow. Perhaps if she scooted the bed over to the wall, she could stand upon it and reach the window. However, it was made of glass and appeared to have no way to open.

That probably wouldn't stop Ally, but although Sophie had come a long way, she still wasn't Ally—despite her newfound sexual awakening.

Jake barged back through the door. "Not hungry, my lady?"

Sophie shook her head. "Thank you, no. But if I could have a little more water please."

Jake brought her some water, which she drank greedily.

"Time to use the chamber pot again, my lady, or I can take you out to the privy."

"The chamber pot is fine."

"And no tricks like the last time."

"No tricks. I promise."

Sophie took care of necessities, and Jake returned in a few moments, Harry in tow. A knot gleamed on his forehead above his black mask.

"Go on and take out the chamber pot," Jake said to Harry. "I'll prepare her for the boss."

Prepare her? What did that mean? Sophie shuddered. She didn't want to find out.

Jake walked toward her. "You gave Harry a right good lump on his dome, missy. He's not feeling well or thinking straight."

Was she supposed to care? She wished he were still out cold.

"I'll need you to stand up, my lady," Jake said.

Sophie froze. Why should she? Would they hurt her if she didn't do what they said?

Only one way to find out.

"I will not." She stayed on the bed.

"You'll move, or I'll move you."

Be strong, Sophie. Remember what Ally would do. "You will get no cooperation from me. I don't know who you are or why you've brought me here. I will not help you in any way."

"Have it your way, then."

Jake was not an overly large man like Harry, but he was portly. He grabbed Sophie's arm and twisted her so that she was facedown on the bed. Jake climbed on top of her, straddling her buttocks, and began unfastening her gown.

"No!" Sophie cried into the comforter.

"Stop your struggling, and this will go faster."

Sophie didn't want to go any faster. No one but Zach could undress her. She kicked and screamed, flailing her arms.

Jake finally got her dress unfastened and began loosening

her corset.

"What do you mean to do to me?" A new wave of dread coursed through her. She would not give herself to any man but Zach.

"All I mean to do is undress you. What the boss does is up to him. You have my word I won't touch you inappropriately."

"You're already touching me inappropriately. I did not give you permission to undress me, did I?"

"Sorry, my lady. I've got to tie you naked to the bed for the boss."

Icy talons crept along Sophie's spine. Who was the boss?

"Who do you work for?" she demanded. "My stepfather is the Earl of Brighton, and he will see that you go to the gallows for this."

"I know very well who your stepfather is, my lady. I used to work for him, actually. Of course, a high and mighty lady like you wouldn't know that. We all look alike to you."

"You do when you're wearing a mask. Who are you working for now?"

"You'll find out soon enough." He jerked Sophie off the bed, removing her dress and corset. She stood only in her chemise and drawers. He set her back on the bed and removed her shoes and stockings.

She felt exposed. Completely and totally exposed in front of a masked, deranged man.

"Your chemise, my lady."

Sophie crossed her arms over her breasts. "I will not."

"Then you force me to do it for you." He gripped her chemise and ripped it off her body.

She sat naked, except for her drawers.

"And now the bloomers, miss."

"No."

Quick as a panther, he tore her drawers from her.

He raked his gaze over her, licking his lips lasciviously. "You are fine, truly fine. I can see why the boss likes you."

Sophie slid one hand one arm down, covering her vulva, and crossed the other over her breasts. Still exposed. Raw and exposed and frightened beyond measure.

"Now, my lady, lie down on the bed, on your back."

Sophie stood her ground. "I will not."

He came toward her.

"Don't you dare lay a hand on me!"

Jake was not fazed. He pushed her down onto the bed. She struggled, kicking and flailing her arms. He laid his weight over her body, grabbed one arm, brought it to the bars at the headboard, and fastened her wrist to the bar with rope. She continued to resist, her wrist burning from the coarse binding.

Jake bound her other wrist to the headboard. Still she kicked her feet, screaming and bouncing her derriere on the bed.

"You're just making this harder, my lady."

She landed a pretty good kick to Jake's forearm.

"God damn it, you bitch."

He grabbed her foot, leashed the rope around it, and bound it to one of the bars of the footboard. He moved to the other side of the bed and repeated the procedure.

"You won't get away with this! My stepfather will come for me. My fiancé will come for me."

"Your fiancé?"

"Yes. Mr. Zachary Newland. He and I are going to be married."

"Well, my lady, I suppose it's my duty to tell you that you

no longer belong to Mr. Newland. You're now the property of the boss. He will be here soon."

Jake turned and walked toward the door.

"You can't just leave me here," Sophie screamed.

"I'm only following orders, my lady. I've done what I've been paid to do."

"You stupid coward. How can you leave a weak woman like this?"

Jake turned. "My lady, I advise you to keep your mouth shut. I do my job, but anyone who calls me coward risks my wrath. And right now, my lady, you're in no position to fight me off. I wouldn't mind having a taste of that tight little body."

Nausea rose in Sophie's throat. "What would the boss think if he knew you were having such thoughts?"

"Well, the boss will never know, will he?"

"Certainly he will. I will tell him."

"Not after I cut out your tongue, little one." Jake's eyes glowed red like the devil's.

Sophie recognized that evil gleam. She had seen it in her own father's eyes when he beat their mother, when he beat her, and especially when he beat Ally.

Something in her snapped. Never again would she be cowardly. Never again would she succumb to her own fear. Ally hadn't feared their father, and she had taken plenty of beatings meant for Sophie.

This man would not touch her, and neither would this boss, whoever he was.

"You cut out my tongue, sir, and I promise you my fiancé will come and cut off your cock."

"I will be long gone, my lady, before anyone knows I had any part of this."

She remembered what Ally had said when Evan's employee had beaten her nearly a year ago. She had said she wanted to keep him talking so he wouldn't rape her, that a beating was far preferable to having that slimy wretch inside her body.

Sophie felt the same way. No one would touch her except her true love, Zach.

"Come to think of it, I don't think the boss would mind if I took a little taste of you. After all, we *are* the ones who took you and brought you. We will be handsomely compensated, of course, but what better compensation than a little taste of the goodies?"

"You will *not* touch me," Sophie seethed through her teeth.

"And exactly who is going to stop me, my dear?"

The doorknob clicked, and another masked man entered, eyes glowing.

"*I* will."

CHAPTER TWENTY-FIVE

Jake turned. "There you are, boss."

"Yes, and none too soon. You were really going to touch my woman, were you?"

"No, of course not. But the little lady has a mouth on her, see, and she was pissing me off. I was just trying to scare her a little."

"Scare her? My true love, the love of my life? Why would you want to scare her? This woman is above you in so many ways."

Sophie furrowed her brow. Who was this? It wasn't Zach. She would recognize his voice. Yet the voice did sound slightly familiar. She couldn't place it.

The boss jerked Jake out of the way. "Leave us," he said.

Jake walked obediently out the door, closing it behind him.

The man sat down on the bed and trailed a gloved finger down her cheek. "You are so lovely, Sophie."

Again the voice. Familiar, yet different.

"Mr. Bertram?" she asked.

The boss shook his head. "No, Mr. Bertram is innocent, as he proclaims."

"Then you have to get him released."

"I don't have to do anything. I have come to claim you. You have always been mine, Sophie. I have been worshiping you from afar for nearly a year now, waiting for the time to make my move. I should've made it long ago, before you got involved with Zachary Newland's theatre. Before you got involved with Newland himself. But I had to cover my tracks. I had to make sure no one would trace this back to me." His jaw tensed. "And in the meantime, you let him soil you, you little whore!" Suddenly the lines of his chin softened, and he let out a breath. "Forgive my hasty words. I know he forced you. Someone as perfect as you would not willingly submit to him."

Sophie's mind raced. What to do? This man was insane. "Who are you?"

"I will reveal that in time." He leaned down and pressed his lips against her forehead.

Sophie shuddered. "Leave me. I cannot bear your touch."

"That will change, I assure you. One day, you will realize we are meant to be. That you are mine and no one else's. That on some plane of existence, you always have been mine and I yours."

"You're insane," Sophie said. "Show yourself. If you do not show yourself, you're nothing but a coward, just like your friend Jake out there."

The man stood and stomped his foot on the ground, making the room shake. "You dare speak to me that way? After all I've done for you? I got rid of that stupid suitor Van Arden for you. It certainly wasn't difficult to find a commoner to seduce him and claim to be with child. I killed that harlot Nanette Lloyd for you, so she would no longer bother you. She had the nerve to actually put her hands on you, Sophie. Well, she has met her demise now, has she not?"

Her skin turned cold as ice. "You're a murderer."

"I'm not a murderer. Everything I do, I do for you."

"I never asked you to kill anyone. Who are you?"

"I tried to get rid of Newland too. He was my last obstacle, but I could not finish the job. One of his servants heard the tussle in his bedroom, and I had to leave quickly."

Thank God. If Zach had died... Sophie closed her eyes, and two tears squeezed out. She would not have wanted to go on living. He had become so much to her in so little time. She needed him. And he needed her as well.

So she would fight. Even bound as she was, she would fight with all she had—first, to keep this lunatic out of her body, and second, to stay alive...for Zach.

Keep him talking. Sophie heard Ally's voice in her head. *Keep him talking and focused on something other than you.*

"What do you want with me?"

"You are mine. It is as simple as that."

"I don't even know who you are. Don't you think something of this magnitude should be mutual?"

"It *is* mutual, Sophie. You just haven't realized it yet. You will."

"Why do you want me? Surely there are other women—"

"Not for me!" He stomped his foot again. "All other women are whores. I wouldn't soil myself with them." He sat down next to her on the bed.

She longed to roll away, but being bound, she couldn't.

Another gloved finger trailed down her cheek, her neck, and this time over her shoulder. His touch repulsed her. Bile rose in her throat.

"I have dreamed of this day. You're even more perfect than I imagined. Your nipples are hard for me, Sophie. Did you know that?"

Her nipples were hard because she was scared and cold. But what he didn't know... Would it help if he thought she returned his feelings? She wasn't sure. If her goal was to keep him out of her body, if she acted like she wanted him, he would take her sooner rather than later.

But perhaps he wouldn't. Perhaps if she said she wasn't quite ready...

Oh, Ally, if only you were here to advise me.

She stayed quiet for the time being, gulping back nausea.

His gloved fingertips glided over one of her nipples. She forced herself not to wince or scream.

"So beautiful. Little hard nipples. Tell me, Sophie, is your cunt wet for me?"

She ached to squeeze her thighs together, but bound as she was, she could not. Her nipples might be hard, but her pussy was most definitely not wet. That would not happen, and she could force it.

He trailed his finger down over her abdomen and through her nest of blond curls. His fingertip nudged her clitoris.

Again, she forced herself not to wince. "Would you like to have my mouth on your juicy little quim, Sophie?"

Now or never. "I'm sure that would be...pleasing, but I fear I'm not quite ready yet."

God, she hoped she hadn't just made a terrible mistake.

"Oh, my dear, I assure you I will make sure you're ready for me. Shall we begin now?"

Sophie forced a smile upon her lips. "I think I'd like to wait a bit. Could you unbind me? I really don't like being bound. And what is your name? Surely you'd prefer me to use your given name."

"You may call me Brian," he said. "And I'm sorry, my dear, but I can't unbind you. This is how I want you. You will come to enjoy it. I promise you."

Now what? "If that is what you wish...B-Brian." *Stop stammering, Sophie.* "However, I fear I'm just not ready to be intimate yet. Can we not get to know each other?"

"I know all I need to know about you, my darling Sophie."

"Perhaps you do, if you have been watching me for so long. But I do not know anything about you. Tell me a bit about yourself. Let me get to know you."

He shook his head again. "I don't think so. You cannot put off the inevitable forever, my dear. I will have you. And I will have you now."

Sophie braced herself. No matter what happened, she had to stay alive.

"Could I at least see your face? Don't you think I have the right to see the face of the man who is claiming my body?"

He nodded. "I suppose I can give you that much. After all, you will know soon enough who I am."

He removed his mask, and Sophie gasped.

★ ★ ★ ★

The maid came bustling back to Zach.

"Where is she?" Zach demanded.

"I'm afraid I don't know, sir. Mr. Graves has taken ill and has taken to his chamber. That is all I could find out so far. I have alerted the master, and he is on his way to speak to you."

The Earl of Brighton entered the foyer a few seconds later. "Newland," he said, "you say you're looking for Sophie? I'm sorry, but I've forbidden her to go to rehearsal until we find out who's been sending her those notes."

Zach stiffened. "She got another note?"

"Yes. Two, actually. Haven't the constables informed you?

They think whoever made an attempt on your life might be the same person who's been writing notes to Sophie."

Zach shook his head. "No one has told me anything like that. I thought Mr. Bertram had been incarcerated."

"He was. Still is. But we're no longer sure he is the perpetrator. Seems he might be innocent as he claims."

Zach's mind whirled, his head beginning to ache. "No one told me any of this."

"Blake probably didn't want you worrying while you were trying to recover," Brighton said.

"Yes, maybe." Zach rubbed his temples. "If you please, my lord, I must speak to Sophie."

"Of course. I'll have her maid wake her. I hope you don't mind waiting."

"Not at all." Zach sat down on the settee in the foyer.

"Don't be absurd, Newland. Go wait in the parlor."

Zach nodded, strode into the parlor, and took a seat on the divan. Little elves hammered inside his brain. Sophie. Everything would be fine when he saw Sophie. A quarter of an hour passed before Brighton entered the parlor, the lines on his forehead creased.

"Newland," he said, gulping, "Sophie is...missing."

"What?" Zach shot up from the divan, perspiration beading on his forehead. "Where the devil is she?"

"Her maid says she's not in her chamber, and her bed hasn't been slept in." Brighton raked his fingers through his ample silver hair. "Iris is beside herself."

All those shadows Zach had imagined...all those eyes watching him... His veins turned icy. "We've got to find her."

The earl nodded. "I will find her. I must, for Iris."

"I'm going with you."

"Newland, you're recovering from a head injury. It's not wise—"

"For God's sake, Brighton, I'm in love with that woman." Zach started to sway on his feet a bit. He needed to keep a level head. "I *will* go with you."

"Lord," the earl said. "All this time, Bertram has maintained his innocence, and then those two notes surfaced in the last day or two. It's truly possible we have the wrong man incarcerated."

"We have to figure out who has her and where she is," Zach said, his nerves jumping. "We must find her. I cannot live without her. I need her."

"Yes, yes, of course. I've been told Mr. Graves is ill, but I will go to his chamber and talk to him. He's the one who knows all the comings and goings around here, and he will be able to point us in the right direction."

"If you don't mind, I will go with you."

"I don't mind at all, Newland. You've proved your devotion to Sophie. Let's go see what we can find out."

Zach followed Brighton to the servants' wing, where they knocked on the door to Graves's chamber. No answer.

Brighton knocked harder. Still no answer. "Graves, I know you're not feeling well, but we need to speak with you right away."

Still no response.

The earl turned the doorknob and opened the door. Graves was not in his room.

"Where has he gone?" Zach asked, his heart stampeding.

Brighton shook his head. "I'm afraid I don't know, but I do not like the look of this one bit."

Zach's stomach dropped, and nausea overtook him. "It

was Graves, wasn't it, who implicated Bertram?"

The earl nodded. "Graves has been in my employ for over thirty years. He has always been a gentleman. I can't believe he would do something so despicable."

"I suppose we don't know for sure," Zach said, "but we've got to find Sophie, Brighton. I cannot allow anything to happen to her."

"Nor can I. Her mother would die if something happened to one of her daughters. We went through enough last year, when Sophie was kidnapped and Ally was beaten. And now with Ally nearly losing her life in childbirth..." Brighton shook his head. "Plus, I love these girls as if they were my own flesh and blood. We must find her."

"But where do we start?" Zach's head ached. He had to figure this out. Had to...

"Graves had a brother who was a tenant on the Brighton land years ago. We'll start with that information. Let's go to my office."

Brighton found the requisite information, and he and Zach saddled some horses to ride out to the parcel of land that Graves's brother had once let. They each had pistols. Horses could go faster without pulling a carriage, and they were less apt to be seen. Zach had wanted to ask Evan to join them, but the Earl refused. Evan and Ally had been through so much already.

Zach fought back rising bile the whole way. He could not lose Sophie. She had become so important to him in so little time, and he was not going to give her up without a hell of a fight.

They finally arrived on the parcel of land a half hour later. A small dwelling stood in the distance, and a couple of horses were tethered to a fence post.

"Are there new tenants on this land?" Zach asked.

The earl shook his head. "No. There should not be anyone here. This is an older piece of land and a dwelling that we haven't renovated."

Zach's heart leaped into his throat. Sophie was here. He could feel it in the thick air. And she needed him.

"Be quiet," Brighton urged him. "We don't know how many men he has."

Zach nodded, his hand resting on the pistol in his waistband.

The earl went first, opening the door.

Like a flash of lightning, a man knocked the earl on the head with a candlestick, and he went down.

"I got the other one, Jake," another man said, grabbing Zach, taking his pistol, and throwing it onto a dirty sofa.

"Where is she?" Zach demanded. "Where is Lady Sophie?"

"So you're here for the lady. I was wondering when someone would come for her. She's in the bedroom...tied up at the moment."

Zach seethed. No one would hurt Sophie while he lived. He tried to get away, but the man who had him was bigger and stronger than he was.

"Take him into the bedroom, Harry, and see what the boss wants to do with them," Jake said. "I'll take care of this one." He pointed to Brighton on the floor.

Zach looked quickly at the earl. He was breathing, and no blood was coming from his head, thank God. He was simply unconscious. Zach could do nothing for him now. His focus was Sophie, and unfortunately, Brighton would be no help.

The other man forced Zach into the bedroom.

And he gasped, terror flooding through him.

There lay Sophie, naked, each limb tied to a bedpost. A man dressed in black hovered over her at the foot of the bed. He was tall with a shock of grey-white hair.

Sophie turned her head at the commotion.

The man holding Zach placed his hand over Zach's mouth before he could yell to Sophie.

The grey-haired man turned.

Graves.

"Newland. How in the hell did you find me?"

The man called Harry unclamped his hand from Zach's mouth, still holding him while Zach struggled.

"Sophie, love, are you all right?"

"Don't speak to him!" Graves warned.

Poor Sophie. His love. Bound naked. Zach would see that damned butler dead for this.

"What in the hell are you doing, Graves? You've been a loyal servant to Brighton for how many years now? And you abduct his stepdaughter? What the hell were you thinking? You need to let her go. Now!"

"I don't need to do anything you say, Newland."

"Did you really think we wouldn't find you? You sick bastard. And then implicating that innocent man, Bertram. He's been rotting in a cell for six weeks, constantly proclaiming his innocence."

"He's a stupid kid. A pawn in my game."

"Your game is over. We have people coming right behind us."

Graves laughed. "No, you don't, or they would be here by now."

Zach swallowed. Caught in a lie. "What do you want with Sophie, Graves?"

"Plain and simple. I want *her*. She is the woman of my dreams. I have been worshiping her since I first laid eyes on her, waiting for the right time to claim her."

Feral anger rose within Zach. No one would take his woman. "She will never be yours. She's mine."

"She's not yours, Newland. But you took her anyway, didn't you? Forced yourself upon her virgin flesh!" Graves's eyes glowed with evil. "Since you're here, I'll prove to you who she belongs to. Harry, hold him. He will *watch*."

Sophie screamed. "Help me, Zach! Please!"

"You will not make another sound, my dear," he said to Sophie, "or I shall have to punish you."

Zach fought against Harry's strong hold. "If you so much as touch one hair on her head—"

"You'll do what?" Graves's eyes glittered with malice. "You're in no situation to make any threats, Newland. The woman is mine. And you shall be witness to my claiming."

"No!"

Harry clamped a hand over Zach's mouth again.

"Such a big sensation. Zachary Newland, the toast of the theatre. Seducer of women everywhere. You take whatever you want. You took my woman, and you soiled her. She is *not* yours. She was *never* yours. How does it feel to you, Newland, to stand there and watch me have her?"

Zach strained, trying to yell, but to no avail with Harry's hammy hand locked over his mouth. He had to get to Sophie. *Had to.*

She lay on the bed, her eyes pleading with him. "It's all right, Zach. I'll be all right," she said.

Graves marched toward her head and smacked her hard across the cheek. "I told you not to speak."

Graves might as well have hit Zach. He felt every bit of the sting. That bastard!

Sophie, he said in his mind, *I love you. I love you so much. I am here. Don't give up. Fight this. We will somehow get out of here.*

Yet he couldn't believe the words. To watch another man have his woman was killing him. Rage boiled beneath his skin.

Graves lowered his trousers, his cock springing free like a menace.

"You will be mine now, Sophie, while Newland watches. He will know without a doubt to whom you belong."

Sophie opened her mouth, but before she could say anything, Graves slapped her again.

He claims to love her and treats her thus? Zach strained against the arms holding him, the hand against his mouth.

Graves removed his boots, stockings, and trousers. Naked from the waist down, he climbed upon the bed and hovered over Sophie.

"And now, dear Sophie, you will be mine."

Sophie let out a blood-curdling scream.

And Zach sprang into action. He summoned every bit of strength in his body, mind, and soul and elbowed Harry in the ribs, releasing himself. Quick as a jackrabbit, he grabbed the pistol out of Harry's waistband, ran to Graves, and pistol-whipped him on the head. The butler fell limp on top of Sophie.

Thinking fast, Zach turned to Harry and held him at gunpoint. "You make one move, and I will shoot your fucking head off."

Harry nodded.

"Help me get him off her," Zach said.

Harry and Zach rolled a delirious Graves off of Sophie.

"I'm sorry, Liam," Graves whispered before his eyes shut and he lost consciousness.

Zach then pistol-whipped Harry, and the big man fell to the floor.

Sophie. His Sophie. His heart nearly broke seeing her bound and mistreated. "My God, darling, are you all right?"

Tears streamed down Sophie's cheeks. "Oh, Zach, I was so afraid..."

"No need to be afraid, my love. I will always come for you. I will never let any harm come to you."

He untied the ropes, and once Sophie was unbound, he wrapped her in the old quilt that covered the rickety bed. He kissed her forehead.

"We have much to talk about, Sophie, but first let's take care of this filth so they can never harm you again."

Sophie nodded, tears still streaming down her face. "Bind him. He enjoyed having me bound so much. Perhaps he should see what it's like."

Zach nodded and bound an unconscious Graves's hands and feet, ironically with the rope he had used on Sophie. He tied Harry as well.

"We need to see about your stepfather. One of the thugs hit him in the head with a candlestick."

Sophie gasped. "Will he be all right?"

Zach nodded. "I think so. He seemed to be breathing fine, and there was no blood."

"But the others..."

Zach grabbed the gun. "Wait here..."

"Zach, no!"

Zach put his finger to his lips. "I have this pistol. I will be all right." Zach opened the door to the bedroom and walked out quietly. The earl still lay on the floor, breathing normally. Zach checked the room. No sign of Jake. The coward had run.

He knelt down to Brighton. "My Lord? Are you all right? Can you hear me?"

His eyes fluttered open. "Newland?"

"Yes. I'm here. You were hit on the head. But I found Sophie. You were right. It was Graves. Just lie here. We're going to get some help."

He went back to Sophie, still cuddling in the comforter. He sat on the bed and took her in his arms.

"I'm so sorry, my love. I should've been there to protect you." Tears fell down his cheeks.

"But you did. You came, and you protected me."

"No harm will ever come to you again as long as I live, my love. I will protect you with my life if need be. I can't lose you. You're a part of me now."

Sophie's lips trembled. She opened her mouth to speak, but he stopped her.

"Please don't leave me."

She looked up at him, cupping his cheek, her striking hazel eyes wet and bloodshot. "Never." A small smile curved her parched lips. "How could I? You've uncovered places in my soul where I was afraid to venture. I was alive before I met you, but I wasn't *living*."

Zach warmed against her, holding her tightly. "I love you, Sophie. What we have isn't always pretty, but it's real and solid, and I'd die without it. Please say you'll still be my wife."

Sophie, tears still streaming down her cheeks, nodded. "I love you too, Zach Newland. I would be pleased and honored to be your wife."

FINALE

Bertram had been released, and he returned to the Brighton estate as the new butler. The earl felt so horrible about what happened that he offered Bertram hefty compensation and a chamber on the second level, away from the servants' quarters. Bertram seemed happy at his new post.

Graves, along with his brother Harry, had been transferred to Newgate in London. Graves had begged everyone's forgiveness before he left, and he hanged himself several days later.

Sophie and Zach, after several days off to recover, finished their performances. Healing from their ordeal would take time, but together, Sophie knew they would thrive. After closing night, they were married via special license in a small ceremony at the estate. After a five-course midnight repast, they headed to Zach's townhome—*their* townhome.

Sophie sat in her new bedchamber, dressed in a pink negligee, waiting for her husband to come to her on their wedding night.

The door opened slowly, and Zach stood, clad in a forest-green silk robe.

"My love, you are beautiful," he said.

Sophie gazed at him in appreciation. Her new husband was as magnificent as anything on earth. "As are you, my husband."

"We've been through a lot to be together," Zach said, "but

I would go through it all again a hundred times to be with you. To have you as my leading lady for life."

"As would I." No truer words had ever left Sophie's lips.

Zach was her destiny and she his. They understood each other. They needed each other.

Zach dropped his robe, exposing his naked body. She gulped. He was as handsome as ever, his sinewy muscles apparent in his calves, thighs, abdomen, chest, and arms. Her body warmed all over.

He came closer. His auburn night beard had begun to appear on his jawline. She touched his face, relishing the stubble.

"Ah," he said. "Your touch... Nothing's ever felt so perfect."

Sophie let out a giggle. "Nothing?" She gave him a kiss on one of his copper coin nipples.

Then she stood and dropped her negligee.

"I fear I've been a naughty girl. I think I might need a good spanking."

ENCORE

The Ruby

A House Party at the Estate of Lord and Lady Peacock

Poppea's tongue made Prissy's pussy sizzle.

"Oh, Poppea, no one sucks cunny quite like you." Prissy writhed under Poppea's questing mouth. "Yes, yes, just like that. You're going to make me—"

Prissy burst into an explosive climax, her whole body throbbing in time with the convulsions in her quim.

Poppea inserted two fingers into her channel, prolonging the pleasure as Prissy rode out her orgasm. When she finally came down, she turned to her companion.

"That was lovely, Poppea. Thank you. Might I return the favor?"

Poppea's chin was gloriously shiny with Prissy's nectar. "Oh, I would adore that, Prissy, but what I have a taste for right now is a good flogging."

"You know I would love to oblige," Prissy said, "but I never dole out punishment. I only submit to it. In fact, now you mention it, I could use another spanking as well. Let us find two gentlemen to see to our needs."

The ladies approached the Earl of Peacock, who was just finishing administering a spanking to Sarah Nora.

"I say, Peacock," Prissy said, "Poppea and I fancy a spanking. I fear we've been quite naughty. Could you arrange it?"

"Of course, my dear. As I've spanked you many times and Poppea only a few, might I suggest that I spank her arse this evening? I'm sure Hardwood would be happy to give you a good show."

"Oh, yes," Sarah Nora agreed, nodding. "Hardwood is famous for his floggings. My bum has been sore since we've been together." She gazed around the room. "There he is. It looks like he's just spent his load in Fannie's throat. I shall send him over." Sarah Nora strode away, her well-shaped derriere wiggling.

Prissy heated with anticipation. Hardwood and Sarah Nora had never been to one of their house parties, so she had never been spanked by him. Excitement surged through her, culminating in her sweet spot. Would Hardwood be as good as Peacock?

Hardwood ambled over, his flaccid cock dangling between his well-formed thighs. "Lady Peacock," he said, "Sarah Nora says you're in need of a spanking."

Prissy nodded. "Oh, yes, my lord. I do crave one. Poppea here just gave me an amazing gamahuching. I fear we were very naughty together and must be punished. Peacock is going to take Poppea. So that leaves you for me."

Hardwood laid his palm over Prissy's bottom. "Your arse is quite splendid, my lady, and already a radiant shade of rose. Let's see if we can redden it a bit, shall we?"

Prissy trembled all over. Icy shivers raced across her skin. She was ready for his punishing hand.

"I shall take you across my knee, like the naughty little girl you are," Hardwood said, his eyes twinkling. He walked a few steps to the divan, sat down, and patted his lap. "Come now, Lady Peacock. It's time for your punishment."

Prissy walked slowly toward him. When she got close enough, Hardwood grabbed her arm and forcefully laid her across his lap.

"I'm afraid you did not get here fast enough, my lady. That has earned you an extra form of punishment." He pinched one cheek of her arse between his thumb and forefinger.

"Oh!" Prissy cried out. The pain threaded through her arse cheek, down her thigh and leg, where it began its transformation into pleasure. A pinch. How lovely.

"Did you like that, my lady?"

"Yes, my lord. Please. Again."

Hardwood pinched the other cheek, sending the same spirals of pleasure up and down her leg.

"I'm afraid you might like that too much, Lady Peacock." *Smack!* His palm came down on her bum.

"Oh, my lord, yes! Again!"

Smack! Smack! Smack!

"There's that bright red I want to see." Hardwood rubbed the cheeks of her buttocks. "So stunning."

Smack! Smack! Smack!

Prissy clawed her fingers into the brocade of the divan, the pain permeating through her whole body, exposing her, freeing her, until it miraculously shifted into pleasure, leading her toward another explosive climax.

She moaned and groaned into the divan, wailing, begging for more.

Smack! Smack! Smack!

With the last slap, Hardwood shoved two fingers into her wet cunt, and she broke into an incandescent orgasm. For a moment, she seemed to rise above the commotion, looking down at her guests frolicking. Peacock was thrashing Poppea.

Fannie and Sarah Nora were eating each other's cunnies, Angelica was sucking the cocks of both Beaverhausen and Gutenberg, and of course, McHunt, the voyeur, was watching and toying with his own giant cock.

When Prissy finally came back down to earth, Hardwood gently helped her off his lap.

"Can I get you some ointment for your arse, my lady?" he asked.

Prissy smiled at the handsome gentleman. "That would be lovely, thank you."

She sat, waiting for Hardwood to return with the ointment, and gazed around the room. Beaverhausen, having just erupted all over Angelica's breasts, walked to Peacock, who had finished spanking Poppea.

"Did Peacock give you a good flogging, my dear?" Beaverhausen asked.

Poppea's pretty cheeks flushed. "Oh, yes. I enjoyed it immensely."

Beaverhausen smiled and gave Peacock a friendly pat on the back. "I say, old chap, this is a demmed fine party. Demmed fine indeed."

THE END

Continue The Sex and the Season Series
with Book Five

THE PERILS OF PATRICIA
A SEX AND THE SEASON NOVEL

COMING SOON!

AUTHOR'S NOTE

Physiological Mysteries and Revelations in Love, Courtship, and Marriage by Eugène Becklard is a real book, and Becklard was a physician. The original was published in 1845 and is in the public domain. The excerpts in *Sophie's Voice* are actual reproductions from the Becklard text with all spelling and punctuation intact. Though the book seems ludicrous now, it was highly regarded as the *Everything You Always Wanted to Know About Sex (But Were Afraid to Ask)* of its time. The latter, written by David Reuben, M.D. in 1969, is now considered antiquated on some topics, such as homosexuality.

An Introduction to the Marriage Bed by Lady Margaret Mead is fictional, though I based it on *Instruction and Advice for the Young Bride* by Ruth Smythers. Also in the public domain, it wasn't written until 1894, forty years after *Sophie's Voice* takes place. Today, evidence exists that the entire text was meant as a joke, and it is well known as a humorous work.

Joke or not, both of these texts illustrate the wealth of misinformation and ignorance that our ancestors were exposed to. Is it possible that in another century or two, our descendents will find out that we were ignorant as well? Only time and evolution will tell.

MESSAGE FROM HELEN

Dear Reader,

Thank you for reading *Sophie's Voice*. If you want to find out about my current backlist and future releases, please like my Facebook page: **www.facebook.com**/**HelenHardt** and join my mailing list: **www.helenhardt.com**/**signup**/. I often do giveaways. If you're a fan and would like to join my street team to help spread the word about my books, you can do so here: **www.facebook.com**/**groups**/**hardtandsoul**/. I regularly do awesome giveaways for my street team members.

If you enjoyed the story, please take the time to leave a review on a site like Amazon or Goodreads. I welcome all feedback.

I wish you all the best!

Helen

ALSO BY HELEN HARDT

The Sex and the Season Series:
Lily and the Duke
Rose in Bloom
Lady Alexandra's Lover
Sophie's Voice
The Perils of Patricia (Coming Soon)

The Temptation Saga:
Tempting Dusty
Teasing Annie
Taking Catie
Taming Angelina
Treasuring Amber
Trusting Sydney
Tantalizing Maria

The Steel Brothers Saga:
Craving
Obsession
Possession
Melt (Coming December 20th, 2016)
Burn (Coming February 14th, 2017)
Surrender (Coming May 16th, 2017)

Daughters of the Prairie:
The Outlaw's Angel
Lessons of the Heart
Song of the Raven

DISCUSSION QUESTIONS

1. The theme of a story is its central idea or ideas. To put it simply, it's what the story *means*. How would you characterize the theme of *Sophie's Voice?*

2. It's clear from the first two books that Sophie is more like Rose than like Lily. Compare and contrast Sophie and Rose. How are they alike, and how are they different?

3. Discuss the excerpts from the Becklard text. Becklard was a physician and was quite serious about his findings. What do you think of his book?

4. Discuss the excerpts from the Lady Margaret Mead book. Do you think they make sense considering the era? Why or why not?

5. Why do you think Sophie let Ally take her father's abuse for her? Does this make her weak? Why or why not?

6. What do you think Zach's life was like after his mother died? How might he have survived? How did this contribute to the man he became?

7. Why do you think Sophie allows Zach liberties so quickly? Does this go against her character? Why or why not?

8. Did you enjoy the erotic adventures of Lord and Lady Peacock? Why or why not?

9. What did you think about Brighton's refusal to allow Zach to court Sophie? What might have been going through Brighton's mind?

10. How did you feel when Nanette was murdered? Did you, even for a moment, think that Zach had killed her?

11. Taking into consideration the era and Sophie's personality, why do you think she gave Zach the alibi?

12. We get a bigger glimpse of Ally's stepfather, the Earl of Brighton, in this story. Discuss his character. Do you find him hypocritical? Why or why not?

13. What might the future hold for Zach and Sophie? Will their marriage be successful? How will it differ from her sister's and cousins' marriages?

14. In today's terms, Sophie had a stalker. Were you surprised at the stalker's identity? Why or why not? Discuss his character. Why do you think he acted as he did?

15. Who would you like to read about next in this series?

ACKNOWLEDGEMENTS

To quote George R. R. Martin, "this one was a bitch." Every so often in an author's career, a book comes along that makes walking across hot coals and pulling one's own teeth out seem preferable to finishing it. *Sophie* was that type of book. As much as I love Sophie and Zach, I had a difficult time telling their story. These words were dragged kicking and screaming onto their pages. And then magic happened. As you see Sophie evolve from a timid young lady afraid to venture out into the world to a beautiful and talented woman who finally believes in herself, I hope you feel the magic too.

As always, thank you to my brilliant editor, Michele Hamner Moore, and my eagle-eyed proofreader, Jenny Rarden. Thank you to all the great people at Waterhouse Press—Meredith, David, Kurt, Shayla, and Jon. Your belief in your authors knows no bounds. I'm proud and thrilled to be one of them.

Thank you to the members of my street team, Hardt and Soul. HS members got the first look at *Sophie*, and I appreciate all your support, reviews, and general good vibes. You are all awesome!

And thanks to all of you who read *Lily, Rose,* and *Alexandra* and looked forward to Sophie's story. I hope you find it worth the wait!

ABOUT THE AUTHOR

New York Times and *USA Today* Bestselling author Helen Hardt's passion for the written word began with the books her mother read to her at bedtime. She wrote her first story at age six and hasn't stopped since. In addition to being an award winning author of contemporary and historical romance and erotica, she's a mother, a black belt in Taekwondo, a grammar geek, an appreciator of fine red wine, and a lover of Ben and Jerry's ice cream. She writes from her home in Colorado, where she lives with her family. Helen loves to hear from readers.

Visit her here:
www.facebook.com/HelenHardt

ALSO AVAILABLE FROM
HELEN HARDT

El Diablo strikes no fear in the heart of Dusty O'Donovan. The accomplished rider knows life holds much greater fears than a feisty stud bull. Diablo's owner, Zach McCray, is offering half a million dollars to anyone who can stay on him for a full eight seconds. That purse would go a long way helping rebuild Dusty and her brother's nearly bankrupt ranch.

Let a woman ride his bull? Not likely. Still, the headstrong Dusty intrigues Zach. Her father worked on the McCray ranch years ago, and Zach remembers her as a little girl when he was a cocky teen. Times change, and now she's a beautiful and desirable young woman. A few passionate kisses leave Zach wanting more, but will Dusty's secrets tear them apart?